The Perfect Child

Megan VanLoo

Dedication

To my sister, Brooklyn, I couldn't have done this without your support.

Can Anyone Really be "Perfect"?

Perfection is something you'll never see.
It's an impossible expectation.
It beats us down just like any bully.
This word causes stress throughout the nation.

It pushes all of us to the extremes.
Never relenting until we give up,
Or until it rips open all our seams.
It tries to make us cover with makeup.

The flaws shove onto the scene anyway
With many of us too stubborn to stop.
We strive for it until our lives look grey,
We strive to be perfect, to be on top.

So can anyone really be "Perfect"
Or is it a standard we should reject?

Table of Contents

August 26th

Chapter 1 - Carson

"Honey, it's time to wake up. You have practice in half an hour." I rolled over and saw my mom standing in the doorway, ready for work. Every morning was the same: mom came in, woke me up in her soft voice like she was soothing a baby, and fixed me breakfast before taking me to whatever practice was scheduled for the morning. Today was football. I climbed out of bed, stumbled to my bathroom, and pulled a T-shirt off the floor. It smelled clean enough, and I was just going to sweat through it anyway.

I walked into the kitchen and was greeted by my father's ever-present scowl. "You better eat fast, boy. Practice starts soon, and you need to build all the muscle you can before the first game," he grumbled without ever looking up from his computer. I loaded my football gear into my mom's car, took my swim bag out of the trunk, and threw my backpack in its place.

The Perfect Child

I play four sports a year: baseball in the spring, swimming in the summer and winter, basketball in the winter, and football in the fall. This is my time to prove I am the best. I am determined to show everyone what I'm made of.

I climbed into the car, looked out the window, and ignored the world until I felt the car stop before we arrived at the school. I questioned my mom gruffly, "What are you doing? We're going to be late!"

"Carson, I told you five times. We have to pick up your cousins." As if on cue, my cousins Cooper, Camden, and Casey came strolling out their front door. I usually rode with Cooper and Camden, but the truck they shared was in the shop, and my mom had pleaded for us to let her drive us to school since it's the first day. She always wants nostalgic moments like that, even though Casey or I could've driven today. They got in the back seat like normal people, but Casey opened my door instead.

"What the hell are you doing? Get in the back!" I growled at her.

"Carson, language!" My mom warned.

"Aunt B, don't you think it would be better if I sat up front with you and Carson sat in the back with the boys? It just makes more sense," Casey pleaded with her election-winning smile.

"Of course, Case. Carson, move," my mother stated as if she hadn't just chosen her niece over her own son.

Everyone always says Casey is a politician. She is friends with everyone she meets, and she is the president of almost every club at school. She is also a spoiled brat who got everything handed to her. She wouldn't know hardship if it kicked her in her perfect smile. But she is my family, and I'd do just about anything for her, and she'd do the same for me. When we were little, we were best friends because her brothers didn't want anything to do with us, but now that we're older and I spend most of my time with the guys, we argue anytime we're awake, at least that's how my mom puts it.

"Get out and stop pouting," Cooper said as he shoved open the door I was leaning against. Cooper and Camden are twins, and they are a year older than Casey and me. Our moms are sisters, and since I'm an only child, we have all been raised like siblings: joint vacations, weekly family dinners, and carpooling all the time. I know I'm lucky to have such a close family, but sometimes I'd rather not know them at all.

Cooper and Camden were hustling towards the field, so I grabbed my football bag, yelled a quick goodbye to my mom, and took off after them.

"Hustle boys, I want you in your lines and ready to run in sixty seconds!" Coach Harley demanded. Coop, Cam, and I got in line and prepared ourselves for what we knew would be a grueling practice. We started running drills immediately, and after fifteen minutes, I was dripping sweat. Coach was yelling again, but this time he wasn't calling out our next exercise; instead, he was yelling at a guy who had just run down to the field.

The Perfect Child

"Mr. Daemon, you're late! You're lucky I'm letting you play at all since you weren't at summer practices, but that'll be short-lived if you aren't dedicated enough to show up on time."

Aaron Daemon looked as though he had just run a few miles. He was out of breath, and his shaggy blonde hair was sticking to his forehead. He quickly threw his bag on the ground, muttered "Yes sir, it won't happen again" to Coach, and joined the line next to me.

"This oughta be good; the crackhead's kid is playing football," Cooper snickered behind me. Before I had time to respond, Coach was yelling at us to get ready for sprints. I had already discovered I was the fastest on the team, so sprints were going to be a piece of cake. I got into position, and as soon as Coach blew his whistle, I was off. Out of the corner of my eye, I saw Aaron pulling ahead of me. How is that possible? I have always been the fastest kid in school. I tried to run faster, but my legs wouldn't let me, and then the sprint was over. Aaron had beat me. The rest of the drills went the same: I pushed myself as hard as possible, and Aaron still beat me. We started practicing throwing and catching, so we all partnered up. Cooper and Camden were partners as usual, which left me to find whoever was left.

As chance would have it, Aaron was the last one left. We partnered up without a word. Coach had already told us just to throw back and forth, and then we would run a few plays to finish up. I grabbed a ball, went to my spot, and threw my best spiral. Aaron, who was just getting to his spot, was caught off guard, but he still caught it like a seasoned professional. He returned the ball with his own perfect throw. I have to admit Aaron is good, but I wasn't going to be beaten by some random guy who had never played a real game of football.

We finished practice with running plays. Aaron ran them as though he had been playing for this team for years. As I was going over to pick up my bag, Coach hollered, "Daemon, Nixley, hang back a minute." I walked over to where Coach Harley and Aaron were already talking on the sidelines.

"Yes, Coach?"

"Good job today, boys; keep doing what you did today, and you'll be the best duo in high school football this year. Now get to class."

Coach Harley had been coaching this team for nearly ten years, and I had never heard of him complimenting any of his players. Maybe if I told my dad, he would finally believe I'm a good athlete. With pride swelling in my chest, I walked towards the school for my first-hour class.

Chapter 2 - Aaron

I couldn't believe I was actually going to be on the football team. I had been dreaming of this my whole life. All of the dads in the trailer park had been teaching me how to play since I started walking. Finally, I was going to be able to play because, for the first time since my sister was born, I didn't have to take care of anyone else. My mom was finally clean. She hadn't gotten drunk or high in over three months, so it was her turn to be the parent and mine to be the kid.

After my sister, Ashley, was born, my mom got really messed up on drugs. We live in a trailer park where no one has much money, but they all did as much for us as they could. When I turned seven, I started doing odd jobs for people around town. Everyone tried to find small jobs for me. Some people were nicer than others, sending me home with dinner, toys, or more money than I had worked for. It wasn't the most glamorous life, but as long as I kept my mom out of prison and gave my sister as normal a life as I could, it was worth it. I never hoped my mom would get clean, but now that she was, I couldn't help but hope she stayed that way.

I knew I would be late getting to practice, but I had to walk Ashley to school. I didn't care if Coach was pissed at me or not; she was my priority. As I got in line, I heard Cooper make some asshole comment about my mom, but I knew better than to retaliate. Instead, I just showed them all up in a sport they thought they were gods at.

Carson obviously hated that I was better than him, but I liked making him squirm.

When Coach called us over, I thought we were in trouble for being too aggressive with each other today, but instead, he told us to keep it up. If all I need to do to show Coach I'm committed to playing is get under Carson's skin, then this is going to be easy.

As soon as practice ended, I ran to the locker room, wiped off my sweat, and pulled on some clean clothes. Most of my clothes were old and stained or had holes in them, but the ones I wore today were brand new. Mrs. Clemetts bought them for me just for today. I had on new jeans and a dark blue collared shirt, which Mrs. Clemetts told me matched my eyes.

Rose Clemetts is a sweet older widow whose only child lived in a different state, and she felt bad for my sister and me. She has been helping us out for as long as I can remember. She was also my first-hour teacher this year.

I walked into her classroom, sat down at the table directly in front of her podium, and waited for class to start as my classmates trickled in. However, instead of Mrs. Clemetts walking in, a younger woman, probably in her late thirties. She then walked up to the whiteboard and wrote Mrs. Clemetts in big, black letters.

"Good morning. I'm sure most of you were expecting my mother-in-law, but she has decided to retire, and I will be taking her place," she said it so calmly like she hadn't just told me she was replacing the only mother figure I had ever had. Rose was the only reason I was even taking an art class. Before I could think, my hand was in the air.

"Yes?" she asked.

"I'm sorry, I forgot my question," I replied shyly. I didn't know what I had planned to ask her anyway.

She spent the next hour droning through her syllabus with a concerned look on her face. Every few minutes, I would notice her looking at me like she couldn't understand me.

When the bell rang, she walked up to me quickly and asked, "What's your name?"

"Aaron Daemon, why?"

"You just look very familiar; sorry, I guess I was wrong." And with that, I left for my next class. Hopefully, Mrs. (not Rose) Clemetts won't act weird tomorrow.

Rose had given me her phone number when I saved up to buy a cell phone. I quickly sent her a message while I walked to my class.

"Why didn't you tell me?" I texted.

A few minutes later, she responded, "I'm sorry, dear. It was sudden. My son came back to town a few weeks ago to stay, and I saw an opportunity to leave the school and give them a replacement for me. How did you find out?"

She had to be kidding me. I've talked to her every day at school for the last three years. "You were supposed to be my first-hour teacher. Your daughter-in-law told us you retired at the last minute."

She didn't respond after that. I guess she didn't really have to explain herself; I'm not really her family. Come to think of it, I hadn't talked to Rose much since my mom got sober. I didn't even know her son had come home. I have been so wrapped up in making the best of the time Ashley and I have with my mom that I forgot about the woman who actually raised us. I would have to take Ashley there one day this week.

Chapter 3 - Casey

Carson was being an ass like usual. He has his dad's dark brown, almost black, hair and eyes and his same charming smile - only Danny's was much rarer. At times, like now, Carson also had Danny's stout, passive demeanor, but typically Carson was more carefree. He made jokes every day of his life and didn't care about rules or anyone's opinions. I envy him more than I care to admit. No one expects him to be the president of every club or get into the best schools. All he has to do is play sports and be a goofball.

As he ran towards the field with my brothers, I realized he had left his backpack in the trunk. Aunt B had to get to work, and of course, as my luck would have it, Carson and I have most of our classes together. I slung his bag over one shoulder and put mine on the other.

Our classes went from nine-thirty to four-thirty, so all our practices and club meetings were in the morning. Since it was the first day, I didn't have any meetings, so I went to the library to read. I knew everyone who went to my school, so when I saw a mess of curly dirty blonde hair peeking over one of the bookshelves, I knew I needed to put on my best politician's smile and make a new friend.

"Hi, I'm Casey," I said with a smile to the girl. She was one of those girls who were naturally pretty without any makeup. She was wearing large, round glasses and a T-shirt of some old country singer tucked into a jean skirt. She had headphones in and didn't even acknowledge me. I tapped her on the shoulder, and she turned around like she was afraid she had done something wrong. I reintroduced myself to her, and she slowly lowered the book she was reading.

"I'm Natalie. I just moved here," she said shyly.

"It's nice to meet you. What grade are you in?"

"I'm a junior."

"Oh, awesome. I am too. What's your schedule look like?"

"Ummm, here," she slowly handed me her schedule. It was similar to mine other than a few classes. Maybe I could show this girl around and teach her who to be friends with and who to avoid, namely my brothers and cousin.

"Wow, we have a lot of classes together. We are totally going to be besties," I exclaimed.

"Yeah, right now, I'm just trying to get used to everything and get ahead on some reading. I'm sorry but could you…" she mumbled, and I couldn't hear the end of her sentence, but I knew what she meant. She wanted me to leave her alone.

As she turned her attention back to her book, a phone started ringing. It sounded like it was on me, but mine wasn't ringing. Carson must have left his phone in his bag. I started digging through his bag until I found it. His phone had a notification for a missed call from his dad; I picked it up and slid over on the notification to call him back.

"Boy, why the fuck do I pay for this phone if you aren't going to answer it?" he growled loudly.

"Sorry, Uncle Danny, Carson left his phone in his bag during practice," I whimpered. I knew I sounded like a child, but I did not want to be on Danny's bad side. I have always been a little afraid of my uncle, especially when he's angry. From what I could tell, he had a bad temper, and I didn't want to be on the receiving end of it.

"It's fine, Casey. Just tell him to call me when he gets a minute."

"Yes, sir," I replied, and with that, I heard the click of him hanging up.

I sat in the library until the bell rang for first hour. Very few people got to school early, so I walked to class next to Natalie. We didn't talk as we walked, but I could tell neither of us really wanted to walk alone. As I walked into class, I saw Carson surrounded by his friends and girls who were begging for his attention, so I shoved through his adoring fans, put his phone and his bag in his hands, and said as loudly but subtly as I could, "Your daddy called to see how your first day was going." I could feel him glaring at me as I walked to the front of the room and listened to his friends' snickering. I'm sure he'll scream at me later, but right now, I needed to put him in his place so he doesn't get too cocky.

When he walked up and sat at the desk next to me, he looked mad, but not like he was irritated with me, more like he was angry with whatever his dad wanted.

"What did your dad want?" I whispered to him. I knew he wouldn't answer me, but he is my family, so I had to try to be there for him.

"Do you just want me to tell you so you can embarrass me again? What is your problem with me? I know we tease each other and all, but why do you insist on being such a pain in my ass? I treat you the same way your brothers do." He meant to whisper it, but it came out as more of a loud hiss.

"I'm sorry, you seemed upset. I was trying to be nice, but whatever. If you think I'm a bitch, I'll be a bitch." I couldn't believe he was being so rude to me. I just wanted to make sure he was okay.

As we sat next to each other with a palpable tension between us, Ms. Whethers walked in with a smile on her face so big people would think she was a kindergarten teacher.

"Good morning, class! Happy first day! Quickly everyone buddy up. Don't worry about who it is. You won't be with them long," she rambled off quickly. I stood up, walked over to one of Carson's friends, and put my hand on his bicep. Ben has had a crush on me for as long as I can remember, so I knew he would accept my pass at him. Carson's face lit up with anger. Even though he knew nothing was going on between Ben and me, he hated when I flirted with his friends.

Ms. Whethers piped up with her excited directions again, "Today we are going to be speed dating, so everyone is going to need a class roster. You will have two minutes with each person in the room, including myself. After you talk to them, get their signature and move on to the next person. Ready, set, go!"

This game was made for me. I love talking to people and getting to know them, even though I already know most of the people in my class. I started my way around the room. Carson avoided me at all costs, but that was alright. If I needed to, I could forge his signature. Either way, he was not going to get a rise out of me.

Chapter 4 - Natalie

I think I'm still in shock from moving to a new state without any heads up three weeks before school started. I love being close to my grandma, but I don't like meeting new people, and at a new school, I don't really have any other option. I had pleaded with my dad to let me stay with one of my friends, but he told me Grandma needed our help like she was dying or something. All she was doing was retiring. I think my dad just wanted a reason to come back to his hometown. Criden, Tennessee is not my home, though; San Francisco is.

When I met Casey, I could tell she was Miss Popular around here, but she didn't compare to the popular girls in San Francisco. She seemed kind enough, but it was almost like she only wanted to talk to me because it was her job. Then her bitchy side came out when she was talking to some guy in first hour. I couldn't tell if they were more than friends or not. He was tall, at least six feet, he had dark brown hair that matched his eyes, which looked like they could shoot daggers after whatever Casey said to him. He had a hint of a worry line on his forehead like he was stressed, and he was surrounded by lug head athletes. He was definitely not someone I needed to get to know. However, I didn't have much choice; this school had less than a hundred kids per grade, and they had all known each other since kindergarten. I didn't recognize more than half of the kids at my last school because I was in a grade of almost seven hundred. It was great. Now I had to learn faces, names, and backstories for people I didn't care to meet in the first place.

Thankfully the two-minute intervals didn't feel very long. I stuck to three questions: what's your name, what's your favorite color, and what do you want to be. Then Casey came up to me in her typical Chatty Cathy style and, out of the gate, said, "So is he your type?"

"Who?" I questioned back, surprised.

"My cousin, Carson. You know. Tall, dark, handsome athlete with the bone structure of a teen idol."

"You're cousins?"

"Yes, now answer the question because I could totally set you up with him."

"No, he's not my type."

"Whatever. You were totally checking him out."

"I was n…"

"Time!" Ms. Whethers interrupted.

Casey walked away without another word, and as my luck would have it, Carson was the next person to approach me. I'm sure my face was bright red.

"Nice shirt," he said as he walked up.

"Wh-what?" I stuttered. "You like George Strait?"

"Shouldn't I be asking you that, Miss San Francisco? You are in the country now, honey. Everyone knows The King of country," He replied, seeming as if he didn't notice my blush.

"How'd you know where I was from?"

"Everyone else in this class knows each other. You have been the main topic of conversation, Natalie, whose favorite color is pink, and who wants to be a nurse. Seriously though, where did you get your shirt?"

"My mom made it for me. She's the new art teacher here."

"Someone replaced Mrs. Clemetts?"

"Kinda. Mrs. Clemetts still teaches the class, just a younger version. My grandma was the teacher, and now it's my mom." I don't know why I was telling him this. He didn't need to know anything about me.

"Do I make you nervous?" he asked.

"Time!" Ms. Whethers yelled again. She had impeccable timing.

"Well, as much as I love watching you blush, that's our cue to go our separate ways, Nat. It was nice meeting you." His smile grew with my ever-growing blush. No one had ever tried to flirt with me. Was that even what he was doing, or did he and his friends just want to make fun of the new girl? Well, I'm too smart to be the butt of any joke. From now on, Carson was going to be on my list of people to avoid at this school.

I continued on with the same three questions for everyone else in the class. When the bell rang, I hurried to my next class: Upper-Level Algebra. Thankfully, I had been able to transfer my classes from old school at the last minute, so I could still be in some advanced classes.

"Wow. Pretty, smart, and likes country music, you're a girl after my own heart," Carson said as he sat down on my desk.

"What do you want, Carson?" I replied with an eye roll.

"Oooh, she's feisty too. What's wrong? You don't want to make friends?"

"Not that it's any of your business, but I have friends."

"Who? Casey? She's everyone's friend; it's how she wins elections."

"No, not Casey. I have friends at home."

"This isn't your home?"

"Nixley, get off the desk!" The large younger man yelled as he walked into the room. "You can flirt on your own time."

"Alright, alright, I'm goin', Coach," Carson said as he slid off the desk and into the seat next to me. Mr. Harley, who, judging by what Carson called him and his football room decorations, I assume is the football coach, began his lecture on class expectations.

Halfway through class, I felt a tap on my shoulder. I turned toward Carson just as he pushed a note towards me. *You never answered my question. This isn't your home?* it read. I ignored him and turned my attention back to Mr. Harley.
I couldn't help but think about his question.

San Francisco would always be my home, but my dad makes it seem like we will at least be here for the next two years while I finish high school. My little sisters were ecstatic to be living closer to my grandma, so I couldn't voice my feelings about this move around them. Maybe I did need to make some friends here, so I don't have to be known as the loner new girl. I guess it wouldn't be so bad if I had two places that felt like home. Criden is a small town, but maybe eventually I could learn to love it, if not for me, then for my family. Carson, however, was not going to be one of my new friends.

Class ended quickly, and I hadn't paid attention to anything Mr. Harley had said, but I'm sure it was the same list of rules every other teacher had for their students. I got out of my seat and quickly walked to my next class without a look or a word in Carson's direction. I entered my mother's classroom and walked up to her desk. I hadn't wanted to take art, but I needed a fine art credit, and I had never had my mom as a teacher before.

"Hey, Mom," I said, clearly surprising her.

"Oh, hey, honey. How are your classes going? Shouldn't you be getting to your next class? You don't want to be late on your first day," she rambled.

My mom is amazing, but she is the total opposite of my dad. She is laid back and creative, whereas he is serious and always follows the rules. Even their appearance is opposite: my dad has blonde hair with no volume and blue eyes; my mom has dark brown hair with curls for days with tan skin and beautiful green eyes. They never should've worked, but somehow they have a better marriage than any couple I've met.

"Mom, this is my next class, remember?" I told her, interrupting her next question. She was always scatterbrained when she was thinking about her art. I couldn't help but laugh at her.

19

"I'm sorry honey, yes, I remember I'm just trying to get situated. Why don't you go ahead and sit down," she replied as she began gathering random stacks of papers.

I took a seat at one of the tables close to her desk; typically, I sit at the front of the room, but I didn't really care to be pegged as a momma's girl on my first day at this school. Carson was surrounded by girls at a table across the room, none of whom I recognized other than Casey. She looked as if she was ready to slap Carson for who knows what reason. She must have noticed me looking at her because she walked over, sat down across the table, and said, "I swear I have never met a more irritating guy."

"I agree, but what did he do?" I asked.

"He did that," she said disgustedly while gesturing with her head towards the group of girls crowded around her cousin.

"What about it?" I replied.

"Those are my friends, and ever since Carson and Lindsey broke up, they are always all over him. I don't understand what the big draw to him is. He's a player, and he sleeps with anything with boobs," she explained with an eye roll.

"I don't know. He's been following me around all morning, and I haven't found a charming thing about him yet," I knew my irritation with him was dripping from my voice, but I also knew it was unreasonable. All he had done was try to be my friend, but something in me told me not to trust him.

"Of course, he's been following you. You're the newest piece of meat. He's an attention whore. I'm sorry I accused you of being into him. Thanks for listening to me vent. He just drives me crazy."

"You're fine. Everyone needs someone to vent to."

"Good morning or afternoon or whatever time of the day you all want to call almost lunchtime," my mom snickered. "I would like to introduce myself by introducing your first project. You will all be creating a project to tell me about yourself using whatever media you like. All I ask of you is to be creative. If you turn in a slideshow with a few pictures on it that are probably on your Instagram, I am not going to grade it. Here is what I did."

A video started playing of hand-drawn pictures of my family with my mom's voice talking over it. In the video, my mom introduced my dad, Mike; me; my sister Margaret, or Maggie, who is eleven; my sister, Nicole, who is seven; my youngest sister, Macie, who is three; and my grandma Rose, who used to teach this class. When the video ended, everyone in the class had their eyes on me. I guess most people hadn't put together that I am the teacher's daughter. Or perhaps it was because the portrait my mother had drawn of me made me look a hundred times better than I did in person. There was one person, in particular, grinning at me like a circus clown: Carson. I couldn't help but roll my eyes at him, he knew this was my mother's class, but he still wanted to act surprised like everyone else.

"As you can see, I did not focus on my entire life. I focused on what is most important to me: my family, including my Natalie, who is hiding in the back. Stand up, honey, don't be shy," she instructed me as I turned the color of a tomato. I slowly stood up and faced my classmates.

"Isn't she gorgeous? Okay, hon, you can sit down." I sat back down, mortified, and shot my mom a scolding glare. So much for not being seen as a momma's girl.

The bell rang, and I rushed out of class and to the cafeteria. I wasn't excited about school food, but anything would be better than dealing with embarrassing conversations that were sure to follow that class.

"Hon, slow down," it was the name my mom always uses for my sisters and me, but it was not my mom's voice.

"What the hell do you want, Carson? I'm not just the shiny new toy, okay? I'm not interested in whatever game you are trying to play, so please leave me alone," I hissed in Carson's face. I kept walking towards the cafeteria without waiting for his response.

"Easy there, princess. I'm not playing any games, and even if I was, what makes you think I would pick you to play with. What makes you so special?" He called after me.

Tears threatened to fall, but I urged them to stay in my eyes as I made a sudden turn into the ladies' room, where I allowed them to silently fall until lunch was over. I wasn't just crying because of what Carson said. I cried about missing my friends, about wanting to go home; part of me just cried to cry. When the bell rang to go to class, I grabbed my bag and went on as if nothing had happened.

Chapter 5 - Carson

"What the hell has gotten into you? You sound like your dad," Casey remarked as she brushed past me. It was a low blow being compared to my dad, but maybe she was right. What was I doing yelling at a girl I don't even know? Sure, Natalie is stubborn, but she didn't deserve me taking my anger out on her. Ever since Lindsey and I broke up, it's like I am constantly angry. I don't want to be angry with Natalie, though. I don't want to be someone people are scared of. I don't want to be my dad. I skipped lunch; I didn't care if my stomach growled the rest of the day. I needed to apologize to Natalie.

I waited outside the bathroom for the entire lunch period, but she never came out. When the bell rang, I finally saw her walking through the doorway. Her cheeks were tear-stained, and the sight made me want to pull her into me. I have only had that feeling with three women before: my mom, Lindsey, and Casey. No matter how much she pisses me off, I hate seeing her in pain; I guess it's a big-brother-type thing. Nat isn't my mom, my cousin, or the girl I'm in love with. She is just a stranger, a beautiful stranger who draws me in with her perfect golden curls and captivating blue eyes that are magnified by her glasses.

"Snap out of it!" I thought.

"Nat, please wait. I'm sorry," I said with audible desperation in my voice. She kept walking.

"Nat, please, I shouldn't have snapped. I was upset. I'm sorry. I didn't mean to scream at you. Please talk to me. Nat."

"Stop calling me that! We're not friends. We're not going to be friends, so you can stop with your bullshit apology!" she barked. I followed her into the English classroom without another word.

"Are you fucking kidding me? Don't tell me you're in this class too?" She hissed as she noticed me sitting down at the desk next to her.

"Natalie, please. I know I screwed up, and an apology isn't going to fix it, but give me a second chance to prove to you that that's not who I am." She just stared at me.

"Natalie, I'm begging you. Please give me a chance. That's not me," I pleaded even further.

"Why do you care?" She finally replied.

"Because I was serious about wanting to be friends." Or more, I thought to myself. "I want to get to know you. Yes, at first, it was just because you were a pretty face, but you are also stubborn and smart. You seem like fun. You're different than most of the girls at this school. Please believe me. Please forgive me."

"I don't even know you," she replied as if I hadn't just told her everything I had been thinking since I met her. Well, not everything, but if she knew some of it, she definitely wouldn't trust me to be her friend.

"Fine. You don't have to trust me, just don't hate me," I bargained.

"Class, listen up. I'm Dr. Williams, and I'm your teacher for Junior English. In this class, we will learn how to properly read, write, and interpret English. You all know how classrooms work. You know the rules. Follow them, and we will get along well. We will start out this year with reading *To Kill A Mockingbird* starting tomorrow. Today, I expect all of you to predict what this story is about. I don't care if you write it down or not. We will share our thoughts at the end of class," Dr. Williams seemed unmotivated to teach, but I didn't really care if it gave me time to talk to Natalie.

"What class do you have next?" she asked me.

I wasn't expecting her to start the conversation. She seemed like the type that would want to take assignments seriously, but when I looked down at her desk, I saw she had already written her prediction - it was correct. I assumed she had already read *To Kill A Mockingbird*. I have too because it's my mom's favorite book, even though her husband is an angry drunk just like Bob Ewell.

"I have weights. What about you?" I asked.

"Spanish, finally I'll have a class away from you," she said in a way that even though it was meant to be an insult, I could tell she was partially kidding, and right now, I will take partially.

"Here, let me see your schedule," I said while grabbing it out of her hand.

"What are you doing?" she said with a little laugh. It was small, but it was such a sweet sound, which meant I was making progress.

"I'm marking the classes you'll have to miss me in. It looks like Spanish is the only one, and I think Casey has that. I know she's not me, but hopefully, she'll keep you from getting too sad," I said with my best pouty face.

"You are a mess!" She laughed. Her laugh wasn't the quiet giggle I was used to hearing from Casey and Lindsey. It was loud, unreserved, and goofy like a little girl's and was a huge contrast from the shy, serious girl sitting next to me. It was amazing.

"What are you looking at?" She asked after a few seconds.

"What?" I asked, caught off guard.

"You were staring at me and smiling. Do I have something on my face?" She started wiping at her face.

"No, no, you look beautiful." I could feel myself blush. "I was just trying to figure you out,"

"Umm, okay?"

"You're a Clemetts, right? Do you know Mike Clemetts?"

"Yeah. He's my dad. Why?"

"Are you serious? He's a legend here; his name is everywhere in the trophy case. He was the first four-sport athlete at this school. He holds like every record I've been dreaming of beating," I told her, not trying to hide the shock in my voice. "I grew up hearing stories about your dad. He's the reason I've been pushing myself to be the best athlete at this school. He's my idol."

"Well, I hate to burst your bubble, but your idol is now an accountant."

"I can't believe you don't think your dad is awesome. I'd love to talk to him about his experience."

"Yeah, I'll have to introduce you sometime." She looked like she regretted it right after saying it. She blushed again, and I couldn't help but smile.

"Natalie, I like you, but meeting your family, don't you think that's kinda fast?" I teased.

"I-I, I didn't mean it like that," she stuttered, and her face got even redder. The blush on her cheeks somehow made her look even better.

"Nat, calm down. I'm just teasing."

"Rude!" She said like a kid.

For the rest of the hour, I gave her the low down on every teacher at the school. We didn't argue. Somehow, I didn't flirt. It was just a friendly conversation, but it was one of the best conversations I had had in a long time.

The rest of my classes went by in a blur, as did the rest of the week. My mom asked me every day if anything fun happened at school, and every day, my mind went straight to Natalie, but she isn't mine to bring up. We were still just friends, and the last few days, we were talking less and less. I don't know what I did wrong, but I am going to fix it.

September 14th

Chapter 6 - Casey

My first few weeks of junior year were a breeze. I talked to all of my classmates, and by the end of the second week, I had become the president of my class, the debate team, and the Spanish club. I love being a leader in my school. My mom is the president of every organization she is in. She has always pushed me to do the same. I feel like this is the only way I can live up to her expectations. I learned in elementary school how to make everyone feel like my friend, but I haven't had very many close friends because of it.

I think I am actually making a real friend now, though. Natalie and I talked and gossiped every day in our classes together. We talked about our siblings. She talked about what her life was like in San Francisco. I gave her information about her new classmates, one of the perks of being everyone's friend. It was nice. My brothers and Carson have always been the people I am closest to, even though we fight all the time. I have had a few girls that I was close to in elementary and middle school, but we all drifted apart last year.

Today, Natalie walked into Spanish, sat down next to me, and immediately said, "I'm assuming we aren't doing anything today." She was used to a big, fancy school where kids took classes like Spanish actually to learn. Here Spanish was an easy A class that doubled as a social hour.

"Coach Marran said we are finishing the packet he gave us last week," I told her as she rolled her eyes.

"What's the deal with him?" She asked suddenly.

"Who? Coach Marran?"

"No, of course not. Carson."

"Oh, I knew we'd be having this conversation eventually. So what do you want to know, how many relationships he's had? If he's a player?"

"No, I just want to know more about him. He's terrible at talking about himself."

"I know. If it's about school or sports, he can talk for hours, but not when it comes to personal stuff. Well, as far as his family goes, his dad is a dick and one of the best lawyers in Knoxville. His mom is a saint. She has stood by Danny through every bad case that pissed him off. Carson would stay with us a lot when he was younger because his dad would get irritated at having a kid around when he had a hard case. His mom never wanted him to make his dad mad like that. He doesn't have much in common with his dad other than sports. Danny played a lot of sports in high school; that's why Carson pushes himself so hard. Oh, and don't even get me started on Lindsey."

"His ex?" She asked.

"Yeah, they got together in eighth grade, and she had him on a tight leash their whole relationship. If he so much as blinked at another girl, she was mad at him. Then, last spring, she cheated on him with a guy from a different school. He was a baseball player, and when we played against his school, Lindsey was there watching Carson. The other guy talked to Lindsey about getting together again, and Carson overheard. He was devastated. He wasn't going to end it until my brothers showed him that she had been screwing around with other guys before that. She begged him not to leave her and told just about every girl that has looked his way since that she isn't going to let anyone else have him for anything more than a little fun. She's insane, and now every girl is all over him. He doesn't seem to mind, though."

"Seems like it," she chimed in.

"He really loved her though. I don't know how he's going to move on."

She was pretty quiet after that, and before I got the chance to ask her what was wrong, Ray, one of the few friends I didn't mind sharing with Carson, came over and started putting his best moves on Natalie and me. We couldn't help but laugh at all the corny pickup lines he was using. Then, before we knew it, the class was over.

Tuesday and Wednesday went by like every other day. Natalie hadn't brought up Carson since Monday, but I didn't question it until Wednesday after school. I was walking to my brothers' truck when Carson walked up to me, looking pissed.

"What the hell did you tell Natalie?" He fumed.

I brushed past him, "What are you talking about? I tell her a lot of things."

"Don't play dumb with me, Casey; I know you told her about Lindsey."

"So what?"

"So she hasn't been talking to me much the last few days, and I asked her what was wrong. She got mad and told me she didn't want to be my rebound. Where the hell would she get that idea other than from you? You're the one who thinks I'm still hung up on Lindsey," his talking had turned to quiet shouting just as my brothers came up to us.

"Whoa, man, calm down. What's going on?" Camden asked, grabbing Carson's shoulder.

"Ask your sister," he replied gruffly. I swear he's more dramatic than a woman; nevertheless, my brothers turned their sharp gazes on me. I knew I could get out of this by letting a few tears fall, but then they would all call me a baby. So instead, I put on my strongest face and defended myself.

"She's my friend. I'm trying to keep her from getting hurt," I said with anger palpable in my voice.

"And you think I'm going to hurt her?" Carson said as more of an accusation than a question.

"She has enough on her plate without being in a relationship with someone who isn't over his ex," I replied as we all climbed into the truck. "And just so you know, I didn't tell her not to be with you. I just gave her the facts so she could make her decision."

"Except those aren't facts. For the millionth time, I'm over Lindsey."

"Well, she sure as hell isn't over you. She tries to scare off every girl who comes near you."

"That's not true. I still have plenty of girls around me."

"Great, so you're a player, and she would have to deal with a crazy mean girl."

"Well, she already deals with you." When he said that, I saw my brothers grin, but neither of them joined in the conversation. They knew it was better just to let us fight it out on our own.

"You're such an ass. I'm trying to be a good friend to you and her. You aren't ready for a relationship, and you know Lindsey will make her life hell if you all get together."

"She will not. I'll talk to her and get her to leave Nat alone." He was starting to look desperate for me to agree with him. I don't know why she's so important to him. He hardly even knows her.

We pulled into Carson's driveway a few minutes later. As soon as he was out of the truck, my brothers turned on me.

"Why the hell would you do that?" Camden started at the same time Cooper said, "I think Natalie would be good for him."

"Are you all seriously taking his side again? I am trying to protect my friend. Besides, he isn't ready to be in a relationship again. All he knows how to do is have sex, not real relationships." I said as my blood began boiling. My brothers took Carson's side in arguments ninety percent of the time, and the other ten they just stayed out of it.

"The best way to get over someone is to get under someone else. I've been telling him that since he found out Linds cheated, so I'm glad he is taking my advice," Cooper said, sounding like a proud father. He was the wilder of my brothers. Camden, on the other hand, has always been more mature and responsible when he has to be.

"Cooper may have a point here, Case. Carson needs to figure out what a relationship with someone other than Lindsey looks like. I'm not saying he needs to sleep with her like Cooper thinks is the answer to everything," he said while giving my brother a pointed glare. "But, you keep talking about how good of a person Natalie is, so why don't you let him have a shot with her? She would be good for him."

I hate that Camden can always talk me into doing things I think are a bad idea. Everyone says I got our mom's political side, but I guess Camden did too. He just doesn't use it as much as I do.

When we walked in the house, our parents were swapping spit like two teenagers in the backseat of a truck on a gravel road.

"Get a room!" Cooper yelled at them.

"They are all our rooms. It's our house," my dad said while giving my mom a few more kisses.

My parents are always all over each other. I guess I should be glad that my parents are still so in love after almost twenty years of marriage, but it can be a little embarrassing when they are grabbing at each other in public. My dad is a surgeon. He grew up in New York and met my mom when she was in college up there. She loved New

York because it was a party every night, but my dad didn't want to raise his kids there, so they came back to Criden - my mom's hometown. She is a socialite. She's always pushed me to be just like her, and I have so far, but I don't know how she is going to react when she finds out I want to be a teacher. She never pushes my brothers like she does me. I guess that's because Camden has always been set on being just like my dad, and Cooper doesn't seem to ever want to grow up. I am her only hope, and as much as I don't want to disappoint her, I can't imagine doing what she does. Book clubs, charity dinners, prestigious societies, it's always wearing a fake smile and putting on a show. I want to do something meaningful with my life, but she doesn't understand that, so I'm just not going to tell her.

"Casey!" My mom yelled, snapping me out of my daze.

"What?" I replied, trying to pretend I had been listening.

"How was your day? Your brothers said you're fighting with Carson again," fake concern was etched in her voice.

I rolled my eyes at my brothers. They always share my business with my parents, especially if it has to do with Carson, because then my mom won't let it go until she knows every detail. She believes that we should never fight with family.

"It's nothing, Mom. I just don't think he's ready for another relationship,"

"Now, how would you know that? Are you a mind reader now?"

"Mom! He treats the girls that he messes around with like trash. I'm not letting him do that to my friend."

"He isn't going to do that. He's a good boy."

"But a boy nonetheless," my dad finally chimed in.

"Thank you, Dad" he rarely got into my mom and I's arguments, so any input from him in my favor was great.

"What are you talking about, Mitch?" My mom said with an accusation.

"He's a boy. He thinks with a different head, and it doesn't always think to treat girls well," my dad explained.

"Mitch, he's not like that. He's smart and sweet. He's been through hell, cut him some slack," my mom persuaded. Carson hadn't been through anything, so what if his dad is a drunk? His mom is a saint who always made sure he had everything.

"Honey, he is a teenage boy, but you know what? If you think he isn't going to hurt her, then I'm sure you are right."

Of course, my dad would fold. He always does what my mom tells him to. He treats her like a queen. They are my model of a perfect relationship. I want a relationship like theirs for myself and everyone around me: including Carson and Natalie, separately. It doesn't matter what anyone else wants, though. The ball is in Natalie's court, and right now, I am perfectly happy with her choice of rejecting him.

October 21st

Chapter 7 - Aaron

Football season is going by in a flash. We only have one game left of the regular season, and so far, we are undefeated. This has been the best season the school has had in nearly a decade, and everyone is crediting it to me and Carson. We finally started working together after the first few practices, and now we are unstoppable when we are both on our game. He's one of the first people who has been able to look past where I come from and treat me like an equal competitor and teammate instead of a charity case. This is turning into the best year of my life.

I've always loved watching home football games on Friday nights, but being down on the field is an entirely different feeling. I feel like everyone is cheering for me. Rose has told Ashley and me a million times that this town wants to see us succeed, and when I'm on the field, that couldn't feel more true. Tonight was no exception; my name was announced, and I ran out to chest bump Cooper while the crowd was an eruption of cheers. I took in the moment I could never get enough of: the band blaring the school fight song, the crowd screaming as we took our spots on the sidelines, the bright stadium lights making the fall night sky look like day, and the energy of myself and my team pulsing around me. It was time to get in position for the kickoff.

I watched the first play take place as the other team's kicker kicked the ball perfectly to the point where Carson was waiting. He catches it easily and takes off down the field. Once he reaches the other team's forty-yard line, he is taken down by a lineman twice his size. I ran out on the field and readied myself for the ball to be snapped to me. As soon as it is, I start down the field and look for an opportunity to get the ball back to Carson. I lob the ball towards him a split second before I'm brought down by half of the Newport defensive line. I heard the high pitch of the ref's whistle as I was getting back to my feet. Carson had missed the pass, and Newport had gotten the ball. I ran to the sideline and watched as Newport easily scored the first touchdown of the game. Our next possession was a turnover. Our offense couldn't get very far without being taken down. After Newport scored two more times and we had turned the ball over again and again, I finally decided I needed to figure out what was going on with Carson and why he was playing like he had never caught a football.

"What the hell is wrong with you, man?" Camden said, beating me to the question.

"Nothing, these guys are just on me harder than I expected. I'm working on it," Carson huffed, acting like everything was fine, obviously lying, but he didn't seem like he wanted to be pushed on this.

The rest of the first half went the same way, and by the end of it, the scoreboard showed forty-one to zero. As we took our first few steps off the field, the first few raindrops fell and then quickly turned into a downpour. The thunder and lightning were quick to follow. We hustled into the locker room and plopped down on the benches.

"Perfect, a rain delay. Nixley, maybe this will be your chance to get your head out of your ass!" Coach screamed at Carson when he came in.

"I'm sorry, Coach. I'm working on it," Carson sounded like a wounded animal. He started taking off his pads like the rest of us and revealed a large bruise hiding under the bottom of his shirt.

"What is that, Carson?" I asked, pulling on the bottom of his shirt and showing Cooper and Camden a bruise of green, purple, red, and yellow coloring that was larger than my hand.

"It's just from that hit I took earlier. I swear that asshole, Linds is with has been targeting me all night," Carson growled, pulling down his shirt.

"Oh, so Blasser is your problem? He's an idiot, and so is Lindsey. I guess Case is right about you not being over her," Camden replied in his all-knowing, fatherly tone.

"Are we seriously talking about this, again? No, I am not still hung up on Lindsey. She can date whoever the fuck she wants, okay? I'm tired of her making a fool out of me. If it's not her, then it's her oaf of a boyfriend. I'm moving on; now I just need her to let me. So how about you dumbasses, just leave me alone about it?" Carson snapped loud enough for the rest of the locker room to hear him.

38

"Chill, dude, you've been such a damn hothead since Linds cheated on you. Good luck getting anyone, especially Natalie, to date you when you're acting like that. Are you trying to be more like your dad?" Cooper spit at him, obviously hitting Carson below the belt.

"Shut the hell up!" Carson said through gritted teeth while shoving Cooper into the nearest locker.

"What the fuck, Carse!" Cooper yelled, shoving him back.

After a few more shoves, Carson threw the first punch straight for Cooper's nose. Camden was in the middle of it before anyone else could pull them apart. As I moved to grab Carson, to keep him from beating the shit out of his own family, I felt someone's fist connect with my jaw. It was a few more minutes of fists flying from nearly a quarter of the team before Coach Harley was able to break us up.

"Boys, what is wrong with you?" He yelled. "You all look like you just got done in an MMA fight! I can't let you all play like this!"

He continued cursing as he walked away from all of us while pulling out his phone.

"Look what you did now!" Carson hollered, back on his warpath.

"You know what, Carson? Maybe you should go take a walk." Camden fired back while tending to his brother's injuries. When Carson reached the locker room door, he was met by Coach, wearing a more disappointed look than I had ever seen him wear before.

"Sit down, Nixley," He said as he turned to the rest of us. "I hope you boys are proud of yourselves because we just forfeited the game. All of you boys who think it's funny to play boxing match in the locker room can sit out of next week's game too. You hear that, Nixley and Johnson?"

"Yes, sir," Cooper replied. Carson remained silent.

"Pack up your shit, boys. I'll see you bright and early Monday morning for the worst practice you've ever been through. Now get out!" Coach yelled.

The rain had ended already, so we all made our way out of the locker room in silence and went our separate ways. I heard car doors slamming as many of the guys climbed in their trucks. All of us were pissed about what had happened, but Carson looked like he had never been so mad, even though he was the one who started the problem.

"What the fuck is wrong with you, boy? You're lucky you didn't get expelled! Get your ass in the car; we'll talk about this when we get home!" A man, I assume is Carson's dad, hollered loud enough to be heard by everyone in the parking lot. I had heard Carson's dad was kind of a dick, but I wasn't expecting him to be making a scene like this in the parking lot of a high school football game. I guess that's why it pissed Carson off so much when Cooper said he was acting like his dad. However, it was not my place to get involved in family drama, so I kept my head down until I reached Ashley, who was waiting for me at the parking lot exit.

"Where's mom?" I asked Ashley. She wasn't supposed to be out here by herself.

"I told her to go home. She was drunk," She said at the same time as I noticed that her cheeks were tear-stained.

"Ash, I'm sorry you had to deal with that on your own. I'll take care of it as soon as we get home." I reassured her as I wrapped her in my arms.

"I'm not so sure she'll be their Aaron. She was really messed up and really mad that I was telling her what to do. She said she wasn't going to let her child tell her what to do and that if she wanted to do what she wanted, she would go somewhere she is appreciated."

"Ash, everything will be alright. We've been on our own before, and if this is how she wants to be, we will be on our own again."

Familiar dread filled the rest of the walk home. My mom has been in and out of my life for as long as I can remember, but she has always had a way of hurting Ashley. She always believes the best in our mom, no matter how many times she makes the same terrible decisions. I knew my mom wouldn't be at home when we got there, but that didn't relieve the pain and anger I felt at seeing Ashley collapse in tears into the same old, broken recliner that had acted as her bed when she was a toddler.

"Come on, Ash. Get to bed. We'll go see Rose in the morning and see who she knows that has jobs for us." I reassured her.

"What about football?"

"Football doesn't matter, Ashley! Keeping this damn roof over your head is what matters! Making sure you don't go to school hungry is what matters, but our piece of shit mom doesn't seem to understand that! Now go to bed. We'll deal with this in the morning." I couldn't help but get frustrated with her. For how smart she is, she is incredibly naive when it comes to our mom, and I don't understand why.

I heard my mom stumbling into the house around one in the morning, but I knew that if I got up to check on her, she would turn into a crying mess, begging for forgiveness like she always does after her benders. So I stayed in bed and pretended to be asleep until I heard her bedroom door close. The next morning Ashley was up before I was, and she was already reassuring our mom that what she did was okay.

"Ashley, go get dressed. I want to get to Rose's early, so I can start on whatever she needs," I said gruffly as I walked into the room. She knew better than to argue with me and slowly left the room with her head down.

"I'm so sorry, honey. I got a little messed up last night. I just had a bad day," my mom pleaded through tears that no longer had an effect on me.

"I don't want to hear it, Mom. You screwed up. Again. You hurt Ash and me. Again. You said you were going to stay clean this time, and I guess I'm the idiot because I was actually starting to believe you."

"You don't understand."

"No, Mom, you don't understand. I'm seventeen and know more about being a parent than you do. I'm the reason you still have a place to stumble home to. I'm the reason you still have custody of Ashley and me. So I don't want to hear your excuses or empty promises anymore, Mom." I turned to look at her as she wiped her eyes again, and Ashley peaked her head from behind the corner of the hallway. "You ready, Ash?" With a slight nod of her head, I walked out the door without another word to my mom.

"You didn't have to be so harsh," Ashley said, breaking the silence as we walked toward Rose's house.

"You can't always just forgive her. She is a parent, she needs to act like it, and she needs to be held accountable for her actions. You have to hold your ground with her. I know you don't want to be rude, but she is supposed to take care of us, not the other way around," I could give her the same speech a million times, but she will always find a reason to forgive her. She was silent for the rest of the walk.

"May I help you?" A man who seemed to be around forty asked.

"Is Rose home? Could you tell her it's Aaron and Ashley," I replied quickly. Something about this man seemed familiar like I had met him before.

"Mom!" He called into the house. A few moments later, Rose walked up to the door. Her silver and brown hair was tied up in a bun, and she wore a loose nightgown that hid how skinny she was.

"Come in, get out of the cold. Do you want any hot chocolate, sweetie?" Rose asked as she pulled us both in for a hug. "I haven't seen you in a while. Aaron Daemon, what happened to your chin?" She squealed.

"It's nothing, Rose. Just a little bruise from the game last night." I quickly turned my face away from her before she could ask too many more questions.

"Where's your mom? I haven't seen you two without her in months. She isn't working this early on a Saturday, is she?"

"No, that's actually why we're here. I think she's off the wagon again. Do you have any jobs lined up for me? It doesn't need to be anything big. Just mowing or cleaning. You know what I can do."

"Honey, you don't have to sell yourself to me. I know you are a hard worker, but you don't really have the time for all that right now, do you?"

"Ash, can you give us a minute?" I asked, shooting my little sister a scolding look. She slowly walked out of the room. "I'm gonna quit football. It's the only way I can support both of us. All I'll need is for you to get her to school in the mornings. Please?"

"Aaron, I can't let you do that. You have been so happy playing football. You were born to play. You can't quit."

"I'm not letting her get a job. She's too young, and she shouldn't be walking all over town by herself. She can't protect herself."

"She doesn't have to. I can help you all out for a little while. At least until football season is over."

"I can't let you do that. You've already done too much for us."

"Then let me, it's my job anyway," the man who answered the door said as he walked into the living room.

"Mike, let's not do this right now," Rose scolded as only a mother could.

"I promised I would tell him before he turned eighteen. I might as well do it now while he needs me." The man said, still being vague. He then turned to me with a hand extended as I remembered why this man was familiar to me. He was the one who came and went from time to time in the year after Ashley was born. He was my father.

Before I could stop the words from falling out, I said, "You son of a bitch. Of course, you show up now."

"What's going on, Mike?" the new Mrs. Clemetts said as she appeared in the doorway with five girls behind her: one was Ashley; one was the girl Carson was after, Natalie; and the other three were miniature stair step versions of her. Mike looked as though he was going to be sick.

"Well, young man, you started this, so you might as well tell them all now," Rose scolded her son. "Girls, why don't you go play. Natalie, Norah, you should probably sit down. I'll make some hot chocolate, and we'll settle this. Finally." I sat down on the arm of the recliner Ashley had just sat in. Across the room from us, Mike and his wife and daughter were arranging themselves on the couch, looking at us as if Ashley and I were the ones on trial instead of Mike.

"I guess there's no easy way of doing this. Aaron and Ashley are my kids. I had them with my high school girlfriend after I married your mom. I'd meet up with Hannah every few weeks after your mom and I got married. Then, I found out Hannah was pregnant with Aaron. I knew I couldn't be a good partner to both of them from a different city, and I had just gotten the job in San Francisco, so I left Hannah. A year later, I started taking "business trips" to come to see her again. Then your mom got pregnant with you, so I stopped visiting for a while. When I couldn't stay away from her anymore, she got pregnant with Ashley and told me to pick between you all or her. I picked you all. I had my mom watch over them and make sure their situation never got too bad. I sent them money, and I promised my mom if Aaron hadn't started looking for me by the time he turned eighteen, I would tell him." He then turned to me. "You turn eighteen next month. I know you don't really need me anymore, but I am your father. I have always cared about you and Ashley. I just couldn't be there for you and them."

"So you just picked them? How sweet? You saw that our mom was an addict and wouldn't amount to much, so you picked the children and the wife you thought would make you look better and left us in the dumpster?" The thoughts were mine, but the words came out of my sister's mouth with more bitterness than I had ever heard from her.

"Ashley, no, it was never like that. I was married and starting a career. I couldn't give that up. I know it's not an excuse, but I thought you all would be better off. Hannah wasn't like she is now when you all were born. She was clean. I thought she would find someone who could be a better dad to you than I could."

"And all these years while she was a mess, you never felt an obligation to come back?" I questioned while climbing to my feet.

"Was he just supposed to abandon his family?" Natalie piped up with her voice dripping with anger.

"He did it to us pretty easily," I responded, gesturing to Ashley and myself. I was on my feet now and the anger running through me was making me hot,

"He did what was best for himself," Natalie defended.

"Thank you, Nat," Mike said as he put a loving hand on his daughter's shoulder.

"Don't!" She yelled, standing and pushing his hand off. "You aren't innocent. I know you did what you thought was best, but you still lied to all of us! And you cheated on Mom multiple times! Fuck you!"

As she made her way to what I assume is her bedroom, her father, or I guess our father, called after her. "Honey, stop. I know I screwed up, but I didn't want to lose you and your mom."

"So you just kept fucking some crackhead and lying to us instead?" She sneered at him, cutting him off. I wanted to slap her for calling my mom a crackhead. She didn't know my family or me, and she had no right to talk about her like that.

"Enough!" Her mom scolded. She hadn't said a word this whole time, but the pain she was feeling was written all over her face. "Natalie, we do not use that kind of language in this house. Go cool down. Ashley, Adam, or Asher, or whatever your name is, you all need to leave. This is a family matter."

"Norah, whether you like it or not, these kids are your family now, and his name is Aaron," Rose corrected. "I know these kids better than I know yours, and I love them equally as much, so they aren't going anywhere. Okay?"

"Rose, it's fine. We don't want to be here anyway. Thanks for everything, but I think we're good now," I told her gruffly as I grabbed Ashley's hand and pulled her toward the door.

"Please don't leave. I did everything I could. It wasn't my place to tell you," she called out with her voice cracking. As the door shut behind Ashley, I heard her begin to cry.

It hurt me to hurt the only mother figure I had ever had, but right now, her deceit hurts almost as much as Mike's. She watched us struggle all these years, and instead of telling us about our father, she made us feel like orphans: giving us handouts of food, clothes, jobs, and sometimes money. Knowing that it all came from Mike made me want to burn it all. Did he really think sending money for us made up for leaving us? I was a toddler, and Ashley was an infant, but that didn't matter because we weren't the perfect kids that he had with his perfect wife.

I was so lost in my anger I almost didn't notice Ashley stop and sink to the ground crying. I didn't need to ask her what was wrong. Ever since she was little, she had asked me what our dad was like. He left when I was five, and even then, he was hardly around enough to be considered a dad, so there wasn't much I could tell her; instead, we would make up stories about the perfect dad and why he left. Usually, it was because he was secretly a prince or a spy, not some washed-up high school athlete who became an accountant. She had obviously held onto that fascination, and reality just came crashing down on her. I sat down on the curb with her and just let her cry. The glare she gave me as I sat down was enough to tell me she did not want me to touch her. She was mad at me. I wasn't sure if it was because of how I treated Rose or because she had already forgiven Mike for leaving us. It wouldn't surprise me if she had; I know I haven't fulfilled her need for a father figure.

"It's not her fault," she said after a while.

"She hid it from us. I know she wanted Mike to tell us, but she lied to us. Why do you think she never had pictures of him in the house?" I questioned. "She didn't want us to figure it out. She might as well have abandoned us too."

"But she didn't. She watched over us when no one else did and made sure we didn't starve or freeze. She took us to and from school every day until we were old enough to go by ourselves. She babysat me while you worked. She is my best friend. You are never home, so she is the only person I have," Ashley cried.

I hated knowing that she felt that way. I work all the time for her. It's my job to take care of her.

"I'm sorry," I whispered as I pulled her to my chest. I immediately felt her tears wetting my shirt. She continued to cry until a silver Honda Civic we both knew well stopped in front of us.

"Please come back with me. Just let us explain. He doesn't expect you to let him be your dad; he just wants to get to know you," Rose pleaded. When neither of us moved, she continued. "I'm sorry, I had to let him do this himself. It was one of those lessons that a child had to learn for themselves. I didn't want to lie to you, but I wanted to be part of your lives. I love you both. I never meant to hurt you. I'm sorry. I told Mike when Ashley was born that I was going to be in your life whether he wanted me to or not." She was crying now, and Ashley was crying harder.

"It's alright. We understand, and I'm sorry for what I said. I know you did everything you could, but I can't forgive him." I told her as I stepped up to the car door.

"Aaron," Ashley started, but I cut her off before she could get any further.

"Sending money is not enough to make up for abandoning us with a good for nothing drug addict of a mother, so no, Ashley, don't try to convince me to forgive him. My mind is made up, but I do have some more questions for him and the people he abandoned us for," I spit out at my little sister before climbing into the passenger seat of Rose's old Honda.

"Please, don't take this out on anyone other than Mike. The girls didn't know," Rose reminded me.

I knew she was right, I needed to focus on who I was really angry with: my parents. Both of them had given me up for something else: my dad for his other family and my mom for her addiction. They left me to all of the heavy lifting in raising myself and Ashley. Neither one of them deserve my forgiveness, and I'm not going to give it to them.

Before long we were pulling into Rose's driveway, and my sister was climbing out with her face still stained with tears. I grabbed her hand and gave it a light squeeze before following Rose into the house.

"Are you fucking kidding me? You can't just expect me to accept the kids you have with your mistress into our family!" Norah screamed from the other room. She was obviously just as thrilled with this situation as I was.

"For the hundredth time, she isn't my mistress! We were together long before I ever met you, and before last night I hadn't seen her in thirteen years." Mike explained to his wife.

"You saw her last night?" I asked accusingly.

"You came back!" Mike exclaimed as if he hadn't heard my question.

"Not for you. Now, answer the question. You saw her last night?" I repeated more angrily.

"I ran into her at the grocery store; why?" He acted like he had no idea why I was here in the first place.

"Of course, you were the reason she got drunk last night. I mean, you are the reason she has a problem in the first place." I reminded him. "My mom is a drunk because you left her twice with no money and two kids to raise!"

"That was not my fault! Your mother pushed me away! After you were born, I asked her to come with me to San Francisco. I told her about Norah. I wanted you all to be part of my family, but when she found out I was married, she told me to leave." He explained with pleading eyes. He wanted me to believe him, and part of me did, but how could I believe him over the only parent I had.

51

"And when you got her pregnant again? She just forgave you? What did you do? Tell her you were going to leave your other family for us?"

"It wasn't like that." He said more to his wife than to me. "I came back to visit, to see you. With your mom working three jobs, she had agreed to let my mom watch you over the summer, so she wouldn't have to pay for daycare. My mom made arrangements for me to see you once a month. We hid it well when you were first born. Your mom didn't know until I had been coming to see you until after Natalie was born. You were almost two then. When she found out, she was furious. She was so protective over you. When you all were young, she was such a great mom. She was clean, and she did everything she could for you all."

"So what, she got mad at you, so you fucked her into letting you see your kid? Is that what you're trying to tell me?"

"Good lord, you are so much like her! Could you stop putting words in my mouth for five damn minutes so that I can explain?" he was angry now, and he should be. I wanted him to feel what I was. "No, I didn't just sleep with your mom to get her to let me see you. I was still in love with her, but I was in love with Norah too. After a few conversations, I got her to agree to letting me see you and seeing you turned into seeing her too. I came back every month for more than a year before she got pregnant with Ashley, and I still visited while she was pregnant and for a few months after she was born. Then Norah got suspicious, so I told Hannah I would have to stop visiting because I didn't want to ruin my marriage; she asked me to leave again. I

52

hated leaving you all, but I thought I was leaving you in good hands with your mom. She was stable then, clean."

"Yeah, and once she wasn't, you were too worried about your other family to give a damn about us!"

"Enough! I'm tired of listening to you all bicker! Shut the hell up and come to a compromise already. Aaron, I know you don't want to accept him as your dad, but at least accept the fact that right now you need money, and he has money." Rose said finally. She was fuming, and I had never seen her this upset.

"I don't want his money!" I shouted at her without meaning to.

"Well, too damn bad! I'm not letting you quit football because you are too damn stubborn to accept what's being handed to you." She demanded back.

"Please, Aaron. Let me help you and Ashley. I know I've failed as your father, but this is something I can do. And who knows, maybe this could lead to me actually getting to know you all." My father looked at me with pleading eyes. Maybe I'm just naive, or maybe part of me wanted to believe that the man in front of me really could be the dad I always wanted, so I agreed.

"Fine," I told him. "We don't need much, and I'll work for it. Just a hundred to get us started."

Before I could stop him, he was handing me a check for five hundred dollars. "Maybe you've been away from Tennessee for too long, but groceries don't exactly cost that much, and I don't have enough time to work for that much."

"You want to work for it? Fine. You and your sister have dinner with me once a week, and, as long as you do that, I'll give you as much money as you want. I just want to get to know my kids," he responded sullenly.

"Deal," Ashley interjected before I said anything. "We'll meet you here Wednesday night at seven. No excuses. Now let's go."

Before I knew it, my little sister was leading me out of Rose's house with a five hundred dollar check in my hand.

Chapter 8 - Carson

"You want to explain yourself, boy?" My dad yelled. It was a rhetorical question. He never really cared about anything I did or why, especially if it made him look bad.

"I'm sorry, I just got mad," I mumbled.

"That's not a fucking excuse!" My dad growled as he grabbed me by the collar of my t-shirt.

"Danny!" my mom shrieked as she moved to pull him off of me.

"Stay out of this, Belle!" he grumbled, shoving her off. She stumbled backward into the counter, but I knew she would face worse if she tried to protect me.

"Mom, it's fine. Go to bed. I'll take care of it," I reassured her.

"But..." she began

"Go," I demanded.

My dad wasted no time once my mom left the room. "You think you are so tough," his fist connected with the wall next to my head. "You think you are brave for fighting your cousin in the damn locker room," his next hit was low, a punch to my thigh. It wouldn't leave much of a mark. "You think you are brave facing me on your own," his third shot never missed, a kidney shot, the cause of the easy-to-hide ever-growing bruise on my side.

"Leave her alone, Dad," I grunted through the pain.

"I know, I know. You take the hits for your mom. You think that makes you brave, son? It doesn't. It makes you a fucking fool, and it makes her weak!" He hit me once more, a hard shove to the chest this time, enough to make my head bounce off the wall behind me. "You want to be a man, start fighting over things that matter, you piece of shit!" He whispered, leaning in closer. The alcohol on his breath burned my nose.

He'd hardly remember this in the morning. I would remember it, though; I remembered every hit I had ever taken from him. I would never be able to turn him in, though; I had promised my mom that as long as he no longer hurt her, I wouldn't call the police. Instead, I did the same thing I did every time: made sure he went to bed peacefully, iced my injuries, cleaned up any messes around the house, and then went to bed.

As I expected, the next morning, my dad was at the kitchen table looking at his computer as he did every morning. My mom poured more coffee into the cup that surely had whiskey in it already. To anyone looking in, we looked like a perfect, ordinary family, but I was sickened by the distorted image that my mom and I had so carefully crafted to protect the hateful man we both loved and loathed. I ignored it like I always did. I kissed my mother on the cheek, announced that I was going for a run, and left without another word.

I needed to apologize to Cooper and Camden for the shit I started in the locker room. I walked the three blocks to my cousin's house and knocked on the door. My aunt Alice opened the door.

"Hey Alice, are Coop and Cam awake? I asked her quietly.

"They are, but before you come in, I'd like to chat with you," she said as she stepped outside, closing the door. "What the hell happened last night?"

"Al, I'm so sorry about that. That's why I'm here. I want to apologize. I got upset, and I overreacted. When Cooper brought up my dad, I lost it, and I know it was wrong, but you know how it is with him. I don't ever want to be like him." I rambled with a breaking voice.

She pulled me into a hug. "You will never be like your dad, hon. You are a great young man, way better than your father was at your age. Don't get me wrong, he always treated your mother like a queen, but he was never the people-person you are. He was always so business-focused and didn't realize how poor his temper was. You are not him. Don't let your temper get in the way like he does. I believe in you, honey. Now go talk to your cousins, and trust me, they aren't mad at you." As she let me go, she patted me on the back.

Then she stood and walked with me into the house where all three of my cousins were bickering about what happened last night. Although, I was surprised to find that Camden was the only one not on my side.

"Cooper knew that what he said would set him off. I don't understand why you are so pissed off," Casey defended.

"Wow! I don't think you have ever defended me, Case," I interrupted.

"What the hell are you doing here?" Camden asked through gritted teeth.

"I want to apologize for last night. Cam, I know I was stupid, and I didn't mean for it to go that far," I explained.

"You know what, Carson, I'm not going to keep forgiving you for this shit. You make mistakes and lose your temper, and then you blame it on how you were raised. At least when your dad gets pissed off, he's drunk and doesn't use his fist," Camden fired back. I had never told anyone about my dad being abusive, and I wasn't about to change that even if it would help my case.

"You're right. That's why I'm trying to apologize. I was a dick last night, and I know that. And maybe you were right about Natalie too. I deserve to be with girls like Lindsey who are possessive, controlling, and cheat on me."

"Oh, there you go again with the whole woe is me routine. Grow up!"

"Cam, I am really trying here to tell you that I'm sorry. Do you think I went into that locker room last night and thought, 'I'm going to start a fight with my best friends, with my family? No, I didn't. I'm sorry. Okay?"

"Fuck off," Camden said quietly as he turned his back to me and walked towards his room.

His door slammed shut suddenly, and Casey and Cooper, who hadn't said anything through the whole exchange, looked at me stunned. None of us had ever seen Camden that mad. I hated that I was on the receiving end of it.

"Don't worry about it, man. He'll get over it," Cooper said finally.

"Yeah, he's just being dramatic. You know how protective he gets," Casey reassured.

"I guess I'm just used to being on the other side of it,' I told them.

"Well, we are used to you being protective over us too, but when it comes to your dad, it seems like you'd hurt just about anyone for him," anger was seeping into Cooper's voice as he began defending his brother.

"I'm sorry. I feel like a total jerk right now. I didn't mean for it to get out of hand," I tried to explain again.

"I know Carson. I'm not mad at you. I know I crossed a line, and you were just defending your dad. It's the same thing I would've done if someone would've said something about you, Casey, Camden, my parents, or your parents. We're family, and you were just doing your job in defending our family, even if it was against me," Cooper reasoned with me. "I'll talk to Cam for you," and with that, he headed toward his brother's room.

"So, are you still on my side?" I asked Casey.

"About hitting Cooper? Yeah. About Natalie? No. I still don't think you are ready to be in a relationship with anyone. You need a rebound, not a girl who knows nothing about you. Not my friend," she started.

"So that's what this is about? You don't want me to steal your friend?" I questioned her in disbelief.

"No. As I told you before, I don't want you to hurt my friend. You getting mad at the game last night just proved that you are still hung up on Lindsey. Cooper told me it was about Lindsey's boyfriend playing rough. I trust you, but"

"But not with her. Right?" I interrupted.

"Carson, I know how you are with girls. You treat them like play-things until you get bored. Hell, it's hard to say how many girls in our school you have slept with. She's not a toy Carson!"

"You think I don't know that?"

"Please, Carson, just stay away from her."

"Fine," I said, ending the conversation just as my parents walked in the front door. "What's going on, Mom?"

"Family meeting!" she called out and then waited as my aunt, uncle, and cousins trickled in from their rooms.

"Mom?" I asked again, my voice shakier this time. She was worrying me. My mom never hid anything from me. "What's going on?" I said for a third time as everyone settled in.

My parents stood in front of us, looking closer than ever. "We're moving," my dad said as if he had just told us it was raining outside.

"What?" I asked, rising to my feet.

"Just for a few months. Your dad has a case in Nashville, so we are going to rent a house down there," my mom soothed.

"Where is this coming from? What about your job? What about Carson? Bee, have you thought this through?" Alice questioned without giving my mom a chance to answer. Alice had always been in the big sister role, even though she and my mom are twins.

"Alice, will you please calm down. Yes, I have thought this through. I quit my job. Danny makes enough money to support us, and he asked me to come with him. As for Carson, I was hoping he could stay with you," she answered, eyeing my aunt and uncle pleadingly.

"Belle, don't you think that is something you and I should have discussed in private? Of course, you didn't! This affects my family too, Belle! How could you be this selfish? What the hell are you thinking?" Alice snapped. She and my mom rarely fought. They are best friends as much as they are sisters, so seeing them upset with one another was surprising. "Kids, go downstairs," Alice ordered.

"Mom..." Casey began.

"Now!" We all rose from the couch at my aunt's demand and quickly made our way down the stairs.

Once we reached the basement living room, where we had spent many hours playing house, making pillow forts, and wrestling, the yelling began. However, our parents weren't the ones yelling.

"I can't believe they want you to live with us! They have to be kidding," Camden exclaimed as I paced around the seventies style plaid couch that sat in the middle of the room. The entire main floor of their house looked like it belonged in a magazine, but the basement was specifically for us kids, so my aunt and uncle used all the furniture from their first house to furnish it.

"Chill out, Cam!" Cooper scolded him as he grabbed a beer out of the mini-fridge Alice used to stock with soda and snacks for us.

"Seriously, I'm no happier about this than you are. It's my living situation that they are talking about. I should be a part of the conversation." It came out as more of a whine than assertion.

"Will all of you shut up!? I am trying to hear what's going on!" Casey hissed from the middle of the staircase. We all fell silent, which is all we could hear from upstairs as well. Then my dad's voice boomed.

"She's my wife. She's not fucking staying here!" I winced at the sound. He was obviously mad, and I had no doubt that he would have a tight grip on either her wrist or her side if we were at home. I couldn't let him be alone with her for months; there's no telling what he would do to her, especially when he's under the stress of a big case. I started up the stairs, and before my cousins could stop me, I had reached the top.

"Don't you think I should get a say in this?" I interrupted whatever Uncle Mitch was saying.

"Carson, go downstairs!" my dad demanded.

"I'm not a little kid anymore. You can't just pawn me off on people when you go on business trips. I'm sixteen. I can stay home alone." I argued, never looking my dad in the eyes.

"No, you can't. That's called abandonment, and last time I checked, you can't do anything for yourself. You can't cook, or clean, or pay bills!" He said with his voice rising as the list went on. "So no, Carson, you can't stay home alone, and unless you want to go with us and move away from the school you have been at for ten years, I suggest you go back downstairs and don't interrupt us again. Alright?" By this time, he was in my face. I am six foot three, taller than him, and I have twenty-five pounds more muscle than him, but no matter how old I get, he always makes me feel like I am still five years old. I peered over his shoulder at my aunt, uncle, and cousins, all looking horrified; he never yelled at me like this outside of our house. Out of the corner of my eye, I saw my mom pleading with her eyes to let it go so he would calm down.

"Fine," I muttered, shoving past him as I made my way back downstairs. I knew I would pay for it tonight, but it was nice to stand up for myself for once.

"What the hell was that about?" Cooper asked, still questioning my father's outburst. I didn't answer him; instead, I aimed my anger at the punching bag under the staircase. After a few minutes, I was out of breath, and my knuckles were throbbing where they were still sore from the night before. I finally sank down onto the concrete floor without a word. My cousins all stared at me as if I needed an exorcism or something until Casey finally broke the silence with a snarky accusation.

"You really think you'd be able not to hurt her when that's your reaction to your dad?"

"You're fucking joking, right? You want to use me fighting with my dad over where I'm going to live as a reason not to let me date

63

Natalie. She's not your fucking kid. You don't get to make decisions for her," I yelled while my hands slowly balled into fists. I knew better than to ever hit Casey, but that didn't mean I didn't want to sometimes.

"I'm not making a decision for her. I'm just not going to lie to her so you can toy with her!"

"Oh my God! Will you all just drop this already? She's just a girl! Casey stop being a bitch and let Carson and Natalie make their own decisions. Carson grow a pair and stand up to Casey. If you really want to date Natalie, just talk to the damn girl. Just shut the hell up!" Cooper scolded, slamming down his empty beer can. "And you two," he said, pointing his finger at Camden and me. "Just fucking kiss and make up already. Us kids hate seeing Mom and Dad fight." His and Casey's puppy dog eyes made all of us laugh.

"What do you say, Cam? We still brothers?" I held my hand out to him.

He grabbed my hand, pulled me into a hug, and slapped me on the back. "Brothers."

"Aww, it's so beautiful. I think I might cry," Cooper joked while pretending to wipe a tear from his cheek.

"Shut up, you idiot. Can we talk about the fact that I might have to live with you all? That's insane." I plopped down on the couch, and my cousins followed my lead.

"Ugh, it's going to be like a frat party every night!" Casey complained.

Cooper, Cam, and I all turned to each other in unison and shouted, "Yes!" Casey just rolled her eyes. We goofed around for another hour or so before we were called upstairs to join our parents in their family meeting. We all four crammed onto the couch and looked up at our parents standing in front of us. It felt like we were little kids again getting in trouble for something.

"So we've talked about it, and for the next few months, Carson will be staying here with us," Mitch told us what we already knew. I eyed my parents. There had to be something they weren't telling us. "You won't be moving in until next Monday, Carson, so until then, we will work on moving your stuff into the spare in the basement where you will be staying. We can move the least important things first, and of course, we'll get you a bed to keep here, so you don't have to move yours. Same with your dressers. Obviously, you will still have access to the house, too, so it's not a huge deal if you forget something."

"How long are we talking about here, Mom?" I asked, trying to keep my voice from breaking.

"Only about five months," my mom responded as if she had said five days rather than months.

"Five months?!" I gasped.

"Honey, it's going to be okay, we'll still come home to see you, and I'll call you." She knelt down in front of me and talked to me like a child.

I couldn't hold back my tears anymore. My mom is my entire world. It is my job to protect her. "Why do you have to go with him?" I sounded like a little kid now.

"Honey, he's my husband; that's how marriage works wherever he goes, I go too."

"Bullshit! You're lying to me! I know it! What are you not telling me, Mom?" I shouted, rising to my feet. I didn't care if it seemed like I was throwing a tantrum. This whole situation was screwed up.

"Carson, calm down now!" My dad demanded, grabbing onto my wrist.

"Dammit, Dad! Let me go!" I shoved him away from me and rushed out the front door. As soon as I got outside, I started running. I could hear my dad cursing at me, but I didn't stop. I heard his truck start toward me but still kept running.

"Carson, get in the damn truck! You're being dramatic," my dad pulled his truck next to me and got out.

"You really think I'm going to let you take her with you, just so she can be your punching bag?" I accused, still keeping my pace. Running had always been my outlet when I was upset. It kept me from punching someone or screaming.

"Your mother is pregnant, Carson. I'm sorry, but I don't feel comfortable leaving her here for you to take care of." I stopped abruptly

"What?" I sat down on the street in shock. "When did you find out?" Was my mom seriously going to let this man get his hands on another kid?

"Yesterday, that's why I was so upset after your game. I was in shock. I'm sorry about last night, but I promise you I'm going to change. I'm going to be better for you and your mom and this new

66

baby. I was mad at first, but I feel like this is my second chance to be a good dad and husband."

"Do Mitch and Alice know?" was the only thing I could think to ask.

"Yes, we told them this morning, and we are planning to tell the rest of the family tonight at dinner. Would you like to join us?" I didn't answer him. Instead, I climbed into the truck. "You don't feel like running back?" he joked, but I didn't find him funny.

"Why didn't you all tell me first?" I asked.

"You weren't exactly in a mood to discuss things rationally this morning, and we wanted to make sure we had somewhere for you to stay before we told you." I didn't respond. After less than a minute's drive, we were back at my cousins' house. We all quickly said our goodbyes before going back home. My dad retired to his office like he always did, and my mom and I made our way to the living room.

"How far along are you?" I asked as soon as she sat down. She looked exhausted, so I quickly grabbed her a glass of water.

"Three months," she said, calmly taking the glass from my hand.

"I can't believe you would do this! Why would bring another child into this house with HIM?"

"Don't you think I thought about it, Carson? That's why I waited so long to tell him, and trust me, his reaction wasn't very reassuring at first, but it seems like he really wants this baby now."

"Of course he does. He wants someone else that he can take his anger out on because I'm stronger than him now, and he knows I won't let him hurt you."

"He isn't going to hurt me while I'm pregnant."

"Really? You want to take that chance? Who's going to protect you if you're three hours away?"

"Carson, that's enough. I am the parent, and you are the child. Not the other way around. You do not get to question my decisions. I understand your concerns, but I've had enough. Go to your room! I'm not dealing with this." There was no use arguing with her, so I did as she said and went to my room. I stayed there until it was time to go to dinner. About five minutes before we were supposed to leave, my dad informed us that he was too busy to go to dinner. It hadn't even been five hours since my dad had promised he would be a better dad and husband, and he was already failing. How am I supposed to trust him alone with my mom for five months?

We went to dinner, and my mom told my cousins her big news. They were surprised. Casey was excited to have a baby in the family finally, and Coop and Cam were excited to see how I would handle not being an only child. I tried to explain to them that it wouldn't be the same for me as it is for them because of the age gap, but they continued to tell me how much of a pain in the ass younger siblings are.

Sunday was the same as it always was: church in the morning, brunch with my aunt, uncle, and cousins, and then getting ahead on any homework I could. This has been my routine since

Kindergarten. Back then, I had fewer assignments, and after I let my mom check my take-home folder, my dad and I would play in the yard or the living room. That changed when I was ten. My dad got a promotion and started working more, so my mom took over his role until I was old enough to entertain myself.

This Sunday, I used my free time to decide how I was going to go about things with Natalie. I finally decided I was going to let Natalie make her own decision about me. Screw what Casey thinks about how I'll treat her. She can choose for herself, except Natalie wasn't at school all next week.

Instead of focusing on her, I focused on moving. Each night we moved a little more. On Thursday, I spent hours with my mom and Alice shopping for furniture for my new room. It was like nothing else mattered to my mom other than making sure that I had everything at my aunt and uncle's house that I had at home, even though home was only five minutes away. By Sunday night, my first night in my new room, it was almost like sleeping in a replica.

On Monday, Natalie still wasn't at school in the first three hours, so I asked Casey where she was. She told me she hadn't heard from her all week. A few minutes before the bell rang to dismiss us from lunch, I saw her walk in. I immediately got up from my lunch table, not letting my friend Sam finish his story about some girl he hooked up with at his Halloween party on Saturday. I had missed it so I could spend more time with my parents before the move, but that hadn't stopped my friends from giving me shit about it. As I walked down the hallway, I was about to call out to get her attention, but Aaron beat me to it.

"Natalie," he called, but she kept her head down like she hadn't heard him. "Natalie." He called again, with more aggression this time. She kept walking. "Natalie, seriously, just let me talk to you!" He had caught up to her now and grabbed her arm to make her stop walking.

"Stop!" She smacked his hand off of her.

"Then let me talk to you!"

"I don't want to talk to you," Her voice cracked as she said it. She had been crying. Had Aaron made her cry? Was there something going on between them? Either way, she obviously didn't want to be around him, and he wasn't taking the hint.

"Nat, are you okay?" I asked as though I hadn't already been standing there.

"She's fine, Carson. I just need to talk to her about something." Aaron shot me a glare.

"I wasn't asking you, Aaron, and she said she doesn't want to talk to you."

"Carson, stay out of this. It's none of your business," He was getting angry now. There was no way I was going to let him talk to her like this. Just then, the bell rang, but I didn't move.

"Carson, I'm fine. Please, can we just go to class?" Natalie pleaded. When I looked down at her, I couldn't resist doing what she wanted. I nodded at her before we both turned away from Aaron.

"Natalie, I know you aren't happy about this situation either, but we need to talk about it," Aaron called after us as I led Natalie to English with my hand on her backpack.

"Are you alright?" I asked her as she sat down at her desk.

"I'm fine," she seemed annoyed by me asking.

"If you don't mind me asking, what was all that about?"

"Nothing." She glared at me.

"Natalie, I'm sorry. If you don't want to talk about it, that's fine."

"There's nothing to talk about," she snapped, clearly louder than she planned to. She looked surprised by her own voice.

"Okay. It's your relationship. I'm not going to pry."

"It's not a relationship!"

"Carson, Natalie, I'm going to start my class now, so if you need to finish your conversation, step outside!" Dr. Williams scolded. Natalie quickly pulled out her phone and sent a text. A few minutes later, the school secretary, Erica, called over the speaker system that Natalie was to go to the office to leave. I asked to go to the restroom as she was packing her things.

"Nat, I'm sorry. Please, don't leave," I pleaded as she stepped out into the hallway.

"God, Carson, this has nothing to do with you. I just-I can't be here right now. But I can't really deal with being at home either. I thought school would be better, but Aaron is here, and my dad is at home, and it's just too much." She was fighting back tears, and her rambling voice sounded like she was on the verge of a panic attack as she held her head in her hands.

"Do you have a car?" I asked her.

"Yeah... Why?" confusion was written all over her face.

"Go sign out and wait in your car. I'll be out in about ten minutes, okay?" She nodded. "I think I know somewhere that might help." She nodded again and walked towards the office. I went into the bathroom and returned to the class a few minutes later.

"Dr. Williams, I just got sick in the bathroom. I'm going to go to the nurse." Dr. Williams just nodded. I gathered my things and went to the nurse, who, without much questioning, told me to have my mom call the school to let me go home. My mom was concerned, but I told her I was okay and would rather stay at home tonight, so I wouldn't get anyone else sick. As much as I love my mom, she is completely naive when it comes to my lies. She called the school, and within the ten minutes I had promised her, I was sitting in Natalie's car, giving her directions to my house. Her hands shook the entire drive, and every once in a while, I would hear her sniffle. It took everything in me not to reach for her hand to calm her down. Why does this girl have such a strong effect on me?

Before we got to the house, I had her stop at the grocery store. I went in and grabbed all of my favorite comfort foods. When I got back in the car, I had four bags of food.

"What is all of that?" She said with the first laugh I had gotten from her all day.

"Chicken nuggets, potato chips, dip, ice cream, chocolate, soup, fruit snacks, and I found this cute little teddy bear for you," I told her while holding up the pink bear that was the size of my forearm.

72

"This is all the stuff my mom used to buy for me when I was sad or sick. Now, let's go." She smiled at me shyly before putting the car in drive.

When we finally got to the house, I used the keypad to open the garage and had her park inside. She walked into the dark house and made herself comfortable on the couch while I grabbed the groceries and my backpack from the car.

"What are you doing?" I questioned her as I walked into the living room.

"Oh, I'm sorry. I was just…" she looked flustered as she stood up from the couch.

I interrupted her apology. "Everyone knows you have to build a pillow fort when you are trying to get over being sad." I started moving the living room furniture into a smaller square. Then I grabbed all the blankets I could find from my bedroom.

"You're serious about this?" She asked through that loud laugh that never failed to make me smile. Screw pillow forts and comfort food that laugh could fix anything for me. I tossed a blanket at her to distract her from the smile on my face. She laughed again.

"Yes, I am serious. Now, keep working. I'm going to go get the food ready." I went into the kitchen, dumped the entire bag of chicken nuggets on a pan, and started the oven. While they were cooking, I poured the chips and chocolate into bowls and started the soup. I also grabbed two spoons and stuck them into the tub of ice cream. By the time I walked back into the living room, Natalie had built a better pillow fort than my mom and I had ever made. "Damn girl, I was starting to think I was going to have to do this on my own, but you definitely know what you're doing."

"I have three little sisters. This is not my first pillow fort." She placed the last pillow inside the fort and climbed inside.

I followed her in. "What's that like? Having younger siblings?"

"It's like having best friends and children that you can never get rid of. They drive me crazy sometimes, but I love them. Especially Macie, she's three, so it's almost like having my own kid. I've basically raised her, and she likes me more than anyone else." She paused for a second. "You're an only child, right? Casey told me."

"Yeah, I'm an only child... or at least I am for the next five months." This was the first time I had thought about that all day. It was all that had been on my mind for the last week. It had been nice not to think about my parents and the baby for a little while.

"You don't seem too happy about it," Natalie said after a few minutes. I had forgotten she was there.

"It's just a lot to get used to after sixteen years of being an only child. Besides, my dad is crazy busy with work, so it's going to be a lot for my mom."

"I'm sorry."

"It's alright, let's just say I need this as much as you do," I told her as I laid down in the fort. She paused for a minute before laying down next to me. We both had our hands by our sides, but I knew if I moved my arm slightly, my hand would be touching hers. Just as I made the decision to do just that, the timer for the oven went off.

She reached over and playfully smacked my chest. "Go get my chicken nuggets and soup," she ordered with a laugh.

"Yes, ma'am." I grabbed the old serving tray my mom used to use when my cousins and I would have sleepovers. I arranged all of the food and brought it back to the fort. As I made my way in, I caught Natalie wiping away a tear.

"Hey, what's wrong?" I whispered, setting down the tray.

Her tears started to fall faster. "Nothing." I didn't say anything else. I just pulled her closer to me and wrapped my arms around her. She continued to cry for a few minutes, then she looked up at me, let out a pitiful laugh, and said, "You probably think I'm insane. I'm such a mess." I let my arms fall from around her, but I didn't move away. Neither did she. She just reached for the tray of food. I pulled it closer to us. We both ate in silence until we had eaten more than half of the food. For a girl so small, she could definitely eat.

I laid back down when I was finished. This time, she didn't hesitate to lie down too. She was lying on her back while I lay propped up on my side. Suddenly, she turned to face me.

"He's my brother," she blurted out.

With her face so close to mine, I could hardly understand what she had said. "Who is?"

"Aaron, well, my half-brother. We have the same dad."

"Oh, I'm sorry I jumped to conclusions earlier. The way he was acting it seemed like something more. He seems protective over you."

"You mean like you are with Casey?" she started to smile, and I couldn't help but smile back. "Except you've known Casey your entire life. Aaron and I didn't even know we were related until last Saturday. He has no reason to be protective over me" She had started crying again. I reached up and wiped a tear from her cheek. Then as if the arm holding her up had given out, she leaned against me. "My dad had an affair and had two kids." She sounded more angry than sad now. "I can't believe I just told you all of that. UGH!"

She pushed herself off of me and laid flat on her back. I looked down at her. She was still close enough that when I looked down, I was practically on top of her. I could feel one of her breasts pressing against the side of my chest. I wanted to press myself against her and finally kiss her the way I had wanted to since the first day I saw her, but instead, I shifted just enough so I was no longer touching her. Maybe I imagined it, but it looked like her face fell slightly when I moved away. Then she burst out suddenly, "All I am is some rebound girl to you, and yet I just told you my family's biggest secret. What the hell is wrong with me? And what the hell is wrong with you? You act all sweet and pretend to care about my shitshow of a life when all you really want is for me to sleep with you. Don't even try to deny it; Casey already told me all about the little game you play with girls. I bet you do this all the time. You find some damsel in distress and sweep her off her feet. Well, not this time, buddy! My feet are planted. I'm not going to play your game and fall for your shitty sweetness. You are such a player!"

"Are you done?" I asked her after a few seconds.

"Yes, I am."

I sat up, and she did the same. "It's my turn then. Don't get me wrong, I love Casey, but she doesn't know everything about me, and neither do you. Yeah, I was heartbroken when Lindsey cheated on me, but that's not why I was a player. I was a player because I wanted to be. I wanted to go from girl to girl. Hell, there were times when I was sleeping with two or three different girls in a week, but they all knew about it and didn't care. I don't mess with girls without them knowing what they're getting into, but right now, I feel like that's exactly what you are doing to me. I can't tell what the hell you want from me. I like you, Nat. I care about you. Why the hell else would I have left school in the middle of the day? Why would I have spent forty dollars on a bunch of snacks I knew we weren't going to finish? Why would I have brought you to my house, which I planned to avoid until my parents came home? Do you really think I would go to this much trouble to screw you? Is that the picture that Casey painted of me?"

"That's the picture YOU have painted of yourself. You're so proud of yourself for going from girl to girl all the time. How could anyone not see you as a player?" She practically spit the words at me as she climbed out of the fort. I had to laugh at the irony of her anger mixed with the playfulness of the pillow fort. Still, I followed her.

"Wait a second. How is me not flirting with, sleeping with, and hardly even talking to any other girls since the beginning of the year making me seem like a player? I haven't had sex in more than three months because of you."

"Oh, you poor thing. I never asked you to do that. Hell, I've never asked you to do anything for me, so why the hell do you keep chasing me? Is it all about the game? Or is it more than that?" I didn't know what to tell her, so instead, I just stared. "Carson?" I stayed silent. Finally, she turned her back to me with a huff. "That's what I thought. You don't even know why. You just thought I would be a fun new toy."

"Casey would kill me. You know that, right? If anything happened between us, or if I messed around with you? So no, it's not a game because I kinda like having testicles, but it can't really be more either because, again, I like having testicles. So what do you want to do about it?"

Just then, her phone started buzzing. "Dammit, Carson, you can't say shit like that!" She smacked my arm, but this time, it wasn't playful. "Don't tell Casey about this. Okay?" I nodded, but she had already gone in search of her phone. "Dad, I just needed some air," She said into her phone. "Why? Because our family is a mess right now. That's why. I'll be home soon." She started taking pillows and blankets off of the fort.

"What just happened?" I asked her while she continued her destruction. She didn't answer. "Natalie?" She kept her focus on the fort. I lightly put my hand on her arm. She jumped as if she had forgotten I was there. "Natalie, what just happened?"

"My dad is pissed that I didn't come home and that I can't accept our situation. That's what he calls the fact that we all know about his affair now - our situation. So now he wants me home to talk, which will just turn into another yelling match. UGH, I'm so tired of dealing with it!" She was throwing pillows now.

"Nat, it's okay," I told her as I tried to wrap my arms around her. She pushed me away. "Look, don't worry about this stuff. I'll clean it up. Go home and hope for the best." I stepped away from her, and without another word, she left.

Chapter 9 - Natalie

"What the hell did I just do?" I thought to myself as I climbed into my car. What did I agree to? Am I Carson's new toy? Or am I more than that to him? What do I want to be to him? I just spent three hours with a guy, and I don't even know what I want from him. What is wrong with me? I mean, he did spend all day making sure I was okay, but that could've been part of his plan.

By the time I got home, my head was pounding from all the overthinking I was doing, and all the stress that had melted away when I was with Carson was back. I hated that he had made me feel so comfortable. I pulled into my grandma's driveway, which I guess was my driveway now, and was greeted by my dad. He was mad. I wanted to put my car in reverse and go back to Carson's house, so I wouldn't have to deal with him.

My dad threw my door open as soon as the car was parked. "Where have you been? I've been worried sick. I texted you fifteen times."

"I was driving around, and I wasn't checking my phone. I needed some time to breathe, Dad. I'm trying to process everything."

"Well, you need to process faster. You've missed way too much school, and I'm not going to let it slide anymore. Tomorrow, you will go to school, and you will be there all day. Then, on Wednesday, you will go to school. Afterward, you will drive Aaron and Ashley here, and we will have dinner together as a family. Do you understand me? This is how things are now, and you need to get used to it."

I rolled my eyes, walked past him, and went straight to my room to wait for my little sisters to get home.

After about twenty minutes, there was a knock on my door, and my grandma walked in. "He's doing his best, sweetie." She sat down next to me on my bright pink bedspread. She is my favorite part of living in Criden. Even before we moved, I would call her once a week, and we would talk for hours about everything going on in my life. I could always count on her to listen to me, but I could also always count on her to call me out.

"I'm trying too, Grandma. It's too much to deal with." I tried pleading with my biggest puppy-dog eyes, but she didn't budge.

"Don't try that with me, Honey. You have holed up in this room for the last week to avoid it. Yes, your dad had an affair. Yes, you have a brother and sister you never knew about, but don't you think this could be a good thing?" When I didn't respond, she continued. "Look, it's okay to be pissed off at your dad, but don't take it out on Aaron and Ashley. I know you don't know them, but I have known them their entire lives, and they are great kids. They didn't have a choice in this either." My face must have softened from the stony look I had put in place because my grandma smiled at me. "You are a great big sister, and that is exactly what Ashley needs. Take her under your wing like you do with the other girls. And who knows, you might like having a brother." I didn't know what to say to her, so I just hugged her instead. "Your sisters need you right now too. So does your mom. They are having a harder time than you know," she whispered into my hair.

"I'm sorry I haven't handled this very well," I told her as I pulled away.

She held me at arm's length. "There is no correct way to handle this. Now, you look tired. Get some rest before all of your "mini-mes" get home." She climbed off my bed and walked back into the living room, where she would probably go work on knitting a new blanket while she watched old reruns of "The Golden Girls." She didn't look old enough to be sixty-five, but she definitely acted like it.

My mom brought my sisters home about two hours later. Just like I did every day, I got Macie out of the car, and with her on my hip I got snacks ready for each of them. Then Maggie and Nicole played in their room, and Macie would stay with me for the rest of the night. Tonight though, Maggie went to my room and curled up in my bed. She was small for an eleven-year-old, and she looked like a tiny blob with blonde curls in my queen-sized bed.

"What's wrong, Mags?" I asked her as I set Macie down in the middle of the bed.

Little tears started streaming down her cheeks. "Does Daddy like them more?"

"Who? Aaron and Ashley?" She nodded and looked up at me with her bleary, blue eyes. "No, Maggie. Of course not. Why would you think that?"

"You told Dad they were his replacement family." I thought back through all of the screaming matches I had gotten into with my dad over the last week. She was right; I had told my dad that he was using Aaron and Ashley as a replacement family to feel better about his decision to abandon them when they were younger.

"I was angry when I said that. Dad is never going to replace us. I'm sorry I made you think that." Out of the corner of my eye, I caught Nicole peeking her head through the door. "Come here, Nic." She climbed up on the bed next to me. "What do you think about having a new brother and sister?"

She looked up at me and stuck her lower lip out in a pout. "They make you and Mommy sad." I hadn't realized how much my sisters had been paying attention over the last week. I can't imagine how many terrible things they heard me say. Since they were born, all I have done is try to set a good example for them. That's what my parents had always taught me to do. I obviously haven't done a great job of it recently.

"Do you all remember when Macie was born, and we talked about how Mom and Dad were going to spend more time with her than you all?" They both nodded. "This is kinda the same thing, except we are getting a brother and a sister, and they aren't babies, but we still have to welcome them into our family and get to know them. I know I haven't done that very well, but I'm going to do better. This will be hard for all of us, but it's going to be a good thing. Now go play." I don't really know if I was trying to reassure them or myself, but either way, it worked because they got up and went to play in their room, and I started feeling a lot better about the whole situation. Not good enough to talk to my dad about it, though. I spent the rest of my night playing games with my sisters and avoiding my dad.

The next morning, I left for school early for the first time since I found out about my dad's affair. I went straight to the library, where Casey was already waiting for me.

She bombarded me with questions as soon as I sat down. "Oh my God! Where have you been? I've been so worried about you! Are you okay? Were you sick? Why didn't you answer any of my texts? You are going to be so behind in your classes."

"I had some personal stuff going on. Family stuff, but it's fine now. I'm fine now, and I've talked to my teachers. I'm fine." I hadn't meant to sound gruff, but at the moment, I didn't feel like telling Casey everything that was happening with my family.

"Well, good. I thought maybe you were sick like Carson."

"Carson's sick?" The concern I heard in my voice frustrated me. I knew I shouldn't be worried about him, but he seemed fine yesterday.

"Yeah, I guess he got sick during the day yesterday. I don't know if he is here today or not." I felt myself relax a little. He wasn't actually sick; that was just the lie he told his family so that he could deal with me yesterday. I couldn't decide if that was sweet or irritating that he would lie for me. "I hope he isn't sick. That would totally suck for the game on Friday. They really need him and Aaron since it's a District game. He's kinda a cutie, isn't he?"

"Carson? Or Aaron?" I asked, only half paying attention to what she was saying. I was staring at the posters about the benefits of reading and thinking about how I would avoid Carson all day.

"Ew, no! I was talking about Aaron. He gives off the sexy, quiet, bad boy vibes. Don't you think so?"

Her questions about Aaron brought my attention back. "I don't know that I would call him a bad boy. He's more like the sensitive artsy type."

"Really? Do you know him well? Obviously, I know his family is kind of a mess, but like other than that, he's always been so quiet." Just as I was about to answer her, Carson walked in with Casey's brothers, Aaron, and a few other guys from the football team. They walked straight towards Casey and me.

"Hey, lil' sis. What's up?" One of Casey's brothers asked as they reached us.

"What are you all doing here, Cam? This is the library, not the weight room." Casey must have mustered all the sass she could to say that sentence. "Don't you have practice? And Carson, I thought you were sick."

"Coach let us out early, and as thrilled as you seem to see me, I'm fine. It was just a one-day bug." Carson winked at me as he lied with a straight face. It irritated me seeing how easily he lied to people he cared about. What did that mean about everything he said to me yesterday?

He squeezed into the desk chair between Casey and me, and I was hit with the minty smell of his cologne. I wanted to be back in our pillow fort, lying next to him. I hated how much he affected me. He must have been able to tell how much I missed his touch because he spun his seat around a few times before putting his hand on my thigh to stop himself. His touch made me shiver, and I didn't want him to pull away, but I brushed his hand off of me in disgust to turn back to the crowd of guys that had formed around us. Out of the corner of my eye, I could see Aaron. He was standing next to me, looking tense. When Carson's hand dropped, he relaxed. It infuriated me. He has no right to be protective over me. I've been his sister for like ten minutes, and he thinks he has some kind of claim over me. Maybe that's why Carson is interested in me, just to piss Aaron off? Well, I am not going to play either of their games.

"I need to go talk to my mom about something," I told Casey as I stood up and brushed past the crowd. I heard footsteps following after me as I left the library, but I wasn't brave enough to turn around and see who it was. I didn't have to, though; he caught up with me before I could turn the corner towards my mom's classroom.

"You should just ignore him, you know?" It was Zach. He sits behind me in my math class, and he is on the football team. Other than that, I know next to nothing about him, so why does he seem to think he knows me?

"What?" I asked him more defensively than I had intended.

"Carson. He obviously gets on your nerves, so why don't you just ignore him?"

"I don't see how any of that is your business. What makes you so sure I don't just like the attention? You don't know me." I was being a bitch now, and the halls were starting to fill up, but I didn't care. I was tired of people acting like they knew me better than I knew myself.

"I guess you're right. You just seem like a sweet girl that deserves better than being teased for the entertainment of a bunch of other assholes."

"What the hell are you talking about?"

"He's playing you, and everyone sees it. Why do you think the rest of the team follows him around like that? Him playing with his toys is our entertainment, and you're just the newest one. Do you really think he doesn't talk to us about this stuff? About how he is just looking for someone new to screw?" The anger in his voice was rising, but it was nothing compared to the anger I was feeling.

"There you are," When Carson walked up and put his hand on my shoulder, his minty smell didn't give me a giddy feeling; instead, it fueled my anger. I didn't give him a chance to change my mind about what I had just been told. I slapped his hand off of my shoulder and walked away. For once, I was thankful for being the new girl; no one noticed or cared if I stormed through the hallway with tears in my eyes. Well, almost no one.

Carson yelled for me a couple of times as I walked away, but the next voice calling my name made everything worse. "Natalie, oh you poor thing. You're a mess. Here let's get you cleaned up," she cooed to me as if she were trying to soothe a screaming baby. She was tall, blonde, and gorgeous. She looked like a literal Barbie doll. I could see why Carson was so hung up on her. She led me by the arm into the bathroom. When she walked in, she asked everyone to give us a minute.

"Carson?" She asked after everyone left though she clearly already knew. I knew I shouldn't let her see me like this, but all my anger quickly turned to tears at the sound of his name. "Oh, sweetie, what did he do to you?" The way she asked sounded so condescending. "You aren't the first one. This is why I warn girls to stay away from him because if you don't, he'll leave you crying in the bathroom before your first class even starts. So sweet and naive. He must have seen you as the perfect option for his next victim. What did he do? Sleep with you? Make you think he cared? Then cheat on you?"

I was about to respond until I heard him. "Natalie, please come out here, or I'm going to come in."

"It wouldn't be the first time you and I have been in here together," Lindsey teased while I cringed. I may be pissed at him, but I definitely didn't need to hear about his sex with his Miss Teen America ex.

He didn't waste any time barging into the bathroom. "Lindsey, get out. Leave her alone. Okay?" His voice was stern, like he was talking to a misbehaved child. Lindsey knew how to play him, though.

She pouted her lower lip and made puppy dog eyes at him. "You don't want your new hoe to find out about all of your past ones? I mean, you and I have only been apart for what? Six months? And you've been through at least thirty girls?" Her words surprised me. I knew Carson was a player, but thirty girls in six months was

88

ridiculous. Carson was silent for a minute but pleaded to me with his eyes. This was hurting him, and no matter how angry I was with him, I didn't want that.

"Get out!" Carson demanded at Lindsey.

"Carse, I'm just…" He interrupted her.

"Now! I'm not dealing with you right now. I'm so SICK of dealing with you. You wanna keep terrorizing me even though YOU cheated on ME? Fine, go for it. But you need to leave her out of it! Do you understand me, Lindsey?" His voice never shook. He just stared at her until finally, she rolled her eyes at him and walked out. "Are you okay? What happened?" He asked as he moved to put his arms around me.

"Don't!" I hit his arms away from me. "You don't get to play the hero anymore. I know what you're trying to do."

"What the hell are you talking about, Nat? What did she say to you? You can't believe anything she says. Please, Natalie. Talk to me." His voice was soft and matched the desperation in his eyes.

As much as I wanted to ignore him, something about him - probably his perfect brown eyes, tan skin, and deep brown hair - made me not be able to turn away from him. "This isn't about Lindsey!" My voice was weak and strained from crying. "It's about you using girls as entertainment for all of your friends. Zach told me every time you have a new girl, you tell all your friends about everything. You're just using me for locker room talk." I started to cry again, and I wasn't even sure why. Yeah, he had been nice to me for one day, but

89

that didn't mean anything serious. I was still just another girl in his book.

"Natalie, please. Come here." I wanted to stay where I was next to the sink, but he was like a magnet. I took a few steps toward him and stopped. He knew better than to get too close. He put one hand on my arm; when I didn't pull away, he slid his hand down to mine. "I'm not going to use any cliche lines on you, like telling you I'm a changed man or anything like that. What I am going to tell you is that I don't know what Zach said, but I can promise you that there has not been a single time that you have just been locker room talk. Did I talk about other girls like they were prizes to be won? Yeah, I did, but I don't talk about you like that. Hell, the one time your name was brought up in the locker room, I started a damn boxing match with my cousins."

I couldn't help the confused look on my face. I had heard about the fight. It had been all over people's social media, but everyone said it was about Lindsey. "What are you talking about?" I pulled my hand out his and turned toward the mirror to see how much of a wreck I was.

"What the hell is going on?" Casey asked as she walked in. "Carson, what did you do to her? Nat, are you okay?"

"She's fine, Casey. Let me handle this. Okay?"

"I wasn't talking to you." She turned all of her attention to me. "What happened? I was waiting for the bell to ring, and Lindsey came to me freaking out and telling me that you were crying in here because of Carson."

"It's nothing, just stupid rumors. I'm okay, though. You ready to go to class?" I didn't wait for her to answer. I grabbed her arm and started walking towards our first class. I had enough confusion in my life without adding Carson to the mix. From now on, I needed to ignore him as much as possible.

He watched me the rest of the day. In every class, he watched me and tried to get my attention, but I didn't give him a single look. He invaded my every thought, but I wasn't going to give him the satisfaction of one look. He had said the fight was about me. What the hell did that mean? He and Aaron were the only ones on the team who had any connection to me, and Aaron didn't know I was his sister then. This was all so confusing. All I know right now is that Carson is a bad idea. Casey would be pissed if anything happened between us. I need to make sure that it doesn't. I like Carson, but I can't lose my friendship with Casey, and I can't mess up their family.

The next day I ignored him again. I could tell he was getting irritated, but I didn't care. I have more important things to worry about, tonight is our second family dinner with Aaron and Ashley, and according to my dad, 'I have to be better than I was at the last one.'

"Dammit, Natalie, talk to me. I'm losing my mind here. What did I do wrong?" I kept my head down and kept walking as Carson pleaded. He tried to grab my hand, but I shook him off. Every time he touched me, it made it harder to push him away, and the desperation in his voice made me second guess my decision to ignore him. I didn't expect him to be this persistent, but he wasn't giving up. I guess our schedules made that easy for him, though. Whenever Casey or his friends weren't around, he would walk next to me in the hall and sit next to me in almost every class. I wasn't going to give in, though.

At lunch, I sat down at my usual table, but I was by myself today. Casey had a meeting like she did every Wednesday, and my mom was busy, so I couldn't eat in her classroom. I was looking forward to the time to think. Lord knows I have enough to think about anyway. However, my peace ended shortly after it began. He never even asked if anyone else was sitting with me; he just sat down.

"What are you doing?" I practically spit the question at him.

He brushed his blonde hair out of his face and lifted his fork as if to say 'eating,' which obviously wasn't the question I was asking. I continued to stare at him until he answered me with his own question. "What the hell is going on between you two?"

I looked over my shoulder and saw Carson staring at us. I'm pretty sure if looks could kill, Aaron would have been a goner. "Seriously, that's why you're sitting with me? Because I'm pissed off at Carson, and you want to know why?" I couldn't help but scoff at him. Why did he think he had some type of control over me? "You're ridiculous. Did my dad put you up to this? Trust me, I know he wants us to get to know each other, but my personal life is none of your business. However, if you must know, Carson is a piece of shit who doesn't know how to treat a girl right, and I'm not going to deal with it."

"OUR dad has nothing to do with this, okay?" I rolled my eyes at how he said 'our' like he really thinks it means something to me. "I wanted to check on you. You've been upset the last few days, and I didn't know if it was because of me or him. So?"

"You really think that some dumbass jock is going to upset me more than finding out my dad has two illegitimate children." I was yelling at him in a whisper at this point, but he still wasn't giving up.

"Do you think I was happy about this situation? I wasn't, but I was excited to know that Ashley would finally have two things she's never had before: a father and big sister that she can look up to. Mike has stepped into the father role, so now I just need you to step up and be the big sister she needs."

"Number one, it is not my responsibility to take your little sister under my wing just because your mom can't be a responsible adult. Number two, what the hell does any of that have to do with my personal life?" He was being so obnoxious. Between him and the feeling of Carson's eyes still on me, I wanted to shrink under the table and never deal with people again.

"Natalie, I know my mom screwed up, but don't forget that it was YOUR dad who abandoned us." He was in my face now, and he was seething.

"I thought he was OUR dad?" I pushed my chair away from the table and stalked off towards the trash can to throw away my lunch. Aaron stayed where I left him, so I made my way to my mom's classroom as quickly as possible. Mom must have forgotten to lock her door when she went to run errands on her lunch break. When I entered the room, it was empty. This is my favorite room in the school, not because I have any talent when it comes to art, but because it felt comfortable. Most of the decorations in this room had come from either my old house or my grandma's house.

I shut and locked the door behind me, walked up to her desk, and started organizing her papers in the way she liked but never took the time to do herself. When I was younger, I would clean my mom's classroom every morning before school. I washed paint brushes, sorted colored pencils, and put away all of her paints; if I ever missed a day, it wouldn't get done. Now, I come in here once a week in the mornings when Casey has meetings to clean everything up. My mom has told me a hundred times to leave it alone and that she'll get to it eventually, but I actually like organizing. I guess that's something I get from my dad.

After a few minutes of organizing, I heard my mom unlocking the door, so I decided to hide so I could jump out and scare her like I did when I was little. When she walked in, I could see that she had been crying. "Mom, what's wrong?" I walked up and wrapped my arms around her.

"Oh, sweetie, what are you doing in here?" I had obviously taken her by surprise. She hugged me back for a second then let go. When I let my arms drop, she quickly wiped her cheeks and sat down at her desk to try to look busy.

"Mom?" I questioned her again. I knew she would tell me as long as I kept pestering her about it.

"I'm just processing some things, that's all. We've had a lot of change since we moved here, and sometimes I need to process it." I was about to continue pressing the question when the bell rang, telling me that it was time for English. "Get to class, Honey. I'll be okay." Her next class started filing in, and I knew there was no sense and me trying to stay any longer.

"Are you okay? You looked upset when you left the cafeteria." I didn't answer Carson's question. We took our seats, and I continued ignoring him. "I want to punch Aaron for whatever the hell he did to you." Why did he have to care so much? It made it even harder not to care about him. I kept ignoring him, though. Finally, in our last class of the day, he gave up. It made me sad that he wasn't talking to me anymore, but that's exactly what I had been asking for, so I couldn't complain.

Not five minutes after my mom brought my sisters home, Aaron and Ashley were walking up the driveway. I was supposed to give them a ride, but Aaron insisted on walking, and my dad was rushing to meet them at the door. I rolled my eyes at him. He acted like greeting them with a smile would make up for the fact that he left them. Aaron shook his hand, and Ashley gave him a slight hug before they both brushed past him to give my grandma a hug. Honestly, they knew her better than any of us did.

"Can Ashley come play in our room?" Maggie asked Grandma as she was greeting them.

"Of course, girls. Go on ahead." Ashley, Nicole, Maggie ran off in a fit of giggles. I'm glad to see they are adjusting a little better now.

I still hadn't moved from my spot on the living room floor where Macie was telling me about her blocks. Aaron came and sat down next to me.

"Dad wants us to go get dinner sometime so that the girls can see us getting along." The way he said it made it seem like he was afraid of what my response would be. He kept his voice quiet and emphasized that this was not his plan.

"Okay, I'm free Saturday, I guess. You can just meet me here." He looked surprised by my response for a second but then nodded and turned his attention to Macie. I looked past his head and into the kitchen, where my grandma was giving me a proud smile. I know she and my dad want all of us to get along like one big, happy family, but I don't understand why that means I have to practically go on a date with him.

"Blue block," Macie told him matter-of-factly as she sat her blue plastic block in front of him. I have been trying to teach her about colors.

"Very good, Macie. What color is this one?" Aaron asked her, picking up the green block.

"Green!" Macie squealed, grabbing it from his hand.

"She doesn't let people have that one." Just as I told him that, she set the block in her lap. "Except Dad."

He was silent for a minute while he kept stacking blocks with Macie. "I'm sorry about today. You were right. I shouldn't be barging in on your personal business. Your family is taking us in, and I appreciate that, so I wanted to return the favor by looking out for you. I'm protective over people; I've had a lot of practice." He motioned toward Maggie and Nicole's room when he said the last part. I know he has had to do a lot to take care of his sister, but that doesn't make him responsible for me.

"I'm a little past the age of needing a big brother, don't you think? I appreciate you wanting to look after my sisters, but I'm good. And for your information, there's nothing going on between Carson and me." I pulled Macie into my lap and started pulling her thick, dark hair into a little ponytail. "Macie, sit still so I can get your hair out of your eyes." I pleaded with her.

Without asking, Aaron picked her up off my lap and started gathering her hair in his hand at the top of her head. He held one hand out for me to hand him the tie I had planned to use. He had her hair up within a minute before she even had the chance to start crying about it. "You have to move faster so they don't have the chance to squirm away from you. Isn't that right, Macie?" He stood her up and then stood himself up before walking towards the kitchen. Macie wobbled after him.

"Breathe, sweetie." My mom must have seen how tense I got when Macie chose him over me. She always picked me, even over Mom. "He's new, and she's just trying to figure him out. You know, like she did with Bo."

"Mom, Aaron isn't Grandma's twelve-year-old dog. He's Macie's brother. Maybe she can sense that he is someone she is supposed to be around. She has always liked new guys more than girls."

"That's because she's surrounded by girls. Don't get yourself all worked up just yet." I knew she was right, but I still didn't like that he was making my entire family like him.

The rest of the night went fairly smooth. We ate dinner and talked a bit. Ashley seems very sweet, and she is getting along great with Nicole and Maggie. Aaron is quiet like he is still trying to decide if he wants to be a part of this whole mess or not; I can't really blame him for that, though. After dinner, Grandma took Aaron and Ashley back to their house. Everyone seemed exhausted after they left, like we had just finished hosting a party, even though they are technically family. I put my sisters to bed shortly after and then got ready to bed myself.

When I got to bed, I checked my phone for the first time all night - Dad had taken it, so I would be forced to talk to my new siblings - I had three new messages.

"Since talking isn't working maybe you will answer a text" I immediately knew who it was. The second message read, "I stole your number from Casey's phone. She needs a better password :)" As if I would have any suspicion left, the last message simply said, "This is Carson" I couldn't help but smile, and I had to give him points for determination.

I quickly typed out "What do you want?" and hit send before I could think better of it.

He replied quickly. "Why haven't you been talking to me?

Another message came through shortly after. "Did Casey say something to you?"

"No she didn't. I made this decision on my own."

"What did I do?"

"Leave me alone Carson."

"Fine" I didn't respond. Instead, I closed my eyes and tried to sleep.

Chapter 10 - Natalie

"What are you doing tomorrow night?" Casey burst out between bites of apple slices when I walked into the library.

"I thought we were going to the game tomorrow night." I was exhausted and confused. No matter how much I tried to push Carson out of my mind, I couldn't. Why did he have to make this so difficult?

"Okay, good. I was just making sure you were still good with that. Do you want to stay at my house after? Are you even listening to me?"

I wasn't. "Yeah, that sounds good. What time?" My answer must have fit whatever she was rambling about because she kept talking. This is typically how our friendship worked. Casey talked, and I pretended to listen. "I'll ask my mom during class."

"Perfect, you can just take me to my house after school tomorrow then, and I'll leave my car at school." She dropped the conversation after that, and we worked on homework until it was time for class. When I walked in, Carson wasn't there, and I wasn't the only one who had noticed. Casey seemed frantic about it. "Ray? Where's Carson?"

"Uhhh. He said he had something to do after practice." He wouldn't meet her eye.

"Ray, where is he?" Her voice was stern, and Ray looked scared. Just as Ray was about to tell her what was going on, Carson walked in with a bloody nose and a bruise forming around his left eye. "Carson Daniel Nixley, what happened?" Casey practically squealed. His nose was dripping blood into his hand, so I rushed over to him with tissues.

"Carson, you need to put some ice on your eye so the bruising stops. Case, hand me my water bottle and that plastic bag you had for your apples, please." She did as I asked, and I poured some of the ice from my water bottle into the sandwich bag and pressed it to his eye just as Ms. Whethers walked in.

"Carson, do you need to go to the nurse?" She gasped.

He smiled smugly at me. "No, I think I have a pretty good nurse right here." I grabbed his wrist, put it to his ice pack, and went to put on hand sanitizer before sitting back down at my desk. Casey followed me to our seats but continued shooting daggers at her cousin.

"So I have to get hurt to get your attention?" Carson asked me as I walked by him on the way to Algebra. The question stopped me in my tracks.

"You got in a fight to get my attention!" I practically screamed at him in the hallway.

"No, I got in a fight because he pissed me off. It just happened to get your attention." He laughed quickly before touching my arm and walking into class.

I followed him. "Carson, this isn't funny. You can't just go around fighting people. You got hurt. What if it had been worse?"

"It's sweet that you're worried, but trust me, this guy deserved it. And I knew I could beat him." I rolled my eyes at him. He was cocky, and that pissed me off but also made me laugh.

As I sat down at my desk next to his, Zach walked in with two black eyes and a bruise forming on his jawline. I scowled at Carson, who was smiling ear to ear directly at Zach.

"I guess that's what I get for trying to protect a naive little bitch that can't tell when her boyfriend is using her," he whispered loud enough for only Carson and me to hear.

Carson shoved his chair back and stood up. He moved his arm like he was about to shove Zach, but I grabbed his wrist before he could. His eyes met mine as I mouthed, "Don't." He nodded at me, and I released his wrist. He sat down, but his scowl didn't fade.

When Coach Harley walked in, he looked straight at Zach and Carson. "Nixley, Watson, in the hall now!" A few minutes later, the three of them walked back in; Carson smiled, but Zach looked like a kicked puppy. Carson must have noticed the questioning look on my face because he shook his head at me and mouthed, "Later."

After class, he laughed as he pulled me towards my mom's classroom. "That was great. Coach totally bitched Zach out and sat him for tomorrow's game for starting a fight." His smile fell as I shook his hand off my arm and walked into class. I knew that he wouldn't bother trying to talk to me in front of Casey or my mom.

When I reached my mom's desk, Casey was already there, asking if I could stay with her tomorrow. "Of course she can, Casey. You girls have fun." I knew my mom was proud of me for getting so close with Casey, but she didn't need to smile like that to prove it. She looked crazy.

"So I guess Carson got into a fight with Zach Watson over Lindsey. At least that's the story going around," Casey informed me as we made our way to our table at the back of the class.

I tried to act surprised by what she had just told me. She obviously hadn't heard about what Zach had said to me on Tuesday, and I would prefer if it stayed that way. As soon as my mom started her lecture about shadows, Casey was engrossed and stopped paying attention to our conversation. I could probably give this lecture in my sleep at this point. My mom and grandma always used their lectures on my sisters and me when we would try to draw anything. I zoned out like I usually did in my mom's class until I felt my phone buzz. Carson had texted me.

"What's wrong?"

When I looked up, he was staring at me with a confused look on his face.

"I'm glad you think it's funny to get people in trouble, but I don't so leave me out of it."

I shot him a scolding glare as I hit send. It was a look I had been perfecting since Maggie was born.

"I was defending you and I didn't start the fight I just told him to back off and leave you alone. Sorry"

When I looked up, he was rolling his eyes at me. I wanted to throw my phone at him, but I figured that might draw some attention, and I definitely didn't want that right now. People were already talking about the scene I made the other morning. They're saying that I'm crazy and that's why I missed school for a week. Casey has been trying to hide it from me, but I heard some girls talking about it the other day at lunch.

Carson and I ignored each other all day, but this time I was the one who was upset by it. The next day was more of the same, and by the end of the day, I was sick of it. Why was he treating me like I had done something wrong? He was the one who had started two fights in the last month as his way of "protecting me." I wasn't going to let him ruin my night.

Casey and I had it all planned out. We were going to go to her house where I would do her hair, and she was going to do my makeup before the game. She was hoping to impress Aaron, and I didn't have the heart to tell her that it weirded me out. I still hadn't told her about everything that had happened. It isn't that I don't trust her; it's just that I need more time to figure everything out before I talk through with someone. Carson didn't count.

After the game, we would come back to her house and watch sappy movies. She had a study hall during her last hour, so she was waiting for me outside of my history class when the bell rang. "Let's go!" she squealed as she dragged me by the arm out of the building. Winter had hit Tennessee early this year, at least according to Casey it had, and the wind today was especially chilly with the forty-degree weather. I wrapped my arms around myself and jogged behind Casey to my car. When we got in, she blasted the heat and turned on the playlist we had made in Spanish two weeks ago. Her house was less than five minutes from the school, but we screamed to the songs as loud as we could during the short drive.

When we pulled up to the house, Casey's brothers were already there, but she wasted no time saying anything to them. Instead, we rushed to her bathroom, and she started on my makeup.

"Why are we doing this again?" I asked her skeptically as she layered eyeshadow onto my eyelids.

"Because you are a total smoke show, and with makeup, you look like a model. Admit it; you're having fun. Now close your eyes so I can finish this." I laughed and closed my eyes. Once my eyeshadow was finished, she started on my foundation. "Shit, this does not match your skin tone. Let me go check my mom's bathroom for some. Do your mascara and eyeliner while I'm gone." Before I had time to tell her I had no idea what I was doing with this stuff, she was gone. I put the eyeliner on fairly easily and only ended up with a little bit under my eye.

As I was starting on my mascara, Carson walked in. "Casey. Oh, I forgot you were here." He was wearing a tight white t-shirt with blue jeans that hugged him in all the right places.

"Yeah," was the only thing I could think to say as I shrugged with the mascara wand in my hand while trying not to stare at his body.

"Give me that." He took the mascara from my hand. "You don't need this. Trust me. Your baby blues catch enough attention as is."

"Oh, so you're talking to me now?" I didn't want to start a fight, but after the rollercoaster of this week, he deserved it.

"Look, I'm trying here, Nat. Zach was an ass to you, and he said some shitty things about me, so yeah, I went to talk to him, but for the record, he took the first shot. I just took the last."

"What do you want me to say, Carson? Thank you for punching someone for me? Huh? What do you want?" I was trying to keep my voice down so that Casey wouldn't hear us, but he was pissing me off.

"I just want you to trust me. On Monday, we were doing great. Hell, I even thought we were starting something, and now it's like I'm some bug that you can't squash. So which is it?" He sounded hurt. I had never meant to hurt him. He put his hand on my waist.

"Stop." I grabbed his wrist to move his hand, but he wouldn't budge, and I didn't really want him to. "What about Casey? You know she wouldn't be okay with this."

Almost like she knew we were talking about her, Casey hollered as she walked into her bedroom, "I finally found one that should match." Carson dropped his hand just before she entered the bathroom. "Oh, hey Carse, did you need somethin'?"

"Yeah, do you know where your mom keeps the wrinkle spray? I asked Cooper, but he was clueless."

She rolled her eyes as if to say she wasn't surprised and directed him to the top shelf of the laundry room cabinet.

"Thanks. Oh, and don't leave this one alone with makeup. I found her about to stab her eye out with this stuff," He said as he tossed the mascara back to me and left the room. Casey must not have noticed anything off because she went right back to focusing on my makeup. I, however, couldn't stop thinking about Carson's hand on my waist or his tight shirt.

When Casey finished my makeup, I quickly straightened my hair while Casey did her own makeup. I love my curly hair, but Casey wanted to see what it would look like straight. My mom straightened my hair a lot when I was younger because I wouldn't sit still long enough for her to fix it. Once it was done, I started curling Casey's. She had told me she wanted to switch hair for the night, so I put ringlet curls in her hair and straightened mine. We finished getting ready just in time to leave for the game.

When it comes to football, Criden doesn't mess around. The entire football stadium was filled with fans decked out in blue and orange. After I made her wait with me to get popcorn at the concession stand, Casey dragged me to the student section of the bleachers. She used her title as class president to claim what she calls her rightful place in the front row.

So far, I have gone to every game with Casey this season. She spends most of the time socializing while I watch the game. Most of the girls in my class only watch football because they are either dating one of the players or want to be; I watch it because my dad has been teaching me football since before I could walk. He has always wanted a son; I guess now he has one, and one that is a damn good football player. When Aaron ran out on the field, I felt proud of him in a weird way. I hadn't expected to be, but I was proud to see him doing something that he was good at, and that made him happy - no matter how much he annoys me. My attention didn't stay on him long, though, because Carson ran out shortly after him. More than half of the girls in the student section screamed for him. My emotions surprised me again at the amount of jealousy I felt. I didn't have a claim to Carson, so I had no right to be jealous of other girls wanting him. I swallowed down my jealousy and focused my attention back on the field.

By the end of the first half, Criden was beating the other team by thirty-five, and it didn't seem like they were going to have a hard time keeping the lead. But halfway through the third quarter, the other team started playing harder and rougher. A few minutes into the fourth quarter, they scored their fourth touchdown. It had been off a throw to Carson that they intercepted. I hadn't seen the hit Carson took, but it must have been brutal because after they scored, he was still lying on the field.

I looked to Casey to see if she had seen what had happened, but she was engrossed in her conversation with one of her friends from Student Government. "Casey!" I snapped at her.

"What?" She turned her attention back to the field just as Cooper, Camden, and the school's athletic trainer hurried over to Carson. "What happened? Who is that?"

"It's Carson. He got hit, and then one of their players stepped on him." I recognized the guy who said it as one of Carson's friends from our chemistry class, Josh, I think. Carson stayed on the ground for what felt like forever to me before being helped up by his cousins and practically carried back to the bench. Carson sat out the rest of the game. He looked defeated sitting on the sidelines, but Criden still pulled out a win.

There is a tradition at Criden home football games that everyone goes out on the field afterward to see the players. I quickly lost Casey in the crowd as we made our way to the field, but I did find Ashley looking lost as well. I couldn't just let her stand there, so I took her hand and led her down to the field to find Aaron. Before we reached Aaron, I noticed Carson with girls crowded around him. He looked over the head of one of them and met my eyes before I quickly dropped mine to continue my search for Aaron.

When we finally found Aaron, my parents had already beaten us to it. "You lost Ashley," I told them once we were within non-shouting distance.

"I thought she was going to wait with Grandma," My dad explained to me. "The other girls wanted to stay with her since it stinks down here." He laughed and shoved Aaron lightly before turning back to me expectantly.

"You played well tonight, but I think I'm going to have to show you how it's done some time," I challenged.

Aaron looked surprised by my comment but still accepted the competition. "You're on." He gave me a fist bump just as Casey walked up to me.

"There you are. Are you ready to go? Oh, hey, Aaron. Great game tonight. You handled Carson getting hurt so well." She was flirting with him in a way that no one could miss, but Aaron still looked uninterested. When he didn't respond to her, she started pulling me off the field. I waved to my parents quickly and followed after her.

"How do your parents know Aaron?" She questioned me once we got to my car.

I hesitated. I wasn't ready to tell her about everything because she would have questions, probably questions that I didn't know how to answer. "Our families are close." It wasn't technically a lie; it just wasn't exactly true.

"Well, you have to set me up with him. He's cute, and he's smart."

"You've known him longer than I have. Why don't you just try to talk to him?" I didn't know how to feel about Casey's crush on Aaron. I mean, by blood, he was my brother, but I didn't know him well enough to tell her that she couldn't date him - not like she is doing with Carson.

When we got back to her house, it was just past nine o'clock, so Casey and I set up our beds for the night on the couches in their downstairs living room. About five minutes into our first sappy movie,

Casey sat straight up on her couch. "How do you handle these curls? They are driving me crazy. I have to wash them out." Once again, before I could answer, she was gone.

"Psst," I heard from under the staircase. I turned my head to see Carson peeking his head around the doorway to the spare bedroom. Casey had shown me it the first time I stayed here, but it was empty then. I climbed off the couch and walked over to him. Before I got to him, he stepped out from behind the doorway. The view of him in nothing but grey sweatpants made me blush. He looked like a Greek god, and his hair was wet like he had just gotten out of the shower. How had I not noticed him come down here?

"What are you doing here?" I asked while still trying to tear my eyes away from his abs. It looked like he had a large bruise on his side, probably from where that idiot stepped on him tonight.

He opened the door to the room wider so that I could see into it. "I live here. My parents are staying in Nashville for a few months, so I'm living here." When I looked into his room, my eyes and my thoughts went straight to his bed, so I looked back at him instead. That wasn't a good idea either. He must have noticed me staring because he laughed as he leaned up against the doorframe. "Still care about whether Casey is okay with this?" He looked smug. He knew exactly what he was doing, and he knew it was working. He looked me up and down slowly.

"Stop looking at me like that. I'm not a piece of meat." He stood up straight and took a step closer to me before using my waist to pull me closer. His chest was only a few inches from mine, and I had to look up to look into his eyes. I gulped. His minty scent was overwhelming; I was completely disoriented.

"Is this better?" Without thinking, I nodded. He reached up and placed one hand on the back of my neck. "You looked beautiful tonight, but this girl, right here, is the one that drives me crazy." As soon as we got back to the house, I had already taken my makeup off, and my hair only stayed straight for about an hour, especially with the wind. "So? You never answered my question from earlier." He let his hand fall from my neck but kept the other on my waist, holding him close to him.

"Carson." He started to pull away, but I put my hand on his shoulder to stop him. "You can't tell anyone, not even your buddies and especially not your cousins. Okay?" Before I knew what was happening, his hand had slipped back up to my neck, and his lips were pressed against mine. I pulled him even closer to deepen the kiss. His tongue parted my lips, and I let mine follow his lead. He pressed his body against mine, and everything about him was hard. I was breathless when I pulled away. "Casey could be back any minute," I told him as I put my hand on his chest.

"Fine." He made a pouty face and laughed. "I'll let you get back to girls' night."

I moved my hand down to the bruise I had noticed earlier. "How are you feeling?"

"I'll be fine. It's not the first time I've been stepped on."

"And your eye and nose, how are they feeling?" I let my hand fall and stepped to the side of him so I could get a better look. "It looks like the ice helped. Hopefully, the rest of the bruising will go away soon."

"You just can't help yourself from playing nurse, can you?" Casey asked as she walked over to us. "Carson's a big boy, he's used to bumps and bruises, and this definitely isn't his first black eye. Let's go finish our movie."

"Okay, well, you should probably take something. That bruise is not going to feel good in the morning," I told him as I followed Casey back to the living room.

"This," she gestured toward the area under the stairs, "is why he won't leave you alone, because you keep showing him that you care," Casey whispered to me after Carson had gone back into his room.

"He's hurt. I'm just trying to make sure he is okay. If I'm going to be a nurse one day, it's part of my job."

"Whatever, I'm just saying, you are sending the wrong message." She didn't bring up anything else about Carson for the rest of the night. Instead, we talked about guys, colleges, dream jobs, and any drama that didn't have to do with me or Carson. Around midnight, Casey was starting to fall asleep, and my phone buzzed.

"Goodnight gorgeous"

"Goodnight" I sent back. I was thankful for the dark, so Casey couldn't see me blushing as I put my phone down and went to sleep.

Chapter 11 – Casey

Natalie is right; I like Aaron, so I should just talk to him. First, I need to learn more about him, though. On Saturday, I waited in Carson's room for him to get back from his run.

"Good grief, Casey! You about gave me a heart attack," he yelled when he noticed me sitting at his desk.

"Hush, Natalie's still sleeping. I need to talk to you." He walked over and shut his door before sitting down on his bed. "What do you know about Aaron?"

"Aaron Daemon?" He asked like there were any other Aarons in our school.

"Who else would I be talking about? Yes, Aaron Daemon."

"Okay, geez. Chill. From what I know, he's a pretty good guy. He's really quiet at most of the practices and in any of the classes I've had with him. He's smart, and he can throw a football pretty damn well."

"Is that it?"

"I'm his throwing partner, Casey, not his B-F-F. I'm pretty sure he has a little sister too, but that's about it. Oh, and I think he lives in the trailer park a couple of blocks from the school. Why do you want to know all of this?" When I didn't answer, he gave me a scolding stare. "You have a crush on him, don't you? Oh, sweet little Casey, has a crush," he teased loudly.

"So what? There's nothing wrong with having a crush. Leave me alone."

"It's my room. If you don't want to be teased, get out." He held the door open as I left and shut it behind himself as he followed me to the living room. Natalie was finally awake, probably because of Carson's screaming. She was already dressed in skinny jeans and a v-neck sweater that was clearly drawing Carson's attention. "You staying for breakfast?" he asked her as she packed her stuff.

She didn't look up when she responded to him. "No, I'm heading home." She didn't give him any other details, and she didn't look up until he was upstairs. It seemed my advice last night actually worked.

"Can you drop me at school to get my car?" I turned sixteen at the beginning of June, but I'm not a big fan of driving, so I usually let other people take me places.

"Yeah, no problem. You ready?" she asked me as she zipped up her bag and headed up the stairs.

"You're leaving before the pillow fight? I thought we were going to get to see you runnin' around in your underwear. Who knows, maybe you'll save that for a slumber party with me instead." Natalie stopped abruptly in front of me at Cooper's comment. She never knew how to react to being flirted with, and my brothers found it particularly funny.

"Leave her alone, Coop." Nat started to smile at Carson for defending her, but his next comment made it fall just as fast. "Maybe she's just waiting until Casey's gone to come back for more." They all busted out laughing, and Carson still wonders why Natalie thinks he's an ass.

I was about to tell her to ignore them when she walked straight up to the table, leaned down just enough that all of them could see down her shirt, and grabbed a piece of bacon off of Carson's plate. "I think my date tonight will keep me plenty busy if you know what I mean." She took a bite of the bacon and then headed for the door. I had never seen Natalie act like that. I was just as shocked as the guys who were still sitting at the table, dumbfounded, when I followed Natalie out to her car.

"OMG, that was amazing! Did you see their faces? I did not know you had that in you," I squealed as I climbed into Natalie's car.

"Honestly, I didn't either, but they pissed me off. Why do guys just see girls as a piece of ass? Every time you think you finally found a nice guy, they try to seduce you. They use their sweet sensitivity to pull you in, and then they start trying to undress you with their perfectly sculpted bodies." I had no clue what she was ranting about, but it was obvious she was crushing on someone, hard.

"So? Are we talking about anyone in particular here or just men in general? Maybe this mystery date has something to do with this?"

"What? No. I made that up. I don't have a date. Who would want to date me?" She was rambling; I knew I had caught her in a lie. Was she really dating someone and hadn't told me about it? I'm her best friend. Why would she hide this from me? "I was just trying to get them to stop teasing me. Why are you looking at me like that?"

I was staring at her in disbelief " You're dating someone, and you didn't tell. Who is it? You have to tell me."

She didn't look at me; she just kept driving. "I'm not dating anyone. Here. Turn on some music." She tossed her phone into my lap. The screen lit up, and I noticed she had a message.

Aaron: "Hey, what time do you want to go to dinner? I know you've been wanting to try that pasta place in Knoxville so I'll meet you at your house."

Aaron must be the mystery date; that's why she didn't tell me. She knows I like him, so instead, she just lied to me like that would be better. She let me ramble on about how much I liked him when she was already planning on going out with him. What the hell is wrong with her? As soon as she pulled up next to my car, I wasted no time getting out and slamming the door.

Natalie rolled the window down on her bright red Malibu. "Casey, what's wrong?" I climbed in my car and drove away before she could lie to me anymore. As I pulled out of the parking lot, tears began to fall. I'm not sure if they were from fighting with Natalie or from finding out that the first guy I have let myself like is dating my best friend, but they wouldn't stop. I wanted to avoid my family because I knew they would ask about the tears that were still flowing down my cheeks, so I used the basement door to sneak in. As soon as I opened the door, I was standing face to face with Carson, or face to collar bone since he is a foot taller than me.

"Whoa, Case, what happened?"

I couldn't help but fall apart. "Did you know that Natalie and Aaron are dating? She let me make a fool of myself going on and on about him when she is already dating him. I really like him. He's cute, smart, athletic, sweet, and now I'm losing him and Natalie. Why would she lie to me about this? She told me that they were family friends or something." When I finally stopped to take a breath, Carson looked confused.

"Are you sure they're dating? Did something happen to make you think that?"

"He texted her and asked about their date tonight. He's taking her to get pasta in Knoxville." I must have sounded like a lunatic because Carson still looked confused.

"Maybe they are just going as friends. He might be showing her around and teaching her about the area."

"You didn't see the text. It was flirty." I guess it could have been seen as friendly too, but he didn't need to know that.

"Have you seen them be flirty before or literally anything else that makes you think they are together? This could be all in your head, Casey."

"She talked to him last night after the game, and her family seemed really comfortable with him. Oh, and Sam told me he saw her arguing with him at lunch one day when I was gone. What if that was more than friendly?" Then like a lightbulb turning on, I knew exactly what to do. "Cousins' Dinner."

"What? I thought you were worried about Natalie and Aaron. What does Cousins' Dinner have to do with anything?"

"We'll go to the restaurant, and you can see for yourself. It'll be perfect. I'll go tell Cooper and Camden." I started walking away, but Carson caught my arm.

"Are you sure that's a good idea? Maybe we should just let them have their privacy. Don't you think Natalie is going to be upset when she finds out you are spying on her?"

"Well, if she doesn't have anything that she is trying to hide, then she won't care. Besides, I know you like Natalie. Don't you want to know whether or not she is available?" I don't know if Carson saw my point or if he just decided there was no point in arguing with me, but he didn't object and let me go upstairs.

I wasted no time getting everything ready. I told my carb-loving brothers about the plan to do Cousins' Dinner, I left out the part about spying on Aaron and Natalie, and they didn't have any objections. My parents didn't question the idea either - they loved seeing us bond like siblings; that's why they started these dinners when we were younger. Thankfully, I knew exactly which restaurant they were going to. Natalie had told me a few days ago that she was craving pasta, so I recommended Fazzi's to her. The only problem was that I still didn't know what time they would be there, but I had a plan.

After spending a few hours making myself look perfect, we left for the restaurant around five. Once we got there, I pretended not to know what I wanted to eat so I could waste time until Natalie and Aaron arrived. When they walked into the restaurant ten minutes after us, I finally ordered the same pasta salad I always did. Natalie and Aaron were seated on the other side of the restaurant, near the restroom. I waited a few more minutes before quickly excusing myself from the table. They were sitting in a booth across from one another in deep conversation. I walked a little closer, using the short wall to hide me so I could hear their conversation. I was almost directly on the other side of them.

"Have you told anyone about us?" Natalie sounded serious and almost like she was accusing him of something.

"No, I know you want to keep it quiet. You have enough going on without being tied to the trailer trash kid with a whacked-out mom."

"That isn't how anyone sees you. You're the hot football star and the really smart guy in every class. Hell, the other night, I'm pretty sure more girls screamed for you than anyone else on the team." I could hear the smile in her voice. She was definitely flirting.

"That's definitely not how they used to see me."

"Well, it is now. I may not have known you then, but I know you now, and you are a great guy. Seriously, Aaron, even my sisters love you."

"What is wrong with you? Get up. You look like a crazy person." Carson was standing over me and laughing. "Your food is ready." He didn't wait for me to stand up before he walked into the bathroom. When he came back to the table, he looked angry.

"What's wrong" I texted him quickly as my brothers started rambling about the football game next weekend. Since it's the District championship, it will be a constant topic of conversation in our house all week. Carson finally responded a few minutes later.

"They seem like close friends. You need to give up" I knew he didn't want me to be right about this because then he couldn't use Nat as a new way to fill his time. We didn't talk about it the rest of the night. I knew there was no use in persuading Carson to agree with me. I couldn't stop thinking about it, though. Why else would she lie to me about this? I need to confront her about it.

On Monday, I ignored Natalie until lunch. I had a meeting in the morning, and I always had to focus in class to pass, so it was easy to keep her from suspecting that I was mad at her. Just as we sat down to eat our lunch, Aaron walked by, and I couldn't hold back any longer.

"Look, Nat; there's your hot date from Saturday night." Aaron stopped in his tracks, and people from other tables turned to look at us. Natalie looked at me, confused and maybe a little embarrassed. "Don't even try to play dumb with me. I saw you two at Fazzi's." At this point, Aaron had taken a few steps back and was standing next to Natalie.

"It's not like that, Casey." Natalie's voice was tense, like she was trying to hold back anger and sadness. She had no reason to be angry.

"You are such a liar. I trusted you with…" Aaron cut me off before I could finish my sentence.

"Shut the hell up, Casey. Maybe if you weren't so worried about yourself and your status as president of everything, Natalie would have trusted you more. You're so caught up in yourself that you can't even see when your friend is going through something. Just because Natalie doesn't have three fucking bodyguards to protect her doesn't mean you can just bulldoze her." By the way he was pointing, I could tell that Carson and my brothers were standing behind me. As I looked back to confirm what I already knew, Carson spoke up.

"Lay off her, Aaron. She screwed up. She gets the point. Leave her alone." Half of the cafeteria was looking at us, probably because they knew Carson wasn't the type to back down from a fight, and this time he had back up. I was thankful that Carson had spoken up because I could hardly think about anything except what Aaron was saying. Did everyone see me the way he did? I had been called selfish before, but it was always by my brothers or Carson. As I looked around the room, I noticed how many people were laughing at the situation; they all felt the same way about me.

"I don't think she does get it. How could she when she's spent her whole life being treated like she's some perfect little spoiled brat who gets everything she wants." He turned his anger back to me while I fought back the tears that were threatening to roll down my cheeks. "You might think it's cute to have your family fight your battles for you, but you aren't the only one with a protective brother. All you do is bully Natalie, and I'm done with it." I saw Carson and Cooper take a step forward out of the corner of my eye while Camden kept his guarding position behind me. They were ready to fight, and I probably would have let them, but before they could, Natalie stood up and shoved Aaron.

"I guess that secret's out." She walked away before anyone could ask any questions. I looked at the men standing around me: Aaron was still looking at me like he never wanted to see me again; Carson was watching Natalie walk away like he wanted to run after her; Cooper was glaring at Aaron as if to warn him not to move; and Camden had one hand on my shoulder and was looking at everyone who had watched this scene unfold, including our principal Mr. Folley.

"Are you all done disrupting my lunchroom, or do you need to come sit with me?" He looked at each one of us until Camden finally answered him.

"We were all about to head to class, sir. Isn't that right, Aaron?" Aaron nodded. The answer must have been sufficient enough because Mr. Folley turned on his heel and walked away. The rest of us each went our own way as well. I needed to apologize to Natalie, and I wasn't the only one. Aaron was already standing in the art room when I walked in.

"I'm so sorry, Natalie. I know I shouldn't have jumped to conclusions. Can we please talk this out? I promise I'll listen. I've been a terrible friend," I pleaded as soon as she looked at me.

"Now you realize that," Aaron piped up from next to her and her mom. Natalie had obviously been crying, but she still shot him a sharp gaze.

"It's okay. I don't really have the time or the energy to tell you everything right now. I need to get to class." She brushed past me, and as she walked out of the door, Carson appeared next to her. "I'm fine," she told him as she quickened her pace, but he still followed behind her to their next class.

I was still frozen in Mrs. Clemmetts' classroom when Aaron spoke up yet again. "Happy now? I can't tell if you're upset because Natalie is mad at you or because I'm the first person that had the balls to say what everyone thinks of you." He brushed past me on his way out the door, and I let the first tear fall. It didn't take long before many more followed silently while I walked down the hall. I spent the rest of the day hiding my face as best as possible and focusing on fixing everything with Natalie.

Chapter 12 - Aaron

Natalie hasn't spoken to me since Monday, and it's Friday. She even lied to her parents on Wednesday, saying she was sick so she could stay in her room all night. I've tried to apologize a hundred times, but she won't listen. I know she didn't want anyone to know about our family situation, but I was trying to help her. It probably doesn't help that I ridiculed her best friend in the process, though. To make things worse, Carson has been pissed at me all week, which has been throwing off our game - right before the district championship. I know he's protective over Casey, but this was getting ridiculous.

"Hey, I thought I told you to stop beating yourself up," Lindsey told me as she sat down next to me in Spanish second hour.

Just like everyone else at this school, I've known Lindsey my entire life. Even though I'm a year older than her, her dad would walk us home together every day when we were in elementary school. She lived in a little house right before the trailer park. Most people didn't know we were ever friends because, after about third grade, she started getting popular and didn't want anyone to know that her family didn't have much money. She still babysat Ashley from time to time, and when we'd run into each other away from school and her friends, we would catch up on life. This year though, we have gotten closer than we've ever been - probably because I finally have some status at this school. I was one of the first people she told when she got cheated on by the guy she dumped Carson for, and she was the only person I told when my mom lost her sobriety again.

"Natalie still isn't talking to me. I don't know what to do anymore, Linds. My dad keeps pushing for us to be friends, but how am I supposed to do that if she won't even speak to me? Maybe if I apologize to Casey, she'll forgive me." Coach Marran, the baseball coach and Spanish teacher, walked in before Lindsey could answer. He never actually taught us Spanish. This is my second year of it, and I haven't learned anything. Most days, the whole class spends the hour talking in small groups and working on homework. Today was the same, and Lindsey and I were always our own group - mainly because none of her friends were in this class.

"It's going to be fine. You have no reason to regret what you said to Casey. It was all true, and Natalie will get over it. Whether she likes it or not, you all are family." She put her hand over mine reassuringly. "What are you doing tonight after the game?" Her face lit up with excitement when she asked me. It was the same look she used to have when we were about to do something we weren't supposed to.

"Probably just going home. I think Ashley is staying with my dad again tonight. Why?"

"Jess's having a party, and I want you to come. It starts at…" I didn't let her finish.

"No."

"Please? You can't just sit at home alone on a Friday night."
She made a pouty face, but I have had plenty of experience saying no
to pouting, thanks to Ashley.

"You know parties aren't my thing. Besides, I won't be alone. I
will have all of the *Star Wars* movies to keep me company. There's a
marathon tonight."

She rolled her eyes at me. "You know everyone thinks you are
so cool now that you play football. Why do you have to ruin it by not
doing anything fun?" She lightly punched my arm with a laugh.

"If I remember correctly, you were the first one ever to show
me a *Star Wars* movie, so I'm pretty sure I'm fun."

"Shut up; I have a reputation to uphold, you know?" She
moved her hand to hit my arm again, but I caught it this time and held
it as I teased her.

"Yeah, heaven forbid anyone finds out you are secretly a sci-fi
nerd." I let her hand go, but she left it resting on my desk for a minute
before turning back to her homework. We didn't talk much after that,
just little comments about tonight's game. The rest of the day went by
quickly, and before I knew it, it was game time.

"Nixley!" I called out as I walked into the locker room. Carson
turned around, and I walked up to him and held out my hand.
"Tonight's a big game. What do you say we call a truce? Put our
pettiness aside and work together?"

He shook my hand. "Deal. But from now on, don't talk to me
about your sister or mine." He was still being an ass, but I knew better

than to argue with him before a game, so I let it go. If he wants to act all big and tough, I'll let him as long as he plays like he's supposed to.

We played better than we ever had before, but it was still a close game. We won by six points with a touchdown with only forty seconds left in the game. We would be moving on to state next week.

After the game, the whole team was pumped, and so were all of our fans. My dad, Norah, Grandma, and all five of my sisters came down to the field afterward to congratulate me. Natalie didn't say anything to me, but she did give me a high five and handed Macie to me, so I guess that's progress. Lindsey gave me her famous I-told-you-so smile when she saw Natalie standing next to me before mouthing, "Party?" I shook my head at her, said goodbye to the family I was still adjusting to and headed to the locker room.

I knew my house would be empty when I got there, Ashley was at my dad's, and my mom hadn't been home since the day I found out about my dad, but I still felt a twinge of disappointment when I walked in. I pushed the feeling aside, took a quick shower, and slid on a pair of sweats my dad had bought me a few weeks back. He must feel guilty for missing out on so much, and now he is trying to make up for it by buying Ashley and me everything we never had. I ignored my negative thoughts about dad and made myself a nutritious dinner of ramen noodles and popcorn before plopping down on the couch and starting my movie marathon.

About forty-five minutes into what was mostly just me dozing on and off on the couch, there was a knock on the door. I looked through the peephole before opening the door. She was wearing leggings and an old Criden sweatshirt with blue fuzzy socks and sandals. Her hair was messily arranged in a bun on top of her head, and her face was wiped clean of makeup. She had her arms wrapped around herself to protect her from the cold and an unpopped bag of popcorn in one hand.

I quickly unlocked the door to let her in. "Are you crazy? Get in here before you catch a cold. I thought you were going to Jess's?"

"I did; it was boring. Jess wasn't even drinking, and I wasn't really feeling it, so I came here." She looked at me innocently like I was supposed to believe that.

"Lindsey, you know I can take care of myself, right? I don't need a babysitter. Seriously, you didn't need to leave the party just to check on me." She wasn't paying attention to me; she was too busy settling herself on the couch.

"Come on. I just wanted a chill night. I get tired of parties all the time. Now, come sit." She patted the end of the couch where I had been before. I did as she said and took my seat. When I sat down, she propped her feet up in my lap and laid back.

"You can't even see the TV when you lay like that," I lectured, but she didn't move.

"Aaron, I've seen this movie a hundred times. I don't need to actually watch it."

"Whatever." I rolled my eyes at her and placed my hand on her ankle. We sat in silence for a few minutes before she sat up and spun her legs around to put her feet on the floor.

"I forgot how uncomfortable this couch is. I can't believe I slept on this thing so many times when we were little. Do you remember that?" I nodded at her. She would sleep on the couch, Ashley in the recliner, and I would sleep on the floor between the two to make sure they were safe. "Even then, you were a protector. I'm sorry I didn't realize how bad you guys had it." She sounded sad. Didn't she see that there was nothing she could have done?

I sat up next to her and put my arm around her shoulder. "We were kids. I didn't even realize how hard-pressed we were. How could we at six years old?" She didn't say anything; she just laid her head on my shoulder. We didn't talk for a while, but every few minutes, one of us would let ourselves lie down further. Before I knew it, I was propped up on my side; Lindsey was lying in front of me, pressed against me, and her head was against my chest. She was struggling to stay awake, and so was I.

"Don't you think you should get home so your parents don't worry?" I asked her as I cupped the side of her face.

"They think I'm staying at Jess's." Her voice was tired. She sounded like a little kid being told to get up for school.

I rubbed her back. "Then at least go get in Ashley's bed. You can't sleep on this couch all night."

"No. I want to sleep next to you." Her eyes sprung open as if she had just realized what she had said.

"Okay." I started sliding myself out from beside her.

"Aaron, where are you going? I-I I didn't mean to…"

I slid one of my arms under her back and the other under her knees before stopping her. "I'm not sleeping on this couch all night either." I hoisted her up before she could argue with me. She flung her arms around my neck and laughed as I carried her like a child. The sound so close to my ear gave me chills; I wanted to hold her closer to me. Lindsey was a safe place for me. She reminded me of innocence and simplicity. As I laid her on my bed, I noticed that she was watching me with wide eyes. "What's wrong? Why are you staring at me?"

"You've changed a lot. Grown-up, I mean." I sat down next to her, and she put her hand on my arm. "You used to be so scrawny; now you can carry me like I weigh nothing." She let her hand drop as I settled beside her. We were both propped up on one arm facing each other. I didn't know what to say, so instead, I scooted closer to her and used the hand that wasn't holding me up to undo the bun in her hair.

I let my fingers brush through her hair for a little bit before looking back at her. "You've grown up a lot too, you know? You're strong, kind, beautiful." My eyes were drawn to her lips. I needed to focus anywhere except her face, so I stared at the wall behind her.

She must have noticed that I wasn't looking at her because she put her hand on my cheek to turn my face back to hers. I was drawn to her lips again. I let my eyes meet hers for a second, and it was all I needed to make my decision. I met her lips with mine. My hand was still tangled in her hair, and I used it to deepen the kiss. She wrapped her free arm around me, pulling me as close as possible. We stayed that way for a few minutes, each one following the other's lead, matching their rhythm. Then she slowly pulled away. I collapsed on my back and unwound her hair from my hand in shock. I had just made out with the girl whose hand I first held at five years old. She leaned over me with a big smile and gave me another quick kiss. I hugged her to my chest, and she laughed.

She was quiet for a moment. Then she looked at me from where she was lying on my chest; she had tears in her eyes, and her voice was strained. "Why did you stop talking to me when we were little? You were my best friend, but when I started hanging out with other girls, you stopped talking to me."

I stroked her hair to try to calm her down. "I thought you were ashamed of being best friends with a kid from a trailer park."

She sat up next to me, and I followed her lead. "I never saw you as poor, Aaron. Are you forgetting that I didn't exactly grow up in a gated community either? You knew everything about me, but it wasn't until you finally started getting popular this year that you were even willing to have non-small-talk conversations with me. Did you really think I was that shallow?" She had tears rolling down her cheeks. Combined with the tiredness in her eyes, she reminded me of when we were kids, and her dad would make her come home when she had been here too late.

I pulled her into my arms and whispered into her hair. "Shhh, no, I didn't think you were shallow, but I knew your friends made you happy, and I didn't want you to lose that. Trust me. You were the last person I wanted to stop talking to. I mean, hell, I've had a crush on you since I was six."

The sweet look in her eyes when she looked up at me made me want to kiss her again. "Really?" I nodded, and she pulled my lips down to hers. This kiss wasn't like the first; it wasn't full of wanting and lust. This kiss was slow and meaningful. It was clear we had both been waiting for this for too long. When we finally pulled apart, I rested my forehead against hers and smiled.

"So, what does this mean?" I asked her once I had slowed my breathing.

"Well, I don't know what it means to you, but to me, it means I can finally date the guy I've had a crush on for ten years." She gave me a flirty smile as she laid back down in my bed.

"You want to date me?" I couldn't hide the surprise in my voice. This was the girl who I had watched run around with Golden Boy for a year and a half, and now she wanted to be with me.

My surprise made her smile drop. "Is that not what you want?"

"No, no, no, no. Linds that is not what I mean. Of course, that's what I want. But, I'm not your normal type." I laid down next to her, but she turned away from me. I scooted closer to her and put my arm over her waist. "You are what I have always wanted." I kissed the top of her head and waited for her reply.

She waited a few seconds before grabbing my hand. "I guess this means we're dating then." She yawned as she rolled over to face me.

I ran my hand through her hair and planted a kiss on her forehead. "We should get some sleep." As if we had laid like this a million times, she curled up next to me, and my body curved to fit hers. I've never fallen asleep as fast as I did with her in my arms.

I woke to Lindsey stirring with her head on my chest the next morning. If she hadn't been the first thing I had seen, I would have thought last night was all a dream.

"Good morning, Beautiful," I said as she slowly sat up with a smile.

She gave me a quick kiss. "Good morning."

"Did you sleep okay?" I asked her as I climbed out of bed. For the first time since Lindsey had gotten to my house, I was suddenly very aware of the fact that I was not wearing a shirt. I quickly stumbled around my room until I found a half-clean shirt lying at the foot of my bed. I pulled it over my head as Lindsey walked over to me.

"I slept great, but I would have preferred to stay in bed longer."

"Trust me, babe, I would have too, but I probably need to get to my dad's before noon." She gave me a slight smile when I called her babe, which was enough to tell me that it was okay. I grabbed her hand and walked her down the hallway to the kitchen.

"I'm surprised you call him your dad. That seems a little too accepting for someone as skeptical as you." She jumped a little to boost herself up onto the counter next to where I was starting a pot of coffee.

I stood in front of her and put my hands on the counter on either side of her. "Ashley calls him Dad, and it's less confusing for her if I do the same. She needs someone like him, so I'm trying to just accept it."

"I could've used a protective big brother like you when my parents were getting a divorce." Her fingers laced behind my neck.

"I guess I forgot about that. You and I weren't really close at the time. It was four years ago, right?"

"Yeah, my mom took half of everything except time with me. She moved to Chicago with some hotshot businessman. I think I've seen her eight times since the divorce. She sends money, but that's about all she's good for."

"I'm sorry I wasn't there for you, Linds." I stepped in between her legs so that I could pull her into a hug.

"It's fine. We're better off. My dad has Lorie now, and he's happier than ever."

I pulled away a little. "What about you?"

"I miss my mom, but my dad has always been my rock. I can't tell him that everything he's doing isn't enough."

I put my hands on her cheeks. "You can't be unhappy, though, either."

"Do I seem unhappy to you?" She leaned in and kissed me. Her kiss was hungry. I knew she was using it as a distraction, but in the moment, I didn't care. Kissing Lindsey was finally more than an unrealistic dream, so I wasn't going to give her any reason to stop. My phone didn't get the memo; it rang just as I deepened our kiss by pulling her closer to me. I pulled away from her and saw my dad's name flash on the screen. I answered and put him on speaker as I poured two cups of coffee.

"Hey, son, what are you doing?"

"Making coffee. It's eight in the morning. Did you need something?" I tried to make my voice sound more tired than I actually was.

"Listen, I know it's early, but Norah and I have something we need to talk to you about."

"And it can't wait?" I knew he could hear the aggravation in my voice because I wasn't trying to hide it. I wanted to spend this morning with Lindsey.

"I promise it's important. I'll pick you up in ten minutes." Then my phone was silent.

Lindsey slid off the countertop, but I was still in front of her, pinning her in. "I guess I need to get going then."

"No. I still have ten minutes." I leaned forward to kiss her, but she pushed me away.

"Nice try, Mr. Smooth, but you still have to get dressed. Besides, your dad might get the wrong impression if he sees a girl leaving your house when he comes to pick you up." She gave me a quick kiss before ducking under my arm.

"Oh, and what impression would that be? That I had my girlfriend stay over because I had the house to myself?" I gave her a mischievous grin before wrapping my arms around her waist and pulling her back to me. I kissed her neck as she laughed and tried to pry my arms off of her.

"That's exactly what it would look like, and I'd rather not have that be the way your dad sees me. Seriously though, I should get home. Call me tonight?" She twisted around in my arms and smiled.

"Of course." She gave me one more lingering kiss before walking out the door. I quickly changed clothes and brushed my teeth and hair. I was about to call my dad again when I saw his black Range Rover pull up; it looked completely out of place in the trailer park. I didn't waste any time after climbing into the car. "So what's this about?

"Aaron, I'd prefer if we talked about this as a family, so let's wait until we get home." I didn't argue with him, but something felt off. He was hiding something from me.

When we got to the house, he didn't lead me into the living room where we usually had family meetings; instead, he led me to his office. The room had five chairs, and three of them were filled by my grandma, Norah, and one other woman. She didn't have to turn around for me to recognize her; her stringy strawberry blonde hair and frail frame were enough.

"Of course, you decide to show up now, Mom." I turned to walk out of the room, but my dad held me in place.

"Please, Aaron, we need to discuss something with you," My dad told me calmly as he gestured to an empty chair.

"Why does she need to be a part of this?" I turned my anger back toward my mother. "How'd you even know we were here? You haven't been home in three weeks."

"I told her on the day you and Ashley found out. She is your mother. She had a right to know, and she has a right to be a part of this conversation if you'll ever let us get to it," my grandma scolded me like I was the one being unreasonable. She shot me a look that said it wasn't a good idea to argue, so I took my seat.

"What's this about?" The anger was still audible in my voice, and I saw no point in controlling it.

"Your mother and I have been discussing legal custody over you and Ashley. She has agreed to relinquish her rights. I've spoken with your grandma, and there is plenty of space in this house for you and Ashley to move in. But, I wanted to talk to you about it first." My jaw must have gone slack. At first, I couldn't find any words.

Then I couldn't stop them from coming out of my mouth at full force. "So after everything I've done to keep you out of jail and to make sure that Ashley and I were taken care of, you're just going to give us up? I paid your bills. I lied to child services for you. I gave up my entire childhood for you, and all you want to do is get rid of us. I could have done that for you a long time ago, Mom. Child services tried to take us from you many times, but you always said we were your reason to get better. I guess you're done with that, though, right? That's why you look like you just came off of a week-long high?"

"Aaron, that's enough!" Norah hollered over my berating. "Your mother is doing what is best for you. You have no idea how hard it is to give up your children."

"Really? Because both of my parents have done it pretty easily," I fired back as I stood up to leave.

138

"Sit your ass back down right now, young man!" I had never heard Rose this mad. "You do not, for even one minute, get to act like you know what this has been like for your parents. Your dad cried every time he came to see you when you and Ashley were babies. And your mom, well, over the last eighteen years of your life, she must have come to me a hundred times telling me how bad of a mother she was. So no, Aaron, this has not been easy for them, but they are doing what they believe is best for you. Yes, your mom has messed up because she is human, but right now, she is sacrificing her own happiness for you and your sister. So, instead of tearing her down for her mistakes, be grateful that she is strong enough to admit them and make adjustments to no longer hurt the people she loves."

"You know what? Being here is better for Ashley, and I don't have the time to take care of everything at the trailer, so yeah. It's fine with me." I didn't wait to hear their response before I stalked out of the office and out of the house in general.

"You have quite a flair for the dramatics, don't you?" Natalie taunted as she followed me out the front door. "You know, if you want a ride somewhere, you can always just ask."

"Leave me alone, Nat. This is none of your business." I was clearly not in the mood for her jokes.

"Last time I checked, I do live in the house you're moving into, so it is my business." I stopped mid-step on the side of the road and turned to face her.

"They talked to you about it first?" This is about where my sister and I are going to live, not her precious little feelings.

"Actually, Ashley talked to me about it first. It was her idea. My parents wanted to talk to your mom about it instead of using her terrible parenting against her in court. They are trying to do the right thing. Trust me, this isn't what I want either, but Ashley needs parents, not just a brother who thinks he knows best."

That struck a chord. Within a second, I was standing less than a foot away from her. "I have taken care of Ashley her entire life. You do not get to tell me that I don't know what's best for her. We hardly even know you all. It has only been three weeks, and your parents already think they can take full ownership of us. It's ridiculous."

"That's where you're wrong, Aaron. Ashley does know us because she has made an effort. She has stayed here more than half of the nights since she found out we're her family. You haven't stayed here once. You know it's actually easier to trust people when you spend time with them, but that would require you to admit that you can't run a house and take care of a child at eighteen."

"I want another year to adjust before I sign my life away to you all." My dad had appeared behind her and shifted my focus; after all, he was the one I was mad at in the first place.

"How about you think about it and decide by New Year's Day? Look, son, I know this is sudden, but it needs to happen," my dad tried to negotiate with me. "This is what is best for both of you. You need a stable environment to call home."

"And taking Ashley away from the only place she has ever known is stable?"

"Dammit, Aaron, can't you see that this is what she wants? She is the one that asked for this. You don't have to make your decision right now, but Ashley is moving in whether you are or not."

I was furious now and practically shaking with anger. "Like hell she is. That is not a decision that you get to make. Ashley stays with me. End of discussion."

"I don't think you understand how this works, but you aren't her parent. You don't get a say in where she lives. She isn't your child."

"No, but I raised her because her parents wouldn't. One was too strung out on drugs, and the other had another family that he cared about more. So maybe I'm not her dad, but I've done a whole hell of a lot more than you have for her. My name might not be on her birth certificate, but I am her parent. All you've done is spoil her because you feel guilty that you abandoned us."

"I chose this, Aaron. I want to live here. I'm tired of being the girl with no parents who lives off cheap cereal and donations. I want a family." Ashley's voice was firm. She had clearly been listening to the entire conversation, but her words stung. I hadn't been enough for her.

"Fine. Congrats, Dad. You win. I raised her, fed her, clothed her. I held her when she cried, and she wants you. Enjoy your family; just know that I won't be a part of it." Lindsey pulled up next to me just in time. I had texted her to come get me after the little ambush in the office; I hadn't been expecting them to follow me out onto the street. I climbed into her car without looking back at my so-called family.

The Perfect Child

There were a few minutes of complete silence while Lindsey drove until I couldn't hold back my anger anymore. "What the hell did I do wrong? I gave her everything she needed. Sure, it wasn't always the fanciest stuff, but it was enough. I sacrificed everything I had for her. Every dollar I've ever made went toward taking care of her, and now she acts like it doesn't mean anything. She wants his money, and his big house, and fancy car, and everything that I can't afford. We were finally happy, you know? Me, my mom, my sister, we were doing good for the first time in a long time, and then he showed up and ruined it. But it wasn't enough for him to make my mom relapse. Now he has to take my sister away from me too." When I finally stopped to breathe, I noticed that my cheeks were wet, and Lindsey had worry etched all over her face.

"I don't think that's what he wants, Aaron, and Ash loves you. She isn't going to abandon you for someone who doesn't make her feel just as loved as you do. I think you are just overreacting right now because you've never had to share her with anyone. They aren't trying to take her; they just want to take care of her. There's a difference." Her voice was calm, but I could only focus on one thing: she was on his side.

"You think I'm overreacting? Seriously, Lindsey, don't you know what it's like to have someone come in and take what's yours? She's my little sister. She's my responsibility." I couldn't hide my anger. How could she act like I was the irrational one here? I was the one being betrayed, not Ashley and my dad.

The Perfect Child

She parked her car on the side of the road in front of my house. "He is her father, Aaron. He isn't some random person coming in and trying to take over. He is trying to help you too, but you are too damn stubborn to accept it. Do you really want to spend your entire life in this town doing odd and end jobs to make ends meet, or would you rather have someone who wants to support you? You act like in order to get that from him, you have to sell him your soul. All you have to do is accept someone else's help and love. But you can go ahead and abandon your little sister if that's what you want, or you can man up and stop being stubborn. Either way, figure it out on your own." She unlocked my door and glared at me.

"I'm sorry, Linds. Come on. This isn't supposed to be a fight between us. I'm just angry. Maybe you're right." I buried my head in my hands. I knew she was right, but that means I'd have to leave the only place I've ever known as home. Lindsey reached over and scratched my back.

"This is a big change for her too. She needs you now more than ever," she whispered before leaning across her center console and giving me a kiss on the cheek. "You've always put her first, don't change that now. And who knows, you might actually like your new family." I shot her a small smile and climbed out of the car.

I spent a few hours thinking about what she had said before I finally texted my dad. "Ashley and I are keeping our last name, but I'll be ready to move by Friday."

November 17th

Chapter 13 - Natalie

My family spent the entire week slowly moving our whole house around to accommodate Ashley and Aaron. Thankfully my room was the only one that didn't change. Aaron and I each had our own rooms, Maggie and Ashley shared one, and Nicole and Macie shared the other. My sisters were all ecstatic to be sharing rooms - hopefully, for my parents' sake, that novelty doesn't wear off. By Friday, we were finally finished, but there wasn't much point in having everything ready as we wouldn't even be staying at the house this weekend.

We would be in Nashville for the state quarterfinals for football. Our whole family is going and staying in a hotel; Aaron and I were staying for the weekend like most kids from our school, and our parents are going home tomorrow night. As soon as school let out, Casey and I were in my car and on our way there. We had patched everything up since the big blowup in the cafeteria, and we had agreed to be honest about everything. I had kept up my end of the deal - except about one thing.

"OH MY GOSH! I almost forgot to tell you! I think Carson has a girlfriend," Casey screamed as I got onto the highway. My hands clenched on the steering wheel. Does she know about Carson and me?.

"Why do you think that?" I tried to keep my voice from cracking. It had been two weeks since Carson and I had decided to give things between us a try (secretly). Since then, we have constantly been texting, flirting subtly in class, and sneaking little bits of time together whenever we can. The only problem has been hiding it from my increasingly nosey best friend, who I promised to be honest with.

"Last night, he wouldn't put his phone down while we were watching a movie, so when he wasn't paying attention, I walked behind him and saw that he was texting some girl named Becca. And she had a heart by her name." She looked at me expectantly like I was supposed to throw my hands in the air in shock. "Nat, Carson is not a heart-by-the-name type of guy when he is just messing around. This girl is something serious! Do you know what this means?"

"That you're nosy?" I joked with a forced laugh. I had no clue what she thought this meant, but to me, it meant that I needed to find out who Becca was.

"No, this means that he is finally done chasing you. We can find you a guy now!" she squealed loudly. "What about Sam?"

"Ugh, are you kidding me? Sam sleeps with more girls than Carson ever has. No way!" We continued laughing about her terrible suggestions of guys until we stopped for gas. Casey immediately ran inside to use the restroom, and I sent Carson a quick text.

"I need to talk to you about something" He replied before I finished pumping gas.

"Everything ok? We can meet up after dinner"

"Sounds good. I'll tell you when and where" I sent the text as Casey came back out to the car.

"Ready to go?" I asked her as I finished pumping gas.

"Yep!" She climbed in the car.

My nerves were on edge as we made the last thirty minutes of our drive. Carson and I had never said we were serious. Maybe he thought I was okay with him seeing other girls. Maybe I should be seeing other guys. Casey had the radio blaring, so hopefully, she hadn't realized how in my head I was.

By the time we pulled up to our hotel, my head was spinning with all the possibilities of Carson and Becca. I needed to talk to him as soon as possible. As if he could tell I was thinking about him, Carson, along with Camden and Cooper, came out to the car.

"Look, our own personal bellboys," Casey teased while she climbed out of the car. As I opened the trunk of my car to get our luggage, Carson gave me a concerned look as if to ask me again if everything was alright. Then, he quickly lifted my duffle bag and Casey's giant suitcase out of my car.

"How much did you pack, Case?" Camden asked before getting distracted by Jess's car pulling in next to us.

"Well, that's new," Casey scoffed as Aaron grabbed Lindsey's hand from the passenger side of Jess's car. Once she was out of the car, she planted a long, obviously for-show kiss on his lips. I looked at Carson to gauge his reaction, but he looked unbothered by it.

"Yeah, she's been at my house almost all week. Case, what room are we in?" I grabbed my duffle bag out of Carson's hand and slung it onto my shoulder. I didn't like seeing Lindsey and Aaron together. Something about her, maybe the fact that she is the ex of the guy I'm with, made me not trust her.

"Three-fifteen, I think. I don't know. My mom booked them." She handed Carson the room key. "Can you take her to the room? I want to get videos of all the fans coming in for the Student Council Instagram." Carson nodded, and we headed towards the elevator without a word.

When we finally got to the room, I couldn't hold back anymore. "Who's Becca? I mean, I know we never said we were exclusive or anything, but after all the chasing you did, I thought maybe we were. I mean, it's fine if we're not. I'm not seeing anyone else, but that doesn't mean you can't." He put a stop to my rambling with a heated kiss.

He was laughing when he pulled away. "You're adorable. I'm not seeing anyone else." He sat down on one of the beds and grabbed my hand to pull me down next to him. "You're Becca, Nat." He pulled his phone out of his pocket, unlocked it, and handed it to me. "Those are our texts. I thought Casey might get suspicious if she saw your name popping up on my phone constantly."

147

"Why did you put a heart on it then? You knew that would make her ask questions."

"If she thinks I have a girlfriend, she won't pay as much attention to us. Trust me on this, Nat. Casey is way more gullible than you think. So? What am I on your phone?" He gave me a flirty smirk.

"Nix, it's what I call my sister Nicole, but I thought it would work for your last name too. That way, I don't give my boyfriend a heart attack thinking I'm talking to someone else." When I said the word "boyfriend," his eyes got big, and I knew I had messed up. "I didn't mean to say that. Oh my God, I'm so stupid." I covered my eyes and let myself fall back on the bed. When he hadn't said anything for a minute, I slowly peeled my hands off of my eyes and sat up. He looked at me and smiled. "I would like to crawl into a hole and die of embarrassment now."

"Come here." He gave me a sweet smile as he pulled me to his side and put his arm around me. I let my head rest on his shoulder. "So I'm your boyfriend, huh?"

"Shut up!" I hit his chest lightly while he laughed. He looked down at me and pressed a kiss to my temple.

"I'm not your boyfriend, Nat. I'm not seeing anyone else. It's you and me, that's it. But until I can have you on my arm for everyone to see, I'm not your boyfriend."

What he was saying was sweet, but it immediately reminded me of Casey. I stood up. "Speaking of people not knowing about us, Casey is probably going to come up soon."

"Hey, hold on. Are we okay? You seem upset." He stood up and clasped his hands behind the small of my back. His six-something figure towered over me as he looked down.

"We're fine. I just don't like lying to her." I stared at my shoes. I knew if I looked up at him, his eyes would make me forget all of my guilt.

"I don't either, but we agreed that it wasn't a good idea to tell her. Right?" I knew he was right, but how long were we going to keep this up? A few weeks? A couple of months?

"The championship," I blurted out before I could think better of it. He looked at me like I had just lost my mind.

He held me at arm's length. "What does that have to do with this? We're at the quarterfinals."

"We'll tell her after the championship. Win or lose."

"What if we don't get to the championship? Nat, she's gonna freak out. Are you sure about this?"

"She's going to find out eventually whether we tell her or she figures it out. Chances are she'll be way less pissed if we tell her." I gave him my best puppy-dog eyes and watched as his frown softened. He hugged me tight to his chest and spoke into my hair.

"If you really want to, we'll tell her, but please don't let her talk you out of this." Just as I was about to reassure him, someone knocked on the hotel door. I hurried over to the door to look through the peephole: it was my whole family. When I turned around to tell Carson to hide, he was already walking through a door that I assumed led to a closet.

"Hey, sweetie, we're going to head to dinner in about twenty minutes. Are you ready?" my mom asked as she walked in. I had almost forgotten that we were going to dinner. The games don't start until tomorrow morning, so tonight we get to hang out in the city.

"Yeah, I just need to change my shirt." I quickly grabbed a sweater out of my bag and went into the bathroom to change. I could hardly focus on anything other than how I was going to get Carson out of the closet without my family noticing.

"Well, I'll be damned. Danny Nixley, I thought this was your boy." Shit, does that mean my dad found Carson? I opened the bathroom door to see Casey, Carson, and Carson's dad all standing in the doorway of what I thought was a closet. It was actually a door to the room next door, the room that Camden, Cooper, Carson, and Aaron were sharing. I couldn't help but breathe a sigh of relief.

"Dad, I didn't know you and Carson's dad knew each other." I eyed Carson to ask him if he knew about this. He shook his head subtly.

"You don't have a boy that plays, do you? I think I would remember hearing about a Clemmetts playing," Carson's dad asked eagerly.

"My son Aaron plays, and these are my daughters, Natalie, Ashley, Maggie, Nicole, and Macie."

"Hannah Daemon, I forgot that you two were a thing. I guess people were right to place their bets on you when she got knocked up." Carson must have noticed the tension of the situation because he elbowed his dad to tell him to stop. "You remember my wife, Belle."

150

Carson's mom stepped through the doorway. She had a hint of a baby bump, and she definitely had the glow that people talk about pregnant women having. She was gorgeous and looked just like Casey's mom.

"You all should join us for dinner. It would be a great way for all of us that went to school together to catch up and for us to get to know your lovely wife. Alice and her kids will be there too. It'll be great." It was clear to see where Carson had gotten his calming side from. His mom had a singsong voice that could soothe anyone. Maybe that's why she and her husband worked; she calmed him.

"I think that's a wonderful idea. I'll let Aaron and Lindsey know," my mom piped in from behind me. This was going to be terrible.

Thirty minutes later, we arrived at dinner. There were nineteen of us all together. I'm not sure what Casey's mom had to do to add ten people to their Friday night reservation, but she managed to do it in a ten-minute phone call. We were seated at two different tables: parents and younger kids at one and high schoolers at the other. Carson, myself, Aaron, and Lindsey were on one side of the table. Directly across from us were Cooper, Casey, Camden, and Jess.

I was surrounded by awkward circumstances. First of all, being sandwiched between Carson and Aaron, who can't seem to get along unless they are on a football field. Secondly, Casey was sitting across from me, which meant Carson and I had to be careful not to make her suspicious. Thirdly, Lindsey and Aaron seemed determined to flaunt their relationship at all times. Lindsey had pulled her chair closer to Aaron's, and she was leaning against him. I knew I shouldn't let it bother me, but it felt like she was trying to make Carson jealous. Carson lightly brushed his hand against the side of my thigh when he saw me glancing over at them with discomfort.

"Natalie." Casey's voice brought my attention back to the conversation. I had been eating in silence practically the whole time.

"What? Sorry, I was in my own world," I told her while trying to hide my embarrassment at having been caught not paying attention.

"Who are you bringing to the Winter Formal? Are you finally going to give Sam or Zach a chance? They're both into you." Casey was grinning ear to ear, but Carson was shifting uncomfortably in his chair.

"Both of those guys are jerks. She's not going with either of them," Aaron told her quickly. I don't know why he always acts like being part of my family is such an inconvenience for him, but then he tries to play the protective big brother.

"Who says you get to make that call? Last I checked, I'm the only one responsible for making decisions about my dating life." My anger was directed toward Aaron, but I was mad at the situation in general. I shouldn't be sitting here lying about a relationship because I'm afraid my half-brother and my best friend will be mad about it, but here I am.

The table was silent for a moment until Casey directed everyone's attention off of me. "What about you Carson? Are we finally going to meet the mystery girl you text all time?" I could see a hint of red shining through Carson's tan skin. I had to fight to keep mine from doing the same.

"Dammit, Casey, I knew you were looking at my phone. Leave her out of this. I'm serious. Don't mess this up for me." The grit in Carson's voice surprised me, as did the seriousness in his eyes when I looked at him. When I looked back across the table at Casey, she looked surprised too.

"Wow, Carson, I haven't seen you this serious about a girl since," she stopped and pretended to think, "me." Lindsey gave him a flirty smile, and I couldn't stop myself from rolling my eyes.

"I'm sorry, but your boyfriend is sitting right next to you, and you're still flirting with your ex. What the hell is wrong with you? And don't act like you haven't been because every time you cuddle up to Aaron or kiss him, you look at Carson to see his reaction." I hadn't expected Casey to confront her like that, but I wasn't upset that she had. "So are you going to cheat on Aaron with Carson to get back at Natalie for not staying away from him? Yeah, that's a bitch move." She looked down at her nails nonchalantly. Lindsey looked dumbfounded. She had obviously never been called out like this before.

"My relationship with Aaron has nothing to do with either of them. I want to see Carson's reaction, so he knows how much of an ass he was to a great guy." Lindsey turned her defensive attitude toward Carson. "You treated him like shit when we were dating, and I couldn't defend him because you were my boyfriend. Don't get it

153

confused, Casey; I cheated on Carson because he's a terrible person, not because I am."

Carson was clearly hurt by what she had said, but Casey wasn't done taking shots, and her next ones were aimed directly at Carson. "Maybe that's what made him go behind my back and date my best friend. Yeah, wipe the surprised look off your face; you're a terrible liar, Nat, and obviously an even worse friend."

Tears pricked the corners of my eyes. I knew Casey would be mad when she found out, but I hadn't been expecting this. She had hatred in her eyes, and the worst part was that I deserved it. I knew I'd screwed up the first time I kissed Carson, but I couldn't stop myself from wanting more with him. He wasn't the guy everyone had told me he was.

"Oh shit, nice job, man!" Cooper exclaimed while congratulating Carson with a slap on the arm. Carson rolled his eyes at him and looked down at me. His eyes were soft and concerned. I opened my mouth to defend myself, but no words came out. I felt frozen until Carson put his hand on my thigh. Without a thought, I brushed it off. When I finally met Casey's eye, she was looking at us expectantly.

"We aren't dating, Casey. We flirt, talk, kiss, whatever, but we aren't dating. I'm not the dating type anymore. Isn't that what you always say about me?" Carson's voice was gruff, and the concerned look that had been in his eyes was now replaced by one that matched Casey's. Carson turned to me suddenly, put his hand on my cheek, and turned my face towards his. Before I could react, he gave me a

"Are you having sex with him? Don't lie to me. Danny slept with everyone in high school even after he and Belle got together. I don't want to see you get hurt." I had never seen my dad like this, but then again, I had never had a boyfriend or whatever Carson is at this point.

"Dad, I hate to break it to you, but Mom already had the sex talk with me; even if she hadn't, this isn't the time or place for this. Also, I'm not having sex with him." Just as I said it, I caught a whiff of mint and knew Carson was standing behind me. Sure enough, when I turned around, he caught my eye, and I felt my face turn cherry red as I walked back to my seat. Carson sat down next to me a few seconds later with a smirk on his face.

"How was your makeout session?" Casey was still seething. "Now that I know..." Carson cut her off.

"Shut up, Casey." She looked surprised by his sudden bluntness. "Yes, Natalie and I are a thing. It means a lot to her that you're okay with this, but if you aren't, it's not going to change anything. So, please, just get over it. I'm sorry we lied to you, but that's all." He put his arm around my shoulders and waited for her response.

When she didn't answer for a minute, I spoke up. "I'm so sorry, Case. I didn't mean for this to happen. I'm really comfortable around him, and he's easy to talk to. He makes me feel safe."

"And he's a great kisser. He looks like a model when he's shirtless. He's good in bed. He's charming. Congrats, Natalie, you fell for the same things everyone does with Carson. But you must not have slept with him yet since he's still with you, or you're just really good, and he's not tired of you yet." Lindsey's words made all the doubt I had buried resurface, and it bothered me that she knew all of this from experience. I couldn't be just another girl to Carson, right?

"Easy there, Linds. Is it so hard for you to believe that Carson could actually like someone other than you? And, Casey, it's not your job to choose who your friend dates. You're judging Carson based on rumors and reputation; even though you know better than anyone, that's not who he is." Camden gave me a sympathetic look before turning his attention back to the food he had been quietly pushing around his plate.

Casey continued glaring at us silently. After another minute, my tears were threatening to fall again, so I left the table and went over to where my parents were discussing the teachers that used to be at Criden. I tapped my mom on the shoulder, and all conversation stopped. "I'm going to head back to the hotel. Do you want me to take the girls?" She gave me a questioning glance when she saw the tears in my eyes, but she knew better than to ask about them in public.

"That's alright, sweetie. Dad and I will take them. All of us should be getting back anyway; we have an exciting day tomorrow." I nodded at her and walked back to the table to grab my jacket.

"I'm leaving. Are you all riding with me?" I looked at Casey, Cooper, and Carson since I had driven them to the restaurant. Carson and Cooper both stood and started getting ready to leave, but Casey stayed in her seat a little longer.

"I guess I don't have any other choice, do I?" she finally sighed and got out of her seat.

"Sure you do. Walk." Carson left the table without another word, and Cooper followed. Casey brushed past me as she trailed behind them.

"This ought to be a fun ride," I thought to myself as I caught up with them. I wasn't wrong. The five-minute drive back to the hotel felt like the longest drive of my life. Carson sat in the passenger seat with Cooper and Casey in the back. We were silent the entire time, with the exception of Cooper's desperate attempts at jokes.

"Casey, can we please talk about this?" I asked her once we got to our room.

"I would've understood. I would've been mad, but it would have been easier to get over if you hadn't lied to me. You promised that we were going to be honest with each other." She started rummaging through her suitcase until she pulled out her swimsuit. "I'm going to the pool. All I ask is that you stay off my bed." She walked into the bathroom and let the door slam behind her.

"Case, I'm sorry. I didn't want to ruin our friendship over something that I wasn't sure would even work. I was going to tell you after the championship game. Carson and I talked about it earlier because it was killing me to hide it from you."

"And what do you think now? Was it worth it?" She stepped out of the bathroom wearing a bright red, cut-out, one-piece swimsuit that my parents would never let me wear. I didn't know what to say. I hated fighting with Casey, but the thought of losing Carson, after how

159

great these last few weeks have been, sounded just as bad. "Wow, he must be something else if you have to think about it that much." She didn't give me a chance to say anything before she left the room.

Chapter 14 - Carson

"That can't be good," I thought when I heard the door slam to Casey and Natalie's room. I listened for their voices for a few more minutes before knocking on the door that connected our rooms. When Natalie opened the door, tears were streaming down her face, and she could hardly catch her breath. My heart clenched at the sight of her in pain, just like it had the first time I'd seen her cry. I walked into the room and pulled her to my chest. No one was in my room, so I didn't bother shutting the door as I led her to the nearest bed to sit down. I sat down next to her and quickly pulled her into my lap as she continued to cry. She had her face in the crook of my neck and her arms wrapped around me; it was the same way Uncle Mitch used to hold Casey when she would get hurt and the way I held Lindsey when she found out her mom was getting remarried. This felt different, though; it hurt more to see her like this. Natalie wasn't a kid like Casey, and unlike Lindsey's, I could've prevented her tears.

I rubbed her back in small circles until her breathing started to slow. "What happened, beautiful?" I whispered to the top of her head. She looked up at me with red eyes and tear-stained cheeks. I wiped a tear from under her eye.

"Don't do that," she said as she sat up.

"Don't do what, babe?" Was it the way we were sitting? Was it that I touched her face? Did I do something earlier? I was supposed to be making things better right now, not worse.

"Don't call me cute names, and hold me while I cry, and wipe away my tears. You make everyone else think you're a bad guy and a player, and then you're sweet to me, which makes everyone think I'm crazy for being with you." Her voice sounded small, and she was sniffling from crying, and I couldn't help but think it made her even cuter.

I put my smiling lips to her temple. "You're my girlfriend. I'm supposed to be sweet with you. Right?" She tensed up a little bit before turning to face me

She was trying hard to fight a smile for a second, and then it fell again. "I thought you weren't the dating type?" She looked down like she was ashamed of what she had just said or like she was afraid of the answer.

"Look at me." I put my fingers under her chin and tipped her face up towards mine. I normally would have taken this opportunity to kiss her, but the sadness and fear in her eyes changed my mind. "There are a bunch of half-naked girls down at the pool right now, and if I went down there, most of them would be trying to get my attention. Instead, I'm sitting here with my arms wrapped around you while you cry because I hate seeing you in pain, and between the two options, I'd pick you every time. Still think I'm not the dating type?" Her eyes started to tear up again, and she buried her head in my chest. "What's wrong, Nat?" I placed my hands on the small of her back and her shoulder and pulled her closer to me.

"You say sweet things; you smell good; you look great; your voice is like butter; you give me butterflies, and your arms make me feel safe, but you have a terrible reputation; every girl wants you or has already had you; Aaron would be pissed; my dad would be pissed, and Casey would hate me."

"You can take me off of that list, and Dad was just in here a minute ago and saw you sitting like that. Since he didn't say anything, you're probably in the clear." I had been so focused on Natalie that I hadn't seen Aaron standing in the doorway. Nat must not have either because she stood up quickly when she heard his voice. "I'll leave you two alone, but I thought I'd let you know that, even though you don't need my permission, you have it, as long as I never have to hear about your sex life."

I laughed as I wrapped my arms around Natalie's waist and pulled her back into my lap. "Deal," I said, resting my chin on her shoulder. He shook his head with a smile and closed the door as he went back to our room. Natalie stood back up after he left and turned around to face me. "Does that mean I can be your boyfriend now?" I asked eagerly. I'm sure she thought I sounded desperate, and she was right: I desperately wanted to date her.

She sat next to me, rolled her eyes, and for the first time all night, she laughed. "Fine, I guess you can be my boyfriend." She laughed again as my lips met hers. I followed her lead and laid back when she did. She was in control this time. One of her legs was wrapped around my waist, and her hands were in my hair and on my back. I put my hand on her lower back to hold her close to me but used everything in me to keep it from moving any lower. If she were any other girl, I would have her clothes off in minutes, but I didn't want that with her. Well, I didn't want just that. After a few more minutes of fighting temptation, I pulled away.

"Put your swimsuit on. I want to show you off to everyone," I told her while still trying to get a hold of myself.

"No, I need to work on some homework." Her face was red, and she looked adorably embarrassed for a reason I didn't understand.

"Bullshit, I watched you do homework all week, and we're in the same classes. Come on."

"Babe, I'm tired. I don't wanna go." The way she called me "babe," like it was completely natural, made me want to give in to temptation all over again. She stood and started pulling clothes out of her duffle bag with her back to me; I had to focus on keeping myself from staring at her ass. "I need to get ready for bed, and you need to get some sleep." She was using a tone that I normally heard from my mom or aunt; it was strong and made her sound in control, which was sexy on a girl who is barely over five feet tall. I stood up and hugged her from behind.

"You're right. It's getting late. I'll let myself out." I let her go and walked over to the door to my room as she went into the bathroom. Then I changed my mind and climbed back onto her bed. I don't know how long Natalie was in the bathroom, but I was starting to fall asleep when she came out. She was oblivious to my presence at first. She had her back turned to me as she put her dirty clothes in her bag. She was wearing an old Criden t-shirt that was far too big for her and pink shorts that hardly stuck out from under the shirt's hem. She had put her glasses on and had taken her curls out of the ponytail they had been in; she looked perfectly natural.

"Oh my God, Carson! What are you still doing here? You scared the hell out of me!" She quickly wrapped her arms around herself and gave me a scolding look. "I thought you were going to the pool?"

"I didn't mean to scare you. I thought laying with you until you fall asleep would be more fun. Is that alright with you?" She eyed me suspiciously, with a conflicted look flashing over her face. For a moment, I doubted myself. We had just started dating, and now I was asking her to let me cuddle with her. Maybe this was too fast for her. My doubt captivated my attention until I felt Natalie's weight shift next to me in the bed. She had a throw blanket in her hands and covered me with it. I adjusted the blanket over myself before pulling her to my chest and covering her with it as well. She pressed her back to my chest, curled her body to fit mine, and laid her head on my arm. I draped my other arm over her waist and, within a few minutes, felt my eyes growing heavy.

I drifted off to sleep and woke up to Casey coming into the room. Natalie was fast asleep in the same position she had fallen asleep in. I slid my arm out from under her, and she stirred slightly. "It's okay, beautiful. Go back to sleep," I whispered before giving her a gentle kiss on her forehead. A hint of a smile formed on her lips as I slid off of the bed. I grabbed Casey's arm from where she was standing near the door and dragged her into the hallway.

"Carson, let me go! What the hell is wrong with you?" Casey squealed as I pulled the door shut quietly.

"Stop screaming; people are trying to sleep. And what's wrong with me is that you and I need to talk, and you can't refuse to talk to me because I'm family." She rolled her eyes and gave me her typical pissed-off glare. No matter how mad at me Casey was, I knew she would still follow the family rule. "You have to forgive her, Case. She hates fighting with you."

"She doesn't seem too bent up about it." She had a snarky tone in her voice that she always used when she was being stubborn. I had come to know that voice very well over the last sixteen years.

"Why? Because she's sleeping? She's exhausted. She cried for over an hour tonight because of this."

"And you got to step in and be her knight in shining armor. You're welcome." She had to be kidding right now.

"You want me to thank you? You made my girlfriend cry. Why would I thank you for that? You were an absolute bitch to your best friend, Casey, and now you're acting like she doesn't even matter to you. Natalie has been sitting in that room crying because she doesn't want to lose her best friend, and you don't give a shit." Casey's stony expression finally softened.

"Of course, I care, but she hurt me too. She lied to me. Why couldn't you have just stayed away from her? She is the only girl I have ever asked you to leave alone, and you can't do it. All I wanted was for one of my friends to not have feelings for you or my brothers, and you ruined it." Pain was creeping into her eyes, and I knew that if she started crying, this argument would be over. No matter how much Casey annoyed me, she was practically my little sister, and I loved her too much to see her hurt.

"Why is it such a big deal? Can't we share her? Just because she's my girlfriend doesn't mean she can't be your best friend."

"It's a little more complicated than that, Carson. She isn't the last piece of cake; she's a person."

"I know that, but why does it matter so much? It's not like you and I hate each other." This seemed like an ideal situation to me. Natalie and I are two of Casey's favorite people, and now we're together.

"Think of it this way. Natalie comes over to spend the night, and you have to go to your house because her parents aren't going to let her stay with her boyfriend. Or Natalie and I are talking about guys, and her favorite topic is now how hot you are. Or you end up hurting her, and I have to pick between my cousin and my best friend. It just makes everything awkward." There it was, the real reason she didn't want me to date Natalie.

"I'm not going to hurt her." I thought of how hard it was seeing her cry tonight. Casey didn't know anything about my relationship with Natalie. She didn't have the right to make assumptions. I couldn't control my anger anymore, and my voice started to rise. "If I wanted to hurt her, I would have left her tonight. I would have told her 'have fun crying' and gone down to the pool to find a new girl. But I care about her, so I held her all night because seeing her like this hurts ME. So, no, Casey, I'm not going to hurt her because all that would do is cause me pain. You can stop being her friend if that's what you want, or you can get over it and forgive her, but either way, I'm not leaving her."

"What's going on out here? It's eleven-thirty," Natalie asked groggily from the doorway. "Casey, what's wrong? Why are you still in your swimsuit?" I looked at Casey. She had tears welling up in her eyes, and she was shivering from the cold. I wasn't sure why Casey was crying or why I didn't feel bad for causing it.

"Everything's fine, Nat. We were just heading in. Right, Carson?" Natalie gave me a sleepy smile before she followed Casey into their room. I went into my own a few seconds to find Cooper, Camden, and Aaron all sound asleep. I crawled into my side of the bed, which I somehow ended up sharing with Aaron, and fell asleep hoping Casey actually paid attention to what I had told her.

The next morning, I woke up more excited than ever. Not only was today game day, but I also had a beautiful girlfriend waiting for me on the other side of the hotel door. I hopped out of bed while my cousins were still sleeping and knocked quietly on the door to Natalie and Casey's room. It opened quickly, but Natalie wasn't standing on the other side.

My face must have fallen because Casey chuckled. "What, I'm not the curly, blonde girl you were looking for? She went to breakfast with her family just like we are supposed to do in about ten minutes, so wake those idiots up and get ready." She shut the door just as quickly as she had opened it.

"She seems like she's in a great mood," Cam mumbled as he sat up and hit Cooper to wake him up. "What happened to you last night when we got back? You disappeared."

"You know what happened to him." Cooper raised his eyebrows and made an obscene gesture with his hips.

I laughed and smacked him with my shirt. "It's not like that, dumbass. She was upset after dinner, so I calmed her down."

"Oh, I bet you calmed her down a few times," Cooper continued suggestively. "How was she? It's normally the smart, quiet ones that surprise you."

"I wouldn't know because I haven't slept with her yet." I pulled on a sweatshirt and sweatpants before going into the bathroom to brush my teeth. I hoped that if I didn't give Cooper any details about Natalie, he would let it go, but he was like a dog with a bone.

"Why the hell not, man? She's hot. I'd smash her." I rolled my eyes with my toothbrush in my mouth as Camden came into the bathroom.

"Coop, leave Carson's girl alone. Not everything has to be about sex. Some of us would rather have relationships with meaning." I told Cam about Natalie after we spent the day at my house. He knew what it was like to be in a serious relationship; he had been dating Jess since he was a freshman, and she was in eighth grade. When I told him about how I felt with Nat, he gave me shit for it but told me to give it a shot.

169

"You're just jealous that Carson and I are still getting laid since Jess cut you off." I practically choked on my toothpaste, laughing. That was news to me. Cam always said that was one of the best parts about being in a serious relationship: the sex is great.

"When did that happen?" I asked while rinsing out my mouth.

"Last weekend at her party," Cooper answered for him in a fit of laughter. "Cam got drunk and wanted to screw, which pissed Jess off, and she told him he wouldn't be getting any for a while. This idiot thought she was kidding and tried again the next day. She just started speaking to him on Thursday, but sex is still off the table."

"I'm so glad my relationship problems are funny to you. Maybe if you had ever dated a girl, instead of just sleeping with them, you wouldn't find it so funny. Come on, Casey is gonna kill us if we're late to breakfast." Casey is a stickler for traditions and eating breakfast as a family when we go on trips together is a huge one for her.

"Nice job, dude. I didn't think anyone was gonna bag her. I'm gonna need details before the game," Sam slapped me on the back as he walked past me in the hallway. I brushed it off as typical guy talk until I got into the elevator with a few other guys from the team. Two of them greeted me with a round of applause, and the other congratulated me on "my newest conquest." I knew exactly who had to be behind this rumor. Sure enough, when I looked at Cooper, he gave me a shy smile and patted me on the back.

I really didn't feel like dealing with this shit today. "I didn't sleep with her," I told them shortly. As the elevator came to a stop at the lobby a few seconds later, I noticed Aaron standing in the corner glaring at me. I needed to fix this fast.

As the rest of the elevator cleared, I grabbed Aaron by the arm and pulled him to the corner of the lobby. "Please tell me she hasn't heard this yet."

"She's in her parent's room trying to convince them to let her go home. You're such a piece of shit. Every time she starts to believe in you, you screw it up."

"Come on, Aaron, you know I didn't start this rumor. I was with Nat all night. Cooper thought it would be funny. Just tell me what room she's in so I can fix this."

I must have sounded desperate enough because he rolled his eyes but told me with a sigh. "One-eighteen."

I practically sprinted to the room while trying to come up with some way to explain this to her without making things worse, but then I was faced with a bigger problem - her dad answered the door.

"I think it's probably a good idea for you to get the hell away from my door, boy." He looked like he wanted to take my head off in one swing. Over his shoulder, I could see Natalie sitting on the bed, wiping her eyes. Maybe Casey was right that all I was going to do was end up hurting her.

"Sir, I know you're pissed. Honestly, so am I because all I've been trying to do for the last four months is show your daughter that I am worth even a fraction of her time, and now she won't even look at me." Natalie kept her eyes on the floor, but I could tell she was listening. I knew if I could just get her to look at me and see how

171

desperate I was for us to work, I could get her to forgive me. My voice had started shaking at some point, but I kept trying to convince him. "Everything that happened between your daughter and me last night was completely innocent, and I've told anyone that's asked me about it the same thing. I don't really care what they think, though. The only person whose opinion of me matters is sitting right there, and seeing those tears on her face is killing me. So please, can I talk to your daughter?" He looked back at where Nat was sitting. She met his eyes and nodded slightly. He stepped out of my way, and I hesitated a second before walking over to Natalie. I knelt down in front of her, but she avoided meeting my eyes.

"I'm so sorry, Nat, but you have to believe me when I tell you that, even if we had hooked up last night, I would never have told people. I know I have a terrible reputation, and I did that with other girls, but I really need you to trust me that I wouldn't do that to you." She finally met my eyes, but they weren't filled with the tears I was expecting; they were filled with anger.

"Did you at least tell them I was good in bed? You made everyone think I'm easy; that's the least you could've done for me!"

I couldn't help but laugh. "Baby, it took me three months to get a kiss from you. If someone would like to show me anything from our relationship that has been easy, they can go right on ahead." She didn't crack a smile, so I tried a more serious approach. "The only period of time when I wasn't WITH you last night was when I was fighting with Casey ABOUT you. You know how Cooper is; it was all a big joke to him."

"Yeah, and this joke is just so funny to you, isn't it?" She wasn't letting up this time.

"Nat, it was stupid guy stuff. If you want me to, I'll tell every person I see that you and I haven't had sex, or we can just ignore them and let them think whatever they want, which is what they're gonna do anyway. Most of these people have already made their minds up about me, and unfortunately for you, dating me paints a certain picture of you too." I had gotten used to people spreading rumors about me, but I hadn't thought about how hard it would be for her. She had enough of that to deal with already with her family's dirty laundry being out in the open. For the second time this morning, I thought about what Casey said about me hurting her. I reached for the hand she was leaning back on, and instead of pulling away like I thought she would, she put it in mine and leaned forward.

"I didn't ruin my relationship with Casey just to start caring about what other people think of you." Her words were quiet, so it took me a few seconds to register what she was saying: she wasn't mad at me.

I threw my arms around her like she had just saved my life and breathed a sigh of relief into her hair. "Thank you," I whispered. I'm not sure if she heard it or not. "I need to go get ready for the game." I planted a quick kiss on her cheek and left the room practically skipping.

"What happened? Did you go for round two?" Sam joked as I walked into my room.

"No, I got her to forgive me for you asshats spreading rumors. For the record, Natalie and I have not had sex, so if you want to tell people something, tell them that I'm taken and not lookin' to screw around with random girls anymore," I told them proudly. I was officially off the market.

"Ugh, what is with your all's little sisters ruining my brothers?" Cooper asked Aaron and Sam while putting Camden and me in a headlock. "This one looks like he's walking on clouds." He pulled my head toward him. "And this one looks like a wounded puppy." He did the same thing to Cam before releasing us both. "They're pathetic. We're supposed to be having fun in high school, not getting into serious relationships."

"Well, right now, we're supposed to be going to a game, so let's go," Camden instructed. There was no telling how many games we would have been late for this year without him there to keep us in line. We all followed him out of the room with our stuff.

"Carson, when're you going to seal the deal with Natalie? She's a pretty hot commodity. I wouldn't wait too long." Sam asked once we were in the hallway.

"I don't know. Why? Are you planning on stealin' my girl?" I knew Sam would never do that. He was a player, but he was always loyal to his friends, which is why he didn't have a problem with Cam dating his sister, Jess.

"I'm not going to, but I know a few other guys had a competition going about who could get into her pants first."

"Why would you tell him that?" Cooper asked through gritted teeth after elbowing Sam in the ribs.

Even though Cooper, Sam, and I had competed against each other like that before, the fact that it was over Natalie irritated me. She didn't deserve to be treated like that, but then again, the girls we had done the same thing with probably didn't either. "They can do whatever they want, but they aren't gonna get in her pants. Honestly, I'm not in a big hurry either. I'd like to actually get to know her first."

Aaron squirmed in front of me. "Can we stop talking about people getting into my sister's pants?"

"Would you rather talk about whose pants you've been in lately, Aaron?" Sam shot me a questioning look as we got on the elevator.

"Lindsey and I have been done for a while now. She can date whoever she wants. There're no hard feelings between Aaron and me. Well, unless he pisses Natalie off."

"And except for the fact that he was a dick to me up until this year." I had hoped he'd forgotten about that. I really need to apologize for that at some point, but right now isn't the time.

When we got on the bus, I kept my head down and ignored my teammates' questions about Natalie. The last thing I needed to be worried about right now is what people thought about me being in a relationship. I needed to focus on our game that started in an hour. My teammates always made fun of me when we were younger because, before the game, I would go into what they named "prep-mode." Now we all try to do it. Starting an hour before the game, we start covering plays in our minds. We rarely joked around on the way to games because everyone was focused on getting ready to play another winning game. This game was no different. As soon as the bus started, we fell almost completely silent. The only conversations were guys of the same line talking about plays.

We only had about a ten-minute drive, but it was long enough for me to get my head cleared of all things Natalie so I could put my best into this game. The hour went by faster than I had expected it to, and before I knew it, we were running out onto the field for the first play with a stadium full of fans around us. It was late November, and even though it was eleven o'clock in the morning, it was cold - probably close to the mid-thirties. I was sure my mom was sitting in the stands with multiple layers on to keep her always-cold body warm. I hated that she was out here in this weather, especially now that she was four months pregnant. The snap of the ball brought my attention back to the game.

This team was supposed to be one of the hardest we had faced all season, and they were proving that to be true. We were struggling to keep them from scoring, but thankfully, Aaron and I were having a good enough game that every time one of us threw the ball, the other was right where they needed to be. Cam, Cooper, and Ray were our three best offensive players, but they were paired almost equally with our opponent. We were down by seven by the end of the third, and we needed to turn it around.

On the first play of the fourth quarter, Aaron was nowhere to be found when I was looking to get rid of the ball. I had a huge lineman headed straight for me, and no one was in his way. As I was taken down, I made a blind throw to Zach, who I had briefly caught a glimpse of before the tackle. I hit the ground hard, but I could tell by the cheers of the fans that Zach had caught my pass. Those cheers had always been my favorite sound because they meant I was one step closer to being the perfect son my dad wanted. Zach had gained twenty yards on that play. "Nice catch," I told him as we huddled up before the next play.

"Yeah, maybe next time you won't be so worried about throwing it to your boyfriend, and you'll actually notice when other people are open." What the hell was his problem? Zach and I had never gotten along, but we could always play as a team when it came to sports. Apparently, he had forgotten that.

The next play proved that Zach was right. They had figured out Aaron was my go-to guy, and they were covering him hard. I looked at Zach, but he was covered too. None of my receivers could get open; I had no other choice but to run the ball myself. I dropped back and faked a throw to Aaron before making a beeline directly for Zach, who was ten yards out. I had covered five before the first hit: a blow to the shoulder. It wasn't enough to knock me off balance, so I kept running. I faked a handoff to Zach and zig-zagged around another lineman as I made my way past the ten-yard line. I could see the endzone clear as day. Just as I was about to score, I was hit square from the side. I kept my focus on the ground to keep myself from stumbling out of bounds and took a large step forward before stumbling into the endzone and falling shoulder first onto the ground. TOUCHDOWN!

I laid flat in the endzone for a few seconds as the crowd cheered. Pain seared through my chest. It was bouncing from the shoulder that had taken two hits to the one that had taken the blow of the ground. My upper body was still screaming when I stood up, but I hustled back to my team. I had no doubt that Sam would be able to nail the extra-point kick, and I was right; it sailed straight between the two goalposts. We were tied.

As I sat on the sideline during the other team's possession, I tried to roll my shoulders around to shake out the pain, but it was relentless. Oh well, I could still make it through the rest of the game. After a few strong plays from my teammates and five minutes left on the game clock, the ball was ours again. We got the ball on their thirteen-yard line and made slow progress in the first three plays to gain ten yards. Coach Harley always told us that half of winning is wanting it more than your opponent, but they seemed to want it pretty bad. Aaron hadn't been open for a single throw, and I couldn't seem to catch Zach at the right time to hit his hands either. They were limiting us to handoffs, and we weren't making much forward progress.

We had run the clock down to one minute and had almost turned the ball over on downs four times, but we had made it to our own twenty-five-yard line. We needed one more long drive to win this game. At the snap of the ball, I started searching for an open receiver without any success. I tucked the ball and headed straight for Aaron while avoiding the lineman. SMACK! I collided with another player, chest to chest, and it sent me falling flat onto my back. I felt a giant breath leave my lung as I hit the turf, careful to keep my head from smacking the ground. That was gonna hurt like hell in the morning, but the ball was still in my arm. We still had a shot at winning.

I stood up as quickly as I dared to move and evaluated my injury as I walked over to my team. I could breathe fine, which meant my ribs weren't cracked. My shoulders were still begging for rest, but I could get over that. As far as I could tell, I wasn't hurt badly enough not to play, and we still had enough time to score.

I dropped back when the ball reached my hands before cutting left and straight down the sideline. The move distracted enough of their lineman that Aaron was left open. I didn't have enough time to stop and aim, so I lined it up as best as I could while running and threw it. The ball was a little in front of where I wanted it to be, but Aaron got there just in time. There were only two quick seconds between the catch and the final touchdown of the game. Sam kicked another flawless field goal before the game clock ran out. We had won the game.

By the time we had finished our end-of-game huddle, all of our fans had made their way to the field to congratulate us. After every game, I was swarmed by my mostly female classmates, and I would flirt and put on a show. Today when they started to surround me, I pushed my way through the crowd and found the only person I was interested in seeing. She was heading towards Aaron with her family but changed direction when she saw me. Even though I was sweaty and probably smelled like an old gym bag, I pulled her into a tight hug and picked her up. My shoulders cried out for me to stop, but I didn't care. Just as she started to laugh, I pressed my lips to hers, and they immediately matched mine in the split-second before I put her down.

"What was that for?" she asked with a broad smile on her face. I was still holding her close to me.

"I've had to see you out on the field after every game and resist the urge to do that. Now that I can kiss you whenever I want, I want everyone to see that I have the most beautiful girl."

She rolled her eyes with a laugh; it made me thankful for the padded pants I was wearing. She clearly didn't know the effect she had on me. "I think your fan club's a little disappointed." I followed her gaze to where several slack-jawed girls were staring at us. Part of me wanted to kiss her again just to show off, but I thought better of it. Instead, I grabbed her hand and led her over to Aaron and the rest of her family.

"Great job today, man." I slapped Aaron on the back and turned my attention back to Natalie. "I'm going to go find my parents. I'll see you later." It wasn't until I was about to lean in to kiss her on the cheek that I realized she might not be comfortable with PDA, so I settled for an awkward side hug instead.

"You did such a great job, baby," my mom cooed as I reached my family. She put her hand on my arm, and I quickly glanced at the tiny amount of skin she was showing. Over the years, I had gotten good at noticing the small marks my dad's anger would leave on her. Her wrist looked clear, and so did her neck. Maybe, my dad really wouldn't hurt her while she's pregnant. I guess my old man finally has a soft spot for something other than his work.

"She's right, Carse. I haven't seen you play like that all season." Cooper gave me a hard nudge that shot pain bouncing between my shoulders. I did my best to hide my grimace so my mom wouldn't worry.

"Honey, are you going to come by the house for a little while? I'll cook you some dinner." I hadn't seen my parents since they moved, but I had talked to my mom on the phone at least three times a week. I missed being around her, and I knew she wanted to spend time with me, but it almost felt like she and my dad had created a new life that I wasn't a part of.

"Sorry, Mom, but the team is supposed to be getting together tonight. I'll see you all next weekend for Thanksgiving, though, right?" My mom nodded solemnly while my dad checked his watch with an annoyed look on his face. "Do you have somewhere you need to be, Dad?"

"Yeah, your mom had a doctor's appointment the other day that I went to, and I took off early yesterday so we could go to dinner with you, so I have some work to catch up on. We should really be going, Belle." My mom looked ready to cry as she hugged me and my cousins goodbye, but my dad continued to hurry her along. My dad gave me a half-hug-half-handshake and began heading off the field with my mom trailing behind him. I knew I should be thankful that he even showed up, but it was hard to when he acted like I was such an inconvenience.

After the game, our team headed back to the hotel. Most of us had gotten permission from our parents to stay an extra night, but others had to head back to school, so they left, along with most of the teachers and coaches. Those of us who stayed had made plans to get together in one of the connecting rooms to celebrate our win.

"Hey, we were going to order pizza before the party tonight. What kind do you all wa…" I started as I opened the door to Casey and Natalie's room. Natalie was searching through her duffle bag in leggings and a sports bra. It took me a moment to peel my eyes away from her breasts, which were spilling out of the small top. "I'm sorry. I should've knocked," I stuttered as I backed out of the room quickly and shut the door behind me.

"What kind do they want? Whoa, are you alright?" Cooper asked. My face must have reflected the embarrassment I was feeling. I definitely could've handled that smoother. Hell, with any other girl, I would've taken it as an opportunity to flirt and get her into bed with me. Why did I act like she was some horrifying monster instead of the girl I can't get out of my mind.

Natalie answered for me from the open doorway; she still hadn't put her shirt on, and my, along with Coop, Cam, and Sam's, eyes were drawn to her. "He's fine, just a little shy about barging in on me without a shirt on." She was acting like everything was completely normal. "I like pepperoni, but I know Casey likes sausage. She is hanging out with some girls from one of her clubs, though." She reached out for my hand. "Can I talk to you for a minute?" My friends "oohed" like I had just been called to the principal's office. I took her hand and walked back into her room. I couldn't tell if she was mad at me or not, but either way, she had my attention.

After closing the door, she pulled a shirt on and turned to me. "You know, for someone who has slept with as many girls as you have, you sure are squeamish about boobs. I mean, what would you have done if I was standing here in a swimsuit? Run away screaming?"

"I'm sorry. I was a little caught off guard, and what the hell are you doing walking into my room with only a bra on? You had all of those guys practically drooling over you." I didn't really have any reason to be jealous, but I hoped it would make her forget about my reaction.

"I had leggings on too. Besides, why does it matter what other people think? Isn't that what you told me this morning?" She had closed the space between us and spoke in a slow, soft voice. "Were you jealous that other guys were looking at me?"

"So what if I was? You are my girlfriend. I shouldn't have to be worried about you walking around half-naked in front of other guys."

"You have no reason to be jealous, Carson." She leaned in and pressed her lips to mine. She tried to pull away far too soon, so I held her in place with my hands on her hips. She deepened the kiss, letting her tongue tangle with mine. I let one hand slide up slightly to the hem of her shirt, my thumb rubbing across a bit of uncovered skin, while the other trailed down to the top of her ass. Her fingers twisted in my hair were making it hard for me to stop myself, but I had to. I pulled away slowly and caught a flash of disappointment on her face.

She sat down on the bed silently. "Am I just really bad at it?" she asked me after a few seconds.

"What?" I had no clue what she was talking about. From everything I knew about Natalie, there wasn't much of anything she was bad at.

"I know you have a lot more experience than me. I mean, I'd never even kissed anyone before you, so if I'm really that bad of a kisser, please just tell me." Her flustered rambling made it clear she was embarrassed by what she was saying, but I was still confused.

"I was your first kiss? Really?" There was no way that I was her first kiss. I had been plenty of girls' first kisses and first times, but none of them had ever been as good of kissers as Nat.

"Unless you count a peck from my friend, Landon when we were like twelve, then yeah, you were my first real kiss." Her voice had switched from shy and embarrassed to defensive. "Is that a problem for you?"

I stood in front of her and put my hand on her shoulder in an attempt to tell her I wasn't looking for a fight. "Of course, it's not. It's just surprising. Nat, I've made out with a lot of girls." She rolled her eyes before I could finish. "BUT none of them kiss like you do."

"Then why do you always pull away first? Every time our kissing starts to get really good, you come up with an excuse to stop."

I couldn't help but laugh. "Baby, I do that because if I don't, I wouldn't be able to keep myself from tearing your clothes off. Trust me, I never wanna pull away, but I lack the self-control to not take things further." I brushed her hair out of her face, so I could look into her fierce, blue eyes. "I don't want to take things too fast, and I definitely don't want to pressure you into anything."

She was looking up at me with a smile playing on her lips. I really needed to stop looking at her lips if I was going to keep myself under control around her. "How about we try something else?" She patted the spot next to her on the bed, and I sat down. "If I don't like something you're doing, I'll tell you. It's this crazy new thing called communication, and I think you and I could benefit from it."

This girl's stubbornness and sarcasm were driving me crazy. I took one look at the challenging look in her eyes before crashing my lips onto hers. It must have surprised her because she let out a small gasp that made me smile against her lips. I let my hand move up her side to where I could feel the band of her bra through her shirt. My fingers grazing the side of her breast made her breathing speed up, but she never told me to stop. She hooked her finger into one of my belt loops and pushed my back down onto the bed. Thankfully, the distraction of her chest pressed against me was enough to keep me from focusing on the pain in my shoulders as they hit the bed. I grabbed the back of her thigh and laid it over my waist.

"Hey, horndogs, pizza's here." I let go of Natalie's leg as Cooper snickered from the doorway. Nat gave me one more long kiss before climbing off of the bed.

"He might need a minute to calm down," she told Cooper as she brushed past him, which sent him into a fit of laughter and made my face flush. One minute she is crying because everyone thinks we slept together, and the next, she is telling my cousin that I need time to take care of the boner she gave me; I can't figure her out, but maybe that's why I like her so much.

Chapter 15 - Casey

"They're never going to work, but they're both way too stubborn to see that. I've told them exactly how this is going to play out, and they won't listen. There're only two ways this is going to end: Carson will get bored and leave her, or Natalie will realize that she's too good for him and break his heart. Either way, one of them will get hurt. How am I supposed to just sit by and watch that happen? UGH!" I thought out loud as I floated on my back. Everyone was at some stupid party in one of the hotel rooms. I had told my brothers that they were going to get in trouble for this, but of course, they didn't care to listen to me. I wasn't in the mood to party, so I told Nat I was hanging out with some friends from Student Government - a complete lie since none of them even came to the game. Watching Nat and Carson hang all over each other was nauseating, but no one else seemed to think so.

"Is that why you aren't at the party, hot stuff?" The voice was muffled by the water drifting over my ears, but I still knew who it belonged to, Ray. He's been friends with Carson forever, but Ray and I became friends when Lindsey and Carson got together. Everyone thinks he has a crush on me, but it's hard to tell because he flirts with anything that has boobs. I let my feet sink to the ground so that I could see him. He was giving me a stern glare with his emerald eyes.

He definitely wasn't unattractive. He had sandy-brown hair that went perfectly with his olive skin.

I swam over to where he was standing on the edge of the pool. "Shouldn't you be upstairs flirting with some poor girl who isn't interested? How'd you even know I was down here?" I had to look almost straight up to meet his eyes.

"I didn't. Cam told me. He saw you leave your room in your suit. Now, come on." I laid my head back in the water and pointed to my ears before shrugging. "Seriously, are you five? I know you can hear me. Casey Jane, do not make me drag you out of this pool." He knew I hated my middle name, but he always used it anyway. I continued to ignore him until I heard a splash near where he was standing. I sat up quickly. Ray was standing in the water in his basketball shorts, and I could see his t-shirt crumpled up on the pool deck. "Now, get out so we can go to the party." I started swimming away from Ray, but it was no use. He had been on the swim team for five years, so catching me wasn't much of a challenge for him. He grabbed my ankle and pulled the rest of me backward. Once I was close enough to him, he pushed down on my shoulders and dunked my head underwater. "That's for making me get in."

I laughed as I came up for air. "You know you'd rather be goofing around in the pool with me than at some stupid party anyway." I knew I was right because when we were younger, Cooper, Camden, Sam, Carson, Ray, and I would spend almost all summer in the pool in our backyard.

"What do you have against this party? Other than the obvious fact that Carson and Natalie will be there?" He asked me as we climbed out of the pool.

"I'm just not in a partying mood, Ray. Is that so hard to believe?"

"Case, you're the president of every club you're in, and your mom is the most well-known person in our entire county. Everything you do is about partying and socializing. What's going on?" He looked down at his phone and then back to me.

"I know I'm popular, and I have a lot of friends, but Natalie's my best friend. How is she supposed to stay that when she's dating Carson? I mean, I can't even give her relationship advice, like a best friend should, because I have to make sure it doesn't hurt Carson. Why couldn't he just keep it in his pants for once? UGH!" He walked over and climbed into the hot tub before gesturing for me to join him. "I thought you wanted to go to the party?" I asked as I turned on the jets and climbed in next to him.

"I do, but first, I have to talk some sense into you." I was about to defend myself, but he put his hand over my mouth jokingly. "Just listen for once." He put his hand back in the water while I gave him a sideways glare. "Carson is my best friend, but you're my friend too. Even though you're Carson's cousin, that doesn't keep him from being friends with me or me from being friends with you." I opened my mouth to argue, but he talked over me. "Before you say that it's different, let me tell you why it's not. I know you, and I aren't dating, but I still talk to Carson about you and ask for advice about you

189

sometimes. Don't you think that took Carson some time to get used to? What about Camden and Sam? It probably took a little bit of adjusting when Cam and Jess started dating. Aaron doesn't seem to have a problem with Carson dating his sister. Just because two people that you love care about each other, that doesn't mean you have to pick between them."

I was silent for a moment. I knew he was right, but I didn't need to tell him that. "You really talk to Carson about me?"

He rolled his eyes. "Is that seriously the only thing you got out of that? I rehearsed that whole thing, and you didn't even listen."

Irritating Ray was one of my favorite things to do because it was so easy. I couldn't help but laugh as he smacked the water like a little kid throwing a fit. "No, I heard you, but I still want you to answer the question." I gave him my most playful smile.

"I talk to him about whether or not the amount of abuse I take from you and the amount of money I spend on you is worth the little amount of joy you bring me."

I reached over to smack him jokingly, but he grabbed my wrist and pulled me closer to him so I couldn't. I tried to stand up to prevent what I knew was coming, but I wasn't fast enough. His hands quickly found my sides and started tickling me. I fell backward, right into his lap, while he continued.

"Mercy!" I finally squealed through a fit of laughter. His fingers stopped moving, but his hands lingered on my sides for a moment longer. Then, I slid off his lap and onto the bench next to him. "Thanks for talking me down, Ray." He put his arm around me, and I leaned my head against it.

"No problem, dollface." We stayed like that for a few minutes until the door to the pool swung open, and a huge group of my classmates poured through it. "You wouldn't go to the party, so I brought it to you." I could tell that most of them were half-drunk as they splashed into the pool, which irritated me even more than Ray scheming behind my back. He was right, I did like going to parties, but I can't stand drunk people. He must have been able to tell that I was annoyed because he leaned over and whispered in my ear, "I'm sorry, but I thought you'd have more fun this way." Then, he put two fingers on the corners of my mouth and pulled my frown into a smile to make me laugh.

Carson was one of the last people through the door, and he was leading Natalie over to the hot tub by the hand. She looked terrified. At every party I had taken her to, she had stuck to me like glue. She might have a big personality in small groups, but she is quiet as a mouse when it comes to crowds. Carson looked backed and forth between Ray and me with a questioning look in his eyes. He's always teased us about our relationship, but we've never been more than friends.

"Dude, you owe me big time. It was hell getting all of these people down here, especially because most of them didn't want to wear swimsuits," Carson told Ray with a laugh.

"Thanks, man. Do you want to grab a beer?" Carson looked nervously at Natalie.

"Go," I told him. "I'll stay with her. Grab me a drink, please." Carson and Nat both gave me a surprised look, and Ray gave me a reassuring squeeze before he climbed out of the hot tub. "Are you alright?" I asked Natalie as she sat down next to me. The hot tub had filled up fast, and she was growing more and more uncomfortable.

"Yeah, I think I'm starting to get a little more used to these. Carson even talked me into playing cards while we were upstairs." She was clearly trying to remain calm, but the face she made when a girl I had never seen before bumped into her gave her away. She was silent for a minute or two while she searched through the crowd for friendly faces. "I'm going to go talk to Aaron and Lindsey." I thought about arguing with her and apologizing for making her more uncomfortable, but instead, I nodded as she got out of the hot tub.

I decided shortly after she left that I still was not in the mood to deal with people, so I started heading for the door.

"Where are you going?" Carson asked me as he made his way back to the hot tub.

"I'm going to go work on some homework, so I don't have to do it tomorrow. Nat is with Aaron."

He looked upset that I wasn't sticking around. "Does Ray know you're leaving? You're the reason he made me bring everyone down here."

"I didn't ask him to do that, and no, I haven't told him. He's a little preoccupied." I looked over to where Ray had his tongue down some girl's throat - I think her name is Erica. Other than the fact that he saw me as a little sister, him being a manwhore was the main reason we had never been anything other than friends. I pushed past Carson and made my way to the hallway.

I worked on homework for more than an hour after I got to my room and took a shower, and there was no sign of Natalie or any of the guys the entire time. I rarely spent this much time by myself, and I was starting to realize why: this sucks. I needed someone to talk to, but Cam was with Jess, Ray was with Erica, Carson was with Natalie, and Cooper was with Sam and beer. They all had someone, and all I had was homework that I didn't even understand how to do. Just as I was about to crawl into bed, Nat came stumbling into the room with Carson guiding her from behind.

"You got her drunk?" I asked incredulously. "What's wrong with you? She's never drank before. Why would you let her get this drunk?" All I wanted to do was go to sleep, and now I had to deal with this shit. "Get out. I'll take care of her. You aren't going to be any help anyway." Carson tried to protest drunkenly, but I pushed him through the door to his room before he could find the words. I sat Natalie down on her bed and pulled her pajamas out of her bag. I quickly helped her change and tucked her into her bed.

"You're the best," she slurred before falling fast asleep. I finally let my head hit the pillow and then heard a knock on the door. I was going to ignore it until I heard another knock.

"Are you fucking kidding me?" I flung the door open to reveal Ray standing in the hallway with my seltzer in his hand. "Wow, did it take you a little while to find the cooler? It probably wasn't in Erica's mouth, was it?"

"Are you seriously about to give me this lecture again? If you are, I don't want to hear it. It's my life, Casey, not yours, so stop making me feel like shit about it." Going to a party and making out with a random girl was a typical weekend for Ray, but I had told him several times that I thought he was disgusting for doing it. I figured he didn't care about my opinion, so I hadn't realized it was hurting his feelings. "I came up to check on you, but obviously, you're still in your bitchy mood." He started walking away, and a pang of guilt hit me.

"Ray, I'm sorry. You're right." I couldn't think of the last time I had said those words, especially to Ray. Ray stopped at the end of the hallway and turned around slowly.

"Did I just hear you right? Did you just say that I'm right? Are you sick?" he teased. I stepped out into the hallway and sat down on the floor outside my door as he made his way over to me.

"Do you ever get tired of being single?" I wasn't planning on asking him that, but the words spilled out of my mouth anyway. He opened my drink and took a sip of it before handing it to me and sitting down next to me.

"I get tired of seeing all of my friends dating someone, but I like being single. I just don't like being single alone, you know?" I had no clue what he was talking about, and it must have been obvious because he started explaining himself. "Think of it this way. When a group of single guys is going around flirting with girls, it seems normal, but when only one single guy is flirting with girls, he seems like a creep."

"I guess I get it. I mean, it's way more fun to check out guys when you can talk about them with people who are actually interested. But mostly, I just want what they have." I took a huge gulp from the can and gave it to Ray, who was staring at me like I had three eyes.

"You want to be stuck with the same person all the time and have to get their approval for everything? It's like having another parent. I don't want to be responsible for making another person happy and fitting their expectations. No, thank you." I didn't know he felt this way about relationships, but then again, we'd never really had deep conversations like this. Ray wasn't the type of person to take things seriously most of the time; I think that's why our friendship surprised so many people. Come to think of it, our most serious conversations were probably when I needed advice or lectured him about his choices.

"You don't want the butterflies just from being around someone or the always having someone to talk to even about the hardest things in life? It's like having a best friend that you can have sex with. I want to fall in love with someone and learn all of the stupid little things about them." Ray was silently shaking his head at me. "What?"

"Why can't you have that without the commitment? When people commit when they're young, someone always ends up getting hurt because people fall out of love, and knowing all of the little stupid things isn't always enough." Ray's parents have been divorced for as long as I can remember, which must be why he's such a cynic about love.

"Commitment is what makes it special. It isn't love if you have the same thing with half a dozen other people. You really don't ever wanna fall in love with someone?"

His answer sounded more serious than I had ever heard him before. "I can be in love with someone and still sleep with someone else." He made it sound like he had experience with it. Maybe, I've read Ray wrong; maybe, he's already been hurt by someone he loves. "I'm going to bed." He got up in a huff. Why was he so mad now? I stood up to go back into my room but realized I hadn't brought my key with me. Shit!

"Ray?" I called down the hallway desperately.

"What now, Casey?" He was pissed, and I didn't want to bother him, but I wasn't about to sleep in the hallway.

"I don't have my key, and Nat's passed out in there."

He let out a deep breath. "Fine, you can crash in my room." I caught up to him quickly and followed him to his room. When he opened the door, I noticed Sam and Eli sprawled out in one of the beds. Great, now I have three roommates. I crawled into the open bed while Ray went into the bathroom. I wasn't worried about sharing a bed with Ray. When we were younger, we would all lay on the living room floor together, and that had never been awkward, so why should this be? I was sound asleep before Ray even came back into the room. I must have been more exhausted than I thought.

On Sunday morning, I woke up to Ray's arm around my waist with his hand on my thigh, my leg across his waist, and my head and hand on his bare chest. I tried to peel his arm off of me slowly, but just as I started to, he squeezed me tight, making me squeal. I heard his deep laugh and looked up to see him wide awake and smiling down at me. He wasn't the worst thing to see first thing in the morning. I looked across the room at Sam and Eli's bed; it was empty. We were alone in his room, and I had to keep my mind from wandering to the things that could mean for us.

I smacked his chest tiredly. "I was trying not to wake you up."

He laughed again and let go of me. As much as I wanted to stay cuddled up to him, I knew better than to cross that line, so I moved away and sat up. "I've been laying here for about an hour doing the same thing. You practically passed out last night, so I wanted to let you sleep." I had just climbed out of the bed when I heard a knock on the door. Without thinking about how it would look, I opened the door.

"There you are. You know, Casey, typically, if you are going to do the walk of shame, you do it before everyone else wakes up." Carson laughed at his own joke.

"Shut up, Carson. You know nothing is going on between Ray and me." I turned to gesture toward the room and ran my hand into Ray's side. At some point, he had gotten out of bed and was now standing behind me, still shirtless.

"Yeah, it was just innocent cuddling and some other stuff," he said suggestively as he put his arms around my ribs.

I slapped his hands away from me. "What?! It was not!"

I spun around to see him laughing at me. "Relax, Cujo, I'm kidding. Don't bite my head off." My brothers and Carson had started calling me Cujo when we were younger, and I would get mad at them; somehow, all of their friends started calling me that too. Needless to say, I don't find it funny.

"Here, let me take a picture. You are going to want to have this for your kids one day, Casey." I tried to grab Carson's phone out of his hand, but Ray had his arms around me again. I fought against him until he started to tickle me again. I laughed just as Carson took the picture. To anyone else, we would have looked like a happy couple who had just slept together, instead of a guy taunting his friend's 'little sister.' Maybe if I hadn't always been around my brothers and Carson and their friends, I wouldn't have such a hard time finding a boyfriend because, at this point, everyone saw me as a little sister.

"Now, go get dressed so we can go home." Ray playfully shoved me out the door, and Carson and I headed back to our rooms.

"So, how did you end up in Ray's bed?" Carson asked while we walked.

"After I put Natalie to bed, Ray and I were talking out in the hallway, and I forgot my key in the room. I didn't want to wake Nat up, so Ray let me sleep in his room. Don't worry; it was completely innocent."

"Hey, I'm team 'Raysey,' so I was kinda hopin' it was more."

"For the last time, there is no 'Raysey!'" I told him as I walked into his room. I was greeted by a crowd of people: Cooper, Camden,

Sam, Eli, Aaron, Lindsey, Jess, and Natalie. I was still wearing my pajamas, which consisted of a thin tank top and shorts; thankfully, since we were in the hotel, I had kept my bra on.

"That's not what I saw when I woke up this morning," Sam announced. "Last time I checked, cuddling like that isn't nothing."

"And we all saw you two in the hot tub when we first got there last night," Cooper added while he raised his eyebrows. They all stared at me for a few seconds expecting an explanation that I couldn't give. Ray and I are close friends, and we are comfortable around each other, but we aren't anything more. Nobody believed us, though.

Lindsey volunteered more evidence against us. "He didn't even have his trunks on last night, and he still got in the hot tub with you."

"Hell, he made us move a whole damn party for you," Carson made the same argument he had last night. "You all argue like you're married, you get mad at him for being a player, and you always have your..."

I felt Ray's hand on my shoulder at the same time I heard his voice interrupting Carson. He was standing behind me again in the doorway. "That's enough, guys. I know we all joke around about it, but Casey and I are just friends. She doesn't need to be badgered about it all the time." They all stared silently as I made my way to my room to get changed.

I quickly brushed my teeth and hair and threw on a pair of black leggings and a navy blue Criden sweatshirt. I noticed that

Natalie had already packed, so I did the same - careful not to forget anything. When I walked back into the guys' room, not fifteen minutes later, almost everyone was gone except Nat, Carson, and Ray.

Ray must have read the confusion on my face because he answered my question before I even asked it. "Cooper took my spot in Sam's car, so now I'm riding with you all. Everyone else is already downstairs loading cars." I nodded and went to grab my suitcase, but Ray was already pulling up the handle on it. I held the door open for Ray and Carson as they carried out mine and Natalie's bags. Then, Natalie and I followed them down to the lobby in silence. This was going to be a long car ride.

Once we finally got on the road, I was proved right. Carson and Ray made idle chatter about random things while Nat and I stayed quiet, except for small comments here and there. After about an hour, I pretended to sleep leaned up against the door so that I could escape the awkwardness. Then, Ray noticed that I couldn't get comfortable, so he took off his sweatshirt and balled it up in his lap for me to use as a pillow. I had my head in his lap for a few minutes before Carson finally made a comment about it. "You two seriously act like you've been married for twenty years. How do you not see it?"

Ray's hand, which had been stroking my hair, stopped. "Why is it such a big deal to everyone whether we're just friends or not? It's our relationship, and if we decide to be more than friends, we will make that decision on our own. Okay?" His reaction surprised me. Ray wasn't the type of person to fight with anyone, especially not his friends, but he must not have been in the mood for jokes. Normally, when people would tease us about this, he would tell them that we were friends with benefits or something like that. I wonder why it was upsetting him so much now.

Chapter 16 - Aaron

On Thursday morning, I was woken up by the sound of my door creaking open and then the weight of Macie and Nicole on top of me. This was their new favorite thing to do when they woke up before me.

"Girls, what did daddy say about waking up Aaron," Natalie asked in the motherly tone she always used on her sisters. They both shrugged at her innocently. "He said to do it nicely. Not jump on him like wild banshees."

"It's fine. They aren't hurting anything. Besides, now I have a reason to tickle them." Nicole and Macie both squealed as I pulled them into my lap and tickled them.

"Whatever, it's your ribs that they're crushing. I'm just looking out for your team."

I let them go, and the girls ran out of my room laughing. "You mean your boyfriend. We haven't really gotten a chance to talk about all of that."

Natalie was extremely defensive about the subject, and I knew better than bringing it up around little ears, which we called all four of our little sisters. "What about it?" she asked with an edge in her voice that told me to tread lightly.

"Well, for starters, how did it even happen? It was obvious that he had a crush on you, but to me, it seemed like you couldn't stand him."

"When I found out about you and Ash, I felt like my life was falling apart, but Carson was there for me. When I left school that first day I went back, he could tell I was struggling, and he took me to his house, made me feel comfortable, and I told him everything. He didn't make me feel like I was overreacting or underreacting. He didn't even try to give me advice or act like he knew what I was going through. He just listened to me."

"And that made you want to risk your relationship with your best friend?" If that was all it took, then maybe her relationship with Casey wasn't as strong as I thought. Maybe I was right to call her out on being a bitch.

"I tried to ignore him, but he wouldn't let me. It was also really nice having someone to talk to, and he's really nice to me. I know he's mistreated other girls, and it's super cliche of me to say this, but he's different with me."

I couldn't help but roll my eyes. "Yeah, he was different with Lindsey too, and you see how that turned out." When he was dating Lindsey, Carson constantly taunted me about my mom being an addict and my family not having any money, so I already disliked him. Then Lindsey told me about how terribly he had treated her at the end of their relationship.

"What are you talking about? Carson loved her." She clearly only knew his side of the story.

I scoffed at her. "Carson practically forgot he had a girlfriend at the end of their relationship. Lindsey told me he was so worried about being the best in everything that he was just about the worst when it came to being a boyfriend. That's why she cheated on him."

"Because she wasn't getting enough attention? Wow, she seems like a real catch, Aaron."

"It was because he treated her like she didn't matter. When his life started getting rough, he stopped caring about hers. He wasn't the sweet, great-listening guy anymore, and all he wanted her for was as a distraction. Is that what you want?"

"Fuck off. I thought you were cool with me dating Carson? I realize he's not your favorite person in the world, Lindsey isn't mine, but I still don't question your relationship with her." She turned and started walking away from my room. "Happy Thanksgiving," she called sarcastically over her shoulder. That definitely wasn't how I had planned on that discussion going. I knew I would need to fix things with her, but I really didn't have it in me to deal with it right now. Honestly, if Carson wanted to deal with her mood swings, then he could be my guest. She was forcing me to remember why I was so thankful for Ashley not being a teenager yet.

I got out of my bed and pulled on a pair of jeans and polo. Norah had told me the night before that she wanted all of us to look dress up today for Thanksgiving. I'm not sure why though. It was only going to be the same nine people that were in this house every day.

"Hey, sweetie, nice to see you finally woke up this morning. Happy Thanksgiving," Rose told me as I walked into the kitchen. It was almost eleven, and by the look and smell of the kitchen, she had been cooking all morning.

"Sorry, I slept so late. I was exhausted." She gave me a sideways glance.

"You were at Lindsey's pretty late last night. Should we be worried about that?" She was about as subtle as a bull in a china shop, but I was not about to have the sex talk with her. I had been at Lindsey's until almost two this morning, but we spent most of the night hanging out with her dad and step-mom. Even after that, everything was mostly innocent and definitely not her business.

I rolled my eyes. "No, Grandma, you don't need to worry."

"I just want to make sure you are being safe. You just got out of one bad situation; you don't need to be getting into another." Was she seriously trying to have this conversation right now?

"Mom, he does not want to talk about sex with you. He's a guy. If he wants to talk about sex, he can talk to his friends, not his grandma."

Rose tried to whisper, but I could still hear every word. "If he is sexually active, then it is your job to make sure he knows how to be safe and respectful."

"He has a smartphone that he can use to learn that stuff. He doesn't want to talk to either of us about it." Rose gave him a stern look, so he turned to me. "Do you know how to use a condom?" I nodded. "Do you know how to ask for consent?" I nodded again. "Do you want to stop having this conversation?" I nodded more fiercely this time, and they both laughed as I walked away from the counter.

I guess since I've already dealt with two awkward conversations today, I might as well make it three and apologize to Nat. "Knock knock," I said as I pushed her bedroom door open. She was sitting at her vanity, straightening her hair. She glared at me with her reflection. "I want to apologize for earlier. Carson and Lindsey have both moved on from their relationship, so I shouldn't keep using it to justify not liking him." Her anger wasn't budging, so I kept trying. "I don't think Carson's a bad person, but you're my family now, and that means I'm supposed to look out for you."

"No, you aren't. You've been my brother for like a month. Stop using the big brother excuse. I don't care if you want to be protective over any of the little girls, but you aren't that much older than me. I don't need your protection. In case you forgot, I've done just fine thus far. I understand that you've always had to take care of Ashley, but this is not the same thing."

I wanted to argue with her and tell her that it didn't matter to me that I hadn't known her very long. She must not understand that family is family, no matter what, and you always have to protect your family. I knew better than to argue with her; instead, I nodded. "I'm sorry. I'm not going to promise that I won't still get a little overprotective sometimes, but I'll try to be better about it." I knew Natalie well enough to know she would try to get the last word, so I left her room before she could.

I was about to go check on Nicole and Macie, who were playing in the toy room, when the doorbell rang. Natalie must have invited Carson over for lunch. I rolled my eyes at the thought and continued to head upstairs.

"Mom?" Ashley's soft voice stopped me in my tracks halfway up the stairs. Why the hell was she here? She had never cared to celebrate Thanksgiving with her children before. Why would she start now? I heard her muffled voice coming from the living room as she greeted Ashley and my dad. "What are you doing here?" Ashley sounded upset, so I hurried into the room.

"Norah invited me over to enjoy Thanksgiving with my children. Isn't that sweet?" She tried to hug Ashley, but she ducked away from her arm. I tried to subtly switch places with Ash and accept my mom's hug, but I'm sure she noticed Ashley's rudeness. I wasn't thrilled to see my mom either, but I wasn't expecting Ashley to act this way towards her. She was usually the one who told me to give Mom a chance, not the other way around.

"Happy Thanksgiving, Mom. You look great." I tried my best to hide my annoyance with her.

"Thank you. I'm clean. It's been almost two weeks now. I'm doing the work this time."

"How convenient that you finally get clean when your children decide to leave you." I hadn't meant to say the thought out loud, but I couldn't stop myself.

"AARON DAEMON!" Rose scolded.

"It's alright, Rose. I expected them to be upset. I know I have a lot to make up for, but Norah has been kind enough to extend an olive branch to me. She's going to help me stay clean so that I can be a better mom for both of you." I tuned out the rest of her apology and explanation. I had heard it a hundred times now, and usually, her sobriety only lasted a few weeks, and then she was back to her typical drunken self.

"So, Norah is this your way of getting rid of us. You get our mom cleaned up and then send us back to her? It's a great plan. I mean, it makes you look like a good samaritan, and then you don't have to worry about your husband's illegitimate children, right?" I knew I was overreacting about the situation, but Norah's kindness infuriated me. Why did she push so hard for my mom to give up her parental rights when she was going to make us work on our relationship with her anyway?

"I thought it would make you happy to have both of your parents. I know you didn't want to move here because you didn't want to abandon her. I'm sorry, Aaron. I didn't mean to upset you."

"Why would I want to be around her after the shit she's put us through? Hell, you've been more of a mom to us over the last month than she was our whole lives. Why do you think Ashley was so quick to trust people she's never even met? Because we never had anyone to take care of us. And to top it all off, she gave up on us, so for once, I'd like for it to be okay for me to give up on her." I could feel tears rolling down my face, but anger was the only emotion in me. When I looked around the room, I saw my mom crying while everyone else looked at me in shock.

"I should go. It was nice of you to invite me, Norah, but my children obviously like you more than me."

My mother turned to leave, but Ashley wasn't about to let her make us out to be the bad guys. "You're the one who didn't want to be with us in the first place. Don't make us feel bad for choosing the people who do." I don't know when she had grown up so much. I used to try to protect her from seeing my arguments with our mom, and now she had a more level head than I ever have.

I didn't care to watch my mom leave, so I retreated to my room with nothing but my thoughts. Even though my thoughts should've been on my mother and the events that just unfolded, they were actually of how normal my new life was beginning to feel. The family, which I had basically been thrown into, started to feel like the people I belonged with. The house that I had spent many days dreaming of living in when I was younger was finally my home.

I don't know how long I spent lost in my thoughts before I heard a knock at my door. It opened slightly, and Natalie walked through. She plopped down at my desk and looked at me. "Well, you and I have already had a few emotionally charged conversations today; how about another one?"

I snickered and sat up straighter in my bed. "Did dad send you to talk to me?" Normally, he would've sent Rose or Ashley if he wasn't going to do it himself.

"No, I think he's figured out that you don't like to talk about this stuff much. Besides, he's checking on Ash."

In all the time I had spent thinking, I hadn't once thought about how Ash might be feeling right now. "How is she?"

"She's fine. She's trying to explain everything to Maggie. She's strong. I would have fallen apart a hundred times with all of the shit she's gone through over the last month. You did a hell of a job raising her."

"There were quite a few things I messed up. I would do anything to go back and protect her from some of the things she saw. I tried to be the perfect role model for her, and now look, she's fighting with her mom on Thanksgiving."

She moved to the foot of my bed and put her hand on my ankle. "Aaron, you kept her safe, fed, and loved. That's all anyone can ask for, and that's more than what most seven-year-olds would've been able to do. Don't be so hard on yourself." She squeezed my leg reassuringly. "Don't forget, now you get to help raise three more."

I laughed. "Thanks for the pep-talk, Nat."

"You're welcome. Can we eat now? I've been smelling Grandma's green-bean casserole for an hour, and I'm starving."

I followed her to the kitchen, where the rest of our family was gathering. Ashley shot a wide smile that assured me that Natalie was right; she was strong. We all filled up our plates and circled around the dining room table. It was the first time I had ever had someone other than Ashley to share a Thanksgiving meal with, and I couldn't be more grateful for the family that surrounded me.

December 4th

Chapter 17 - Carson

Other than my parents driving in from Nashville, Thanksgiving was pretty normal for us. We celebrated at Mitch and Alice's house, like always, and mostly talked about nothing other than sports: including the semi-final game that we won without a problem. Today's game might be a different story, though.

We had finally made it to the championship game. My cousins and I had talked about this day for years. Today, all three of us would play together to win a state championship. The game was in Nashville again, and the whole team was driving up early Saturday to prepare for our game that starts at noon. Our entire team spent most of the bus ride sleeping, but we were ready to play as soon as we walked into the Tennessee Titans' stadium. We spent the next three hours before our game going over plays and watching game film of our opposing team. Then, it was finally game time.

The rush I felt when I ran out onto to field with so many fans screaming around me was definitely something I could get used to. The announcers called my name as part of the starting line-up, and I ran through the tunnel of my teammates to chest bump Eli at the end of it. The adrenaline coming from all of us was remarkable. At that moment, there was nothing we wanted more than to win.

Their kicker sent the ball sailing down the field and straight to Aaron, who was waiting just in front of the endzone. Without a moment of hesitation, he took off with it straight down the sideline and picked up fifty yards before being brought down. The next play didn't run near as smoothly. At the snap of the ball, I threw ten yards ahead of me to Zach, but the ball was intercepted and run back to the fifty-yard line. We were able to keep them from moving the ball too much further in the next four plays, but that didn't stop them from doing the same to us on our possession. Other than a few skilled passes from both teams, the rest of the first half continued the same way.

"What the hell are you boys doing out there? I've never seen a championship game still be scoreless at the half." It was hard to tell if Coach was angry with us or just surprised. Overall, we were playing well, but so were they. "I want you to go out on that field and play like this is your last game because, for some of you, it is." I looked around at the Senior guys, including Camden, Cooper, and Sam, who had taught me most of what I knew about football. They were all concentrating on every word Coach was saying, which meant they were ready to play.

Sam kicked the ball perfectly down to the endzone, where the receiver caught it effortlessly. They had a style of primarily running trick plays that our defense was able to hold easily to force a turnover. Once the ball was in my hands, it was my turn to run it. There was a clear path down the right sideline, so I made a beeline for it. Aaron followed the play perfectly and made his way over to me. When we got to the twenty-yard line, I handed the ball off to him and served as a distraction while he ran it into the endzone. Our team was playing better than we had all year, and luckily for us, theirs was playing worse. They couldn't seem to get around our defense, whereas they were leaving holes everywhere in theirs. We continued making drive after drive down the field, and they couldn't stop us.

We were up forty-two to twenty-one with three minutes left in the game. We all knew we had just won the state championship, but none of us were going to stop giving our best. After another turnover on downs on their side, there was only a minute and a half left. We lined up, snapped the ball, and chucked it to Zach. He took off down the field but got stopped at halfway. We ran two more plays the same way before the clock finally ran out. We had officially won!

Criden fans flooded the field as our team huddled together, cheering for our victory. Before we knew it, our team huddle had become a town huddle, and we couldn't have been happier about it. It was the best feeling in the world; well, maybe second best. When the huddle finally split apart, Natalie quickly found me and pulled my lips down to meet hers in a congratulatory kiss - that was the best feeling in the world. When I pulled away, I realized that her whole family had gathered behind her just as mine had behind me.

"Well, I'm not going to tongue you in the middle of the field, but I would like to congratulate you on a great season." Mr. Clemmetts held his hand out to me, and I shook it with a laugh. I hoped it sounded less nervous than I was feeling. Over the last two weeks, the interactions I've had with Natalie's family haven't been much more than a few words, and I was starting to get the feeling that her dad didn't like me very much. Maybe I was just being paranoid. He seemed perfectly happy with me today, but then again, so was everyone else.

"Well, it's a good thing you aren't a senior this year. I don't think my hormones could handle it," My mom told me after hugging Cooper and Camden.

"Who knows, you might have another little football player in there." I nodded toward her stomach and looked to see her smiling while my dad shook his head.

"I think dance might be the direction this one heads in with how much she moves." She shot me a nervous glance as if gauging my reaction.

"Congratulations, Mom. You're finally going to have a little girl to play dress-up with." I gave her a hug and a reassuring squeeze.

"What's this I hear about you having a little girl? Am I really not going to be the only girl anymore?" Casey asked as Ray carried her over on piggyback.

Natalie gently slipped her hand into mine. "I guess I'll have to teach you what it's like to have a little sister," she told me.

"We have plenty. I'll let you take one for a little bit." I followed the strangled voice to where Aaron had two of his little sisters climbing on his back. "Look what you started, Ray!"

"Guys, we should probably get going. I'll talk to you soon, Mom. Love you, guys." For the first time since they had moved, my dad hugged me before Aaron, Cooper, Camden, Ray, and I headed back to the locker room.

After the long drive back to the school, I headed back to the house with Cooper and Camden to eat some dinner and take a shower. Then, it was party time. The three of us and Casey hopped in the truck and headed over to Sam and Jess's right at eight o'clock.

"Everyone has to take a shot when they come in," Sam told us as he handed each of us a plastic shot glass. Coop, Case, and I took ours without a second thought, but Cam refused, using the excuse that he was driving.

I spotted Aaron and Lindsey shortly after, but Natalie wasn't with them. "Hey, man, where's your sister?" I asked when I got to them. Aaron nodded to the make-shift bar where Natalie was showing off her award-winning smile to Zach. I felt irritation boiling up as I walked over to them. "Hey, baby, what's up?" I put my arm around her waist and pulled a beer out of the fridge. She laughed as I planted a kiss on her lips. I could taste the whiskey on her lips. She decided two weeks ago that straight whiskey is her drink, which made her even hotter to me.

"Zach was just trying to make me feel better about getting so drunk in Nashville by telling me some of his drunk stories."

"I will say, her choice to drink straight whiskey might end up with her having quite a few more stories, though." Zach reached across and put his hand on her arm.

Every bit of me wanted to slap his hand away, but I didn't want to upset Natalie. "Well, I was just coming to say hi and grab a beer." I let go of her waist and headed over to where Cooper was pouring shots for more of the players. "Pour one for me, Coop." I downed the first one and was about to grab the next one he put in front of me, but it was taken off the table before I could. I turned around to see Natalie finishing my shot.

"What the hell was that about? Are you really so insecure that I can't even have a friendly conversation with a guy?" A few people had turned their attention to our argument.

"Come with me." I led her into Sam's room.

"Dammit, Carson, I'm trying to have a conversation with you, not make out." Her voice was dripping anger.

"I didn't bring you in here to make out. I'm trying not to cause a fucking scene and ruin everyone's buzz. Also, I was grabbing a beer and giving my girlfriend a kiss. I wasn't trying to interrupt your conversation."

"Bullshit, you were practically marking your territory, and you know it. Why are you so damn stubborn?"

I scoffed. She's the most stubborn person I've ever met. "You're one to talk. Do you seriously see nothing wrong with talking to someone who lied to you about things I tell my friends?"

"See, I knew you were mad about it. Why can't you just trust me?"

"Because the last person I was in love with cheated on me, so I'm sorry if I'm being a little more cautious this time." It took me a moment to understand the shocked look on Natalie's face. Had I just inadvertently told her I was in love with her? What the hell was wrong with me? We've only been dating for two weeks. Why would I tell her that? And why did I feel kinda relieved about saying it?

"I'm sorry. I know it's hard to trust someone after you've been hurt." She sat down solemnly on the bed. I knew she was referring to her dad and how he hid Aaron and Ashley from her family. She hadn't talked to me about it much since we had started dating, but I knew she hadn't fully forgiven him yet.

"Look, I don't want to fight with you, babe. So how about I try to be a little less jealous, and you try to not talk to Zach anymore."

She rolled her eyes while trying to suppress a smile. She wasn't any good at staying mad at me. I pulled her up by the hand and gave her a long kiss. She pulled me closer to her as her hand found the back of my neck. Just like with everything else, she was in control. "You are extremely frustrating," she mumbled while I moved my lips down to her neck. She clearly had no clue just how frustrating she was, especially when she was wearing skin-tight leggings and a v-neck t-shirt. I started pushing up the hem of her shirt to reveal her small form. "Carson." She was breathless, and the sound made me move my hands farther. "Stop." My hands froze where they were on her bare ribs. She pushed away from me. Reluctantly, I slid my hands back down her stomach and pulled away from her.

"Why? What's wrong?" I tried to hide my disappointment, but this girl was driving me crazy. I plopped down on the bed.

"Seriously? That's how you're going to react to me telling you to stop? Like a child who doesn't get to play with a damn toy? I'm not a piece of ass, Carson; I have feelings. Fuck, you're ridiculous. I don't even know why I try with you." She turned to walk away, but I caught her hand.

"I'm sorry, Nat, I got lost in the moment. It's hard for me to keep my hands off of you." I moved my hand from her wrist to her waist to lighten the mood, but all it did was piss her off more.

She slapped my hand away. "Don't try to be cute with me. Can you not tell that I'm mad at you right now? You said you would respect my boundaries, and now you're pouting about it. Honestly, I don't want to deal with this tonight. I'm gonna go home, and I'll text you tomorrow."

"You've been drinking, and Aaron drove you here. How are you going to get home? I don't even know why you're mad right now. Almost any other girl here would jump at the chance to have me touching them like that." Between the anger and the alcohol, neither of us were thinking clearly.

"Well, then go find one of 'em because I'm not interested. And I'll find someone to give me a ride." She wasn't going to let this go, and there wasn't any point in arguing with her, so when she tried to leave this time, I let her go. I left the room a few minutes later, just as Cooper and Sam were getting ready to shotgun beers. Instead of worrying about where Natalie was, I grabbed a beer and joined them.

About thirty minutes and a few beers later, Ray approached me. "Hey, dude, I'm going to take Natalie and Casey home."

"Well, I'm sure you can get Casey to sleep with you, but good luck getting Natalie to do anything. I know I sure as hell can't." I threw back the rest of my beer.

He laughed at my comment. "Okay, can you tell Cam so he knows where Casey is? She's been sleeping in my truck for the last hour. And your girlfriend seems pretty pissed, so I figured she was ready to leave too."

I don't know why he was telling me all of this. Natalie had made it very clear that I was not her keeper. "Yeah, have fun with that. I'm gonna get another beer." He mumbled some asshole comment to me, but I didn't care enough to listen to what it was.

I had a couple more drinks before the guilt finally hit me, and I decided to sober up. Cooper tried to get me to keep taking shots with him, but I wasn't in the mood to party anymore. I had never gone to a party and stopped drinking in the middle of it, but it was hard for me to have fun when I had screwed up with Natalie again. We had only been together for two weeks, and I had already pissed her off three times. I need to get my shit together before she decides I'm not worth her time. Although, we probably wouldn't fight as much if she weren't so damn stubborn.

"Dude, what's up with you? You stopped drinking two hours ago, and now you're pouting in a corner. If you're done with this, go grab Cooper and let's go." I hadn't noticed Camden standing next to me, probably because he didn't have Jess on his arm like he usually did.

"Coop, let's get out of here!" I shouted from across the room. He gulped down the rest of his drink and came over to us. He never liked to leave parties early, but I think he's learned better than to try to argue when Cam and I are ready to go.

Cooper slammed the truck door after he climbed into the front seat. "What the hell is wrong with you two? I'm trying to have a good time, and you both are acting like lovesick puppies." He pointed drunkenly at where I was sitting in the seat behind him. "You said you didn't give a shit about Natalie being mad at you. What happened to that?" Cooper's most serious relationship was sleeping with the same girl three nights in a row. He didn't understand what it was like to care about a girl's opinion and feelings. Part of me missed being able to do that - it definitely would've made tonight more fun.

"Cooper, cut him some slack. He just got into this relationship; he doesn't want to lose it already. I realize you don't really understand relationships, but some people like to keep the person they like happy."

"You don't even get to talk, Cam. You disappeared for most of the night. Did Jess finally stop being mad and sleep with you?" Cam wouldn't meet his eye. "Ahh, she did, so why did we have to leave early?"

"Because, unlike you, I care about more than just sex and partying. I don't like staying up until all hours of the night. Seriously, man, you need to grow up. What are you going to do when you actually have to be responsible for someone other than yourself?" Cam had given Cooper this lecture a hundred times, but it was almost always when Cooper was drunk and wouldn't remember it the next day. I didn't need to listen to this again, so I closed my eyes, leaned my head against the window, and tuned them out.

"FUCK!" I opened my eyes as Camden swerved to the left to avoid a deer. When he swerved back to the right lane, I felt the truck start to lean while Camden continued to curse. As the truck's passenger side crashed into the ground, my head slammed into the window. Everything went black.

Chapter 18 - Casey

"Casey, get up! We have to go!" I woke up to Ray shaking me
frantically. "There was an accident. Casey, your parents are heading
to the hospital. We have to go!" His words were blending in my head. I
couldn't make sense of anything he was saying, so I continued lying
frozen in my bed. Finally, he grabbed my arm, pulled me to a seated
position, and crouched down in front of me. "Case, I know you're
confused, but we have to go. I'll explain everything on the way there.
Right now, I just need you to get out of bed and get in my truck." I
crawled out of bed slowly as his words finally started to hit me. I
rushed to change out of my shorts and pull on a pair of sweats - not
caring that Ray was in the room the whole time.

"What happened?" I finally got the nerve to ask once I had
climbed into the truck.

My tears had already started falling before he even started.
"After I brought you home, I decided just to hang out until the guys got
home. I was sleeping on the couch when your dad got the call. I
guess Cam rolled the truck. Your parents were both pretty freaked
out, so I volunteered to bring you to the hospital. They didn't know
anything about what kind of condition they're in." The tears were
falling faster now, and I couldn't make them stop. Ray reached across
the cab of the truck and put his hand on my thigh. "We can't freak out
yet. People get in car accidents every day and are perfectly fine. Until

we know something, we have to stay calm. Okay?" I nodded while my tears continued to flow. When I looked over at Ray, I could tell he wanted to say more, but instead, we rode in silence the rest of the way to the hospital in Knoxville.

When I walked through the hospital doors, the first thing I saw was my parents holding each other while they cried. Something was seriously wrong. I had been in the hospital a hundred times to see my dad when he was working, but this time was different. My legs suddenly felt like jello, and I stopped walking. Ray wrapped his arm around me and practically held me up as we continued to walk towards my parents.

My dad stood to meet us. "Sweetheart." Ray passed me from his arms to my father's. "The truck rolled. Carson is in surgery right now for some internal injuries, Cam's legs were crushed, and Cooper…" He looked helplessly at my mom as he started to cry again. "Cooper didn't make it." My entire world stopped. My knees gave out; if not for my dad's arms wrapped around me, I would have crumbled to the ground. I felt like I was underwater; everything was distorted. My parents tried to talk to me, but all I heard was mumbling. Doctors, nurses, and patients walked around the waiting room, but they all looked like blurry blobs through my tears. My mom had stood up to join my dad and me, but they both felt far away.

When we finally separated, Ray guided me to a chair. "Do you need me to get you anything? Coffee? A blanket?" I shook my head and reached my hand out to him. He took it and sat down next to me. "I should probably call Sam and Jess." I nodded, but thankfully, he didn't move. I needed him right now. I spent the next three hours with my hand in his and my head on his shoulder while my silent tears continued to fall. Every once in a while, I would feel a tear fall into my hair - Ray was crying too. Carson, Camden, and Cooper were the closest thing he had to brothers; right now, he needed me just as much as I needed him.

"Where is he? What happened?" Aunt B was already crying by the time she walked in the door. Danny came in behind her with a frantic look on his face. My parents rushed over to meet them. As my dad told them what had happened, Belle started to sob.

"Cooper didn't make it." My dad used the exact words he had used when he told me. He was used to giving people this news, but hearing the words again made it even harder for me. They made it more real, but this couldn't be real. I squeezed my eyes shut as tightly as I could to keep my tears from falling even faster. "We haven't heard anything else from the doctors on how they're doing."

"What can you tell me about my son, Carson Nixley?" Danny asked the nurse at the front desk. His voice sounded like he was holding back tears.

"He's in surgery right now for internal injuries. I can find out from his doctor how much longer they think it will take."

"That would be great, thank you. Could you give me any information on my nephew, Camden Johnson?"

"I'll find out what I can." The nurse seemed intimidated by Danny's stern demeanor, but then again, most people were. The nurse made a few quick phone calls and then looked back to Danny.

"The doctors are just finishing up your son's surgery; they'll be out to talk to you soon."

"How soon is soon? He's been back there for three hours." Danny was starting to raise his voice. "My wife is five months pregnant, one of our nephews just died, and no one is updating us on our son." For the first time in my life, I saw tears rolling down Danny's face. The sight sent me over the edge. I stood up from my chair and stalked out of the hospital. The blast of cold air took my breath away as I walked through the door. It felt like a slap in the face that finally made the last few hours feel real. My legs collapsed under me, but a pair of arms wrapped around me before I hit the ground. He lowered me to the ground and held me close to him while I sobbed.

"Just let it out, Casey Jane. I've got you. Just let it out." On the ground outside the hospital with my head buried in Ray's chest, I cried harder than I ever had before. I don't know how long we stayed like that, but Ray never let go of me.

"We should probably get back inside," I finally told him when my breathing had slowed. It was the first thing I had said since we got to the hospital. "Carson is supposed to be out soon." I didn't want to leave his arms, though. He was protecting me from everything bad that could happen when we walked back through those doors.

"Yeah, I don't want you to get sick." I nodded, but we still didn't move away from one another. I was curled in a ball with Ray's legs and arms holding me close to him.

"Carson's out of surgery!" My mom's shaky voice made both of us stand straight up. We practically sprinted inside to where my dad

225

was talking to Dr. O'Neal, one of his colleagues, and Carson's parents. Ray slipped his hand into mine as we prepared ourselves for the news.

"Carson's injuries were severe. He had multiple broken bones, including ribs, a pierced lung, and major head trauma. We were able to repair his ribs and repair his lung. Right now, he's on a ventilator to make sure that his lungs are getting enough oxygen. He should be able to come off the vent after a few hours, and he might have to undergo more surgery to repair the other breaks," Dr. O'Neal explained to us.

"As for his head, we won't be able to tell what kind of damage has been done until he wakes up. They had to stop a few bleeds in his brain already, but it's possible that they will have to go back in as he recovers." My dad had clearly already spoken with Carson's team before he and Dr. O'Neal had come to talk to us.

"You said when 'he wakes up,' what do you mean? When will that be?" Belle's words were hardly audible.

"Belle, he's in a coma. His body went into shock. He's going to have to fight to wake up, but we have to be positive right now." Danny walked away from us. "Danny, come on." My father called out to him. "Carson's a fighter. You raised him to be a fighter." Belle moved to hug Danny, but he shoved her away. She started to stumble back, but he caught her.

"Belle, I'm sorry. I didn't mean to." He wrapped his arms around his wife as he pleaded with her.

"Mitch, when can we see him?" Belle asked. "I-I need to see him."

"Visiting hours don't start until six a.m., but since he's a minor, you all can go in and see him." Danny and Belle followed Dr. O'Neal into the ICU.

Ray dropped my hand, and I felt the urge to grab his back. "Now that we know what's going on, I'm going to call Sam and my mom. Are you going to be alright here for a few minutes?" I stared at him blankly. He put his hand on my shoulder. "Casey? Are you okay?" I nodded slightly. "Okay, someone needs to call Natalie. It should be you, Case. You're her best friend." He didn't let me respond before clicking on his mom's number and putting the phone to his ear.

How could he expect me to be the one to call her? I had hardly talked to her over the last two weeks. I can't call her out of nowhere and tell her that her boyfriend is in a coma. He was right though. She needed to know, and I can't leave it up to Carson's parents to do it. I picked up my phone to call her, but I couldn't bring myself to do it. I couldn't say the words out loud because that would make them real. I couldn't tell Natalie that her boyfriend was fighting for his life because of a car accident that killed my brother. Instead, I opened the last text I got from Cooper.

"Stop being a downer." I had ignored it when he had sent it to me at Sam's house. Seeing the words now made everything worse. How could I not be a downer right now? My world was falling apart. Everything in me was either numb or hurting. This wasn't fair. Cooper was the person that could be solid and upbeat even in the most challenging times. I threw my phone onto the shiny, white hospital floor. Ray and my parents quickly looked at me and my shattered phone.

"IT'S NOT FAIR! THEY DIDN'T DO ANYTHING WRONG! PEOPLE GET IN CAR ACCIDENTS ALL THE TIME! IT'S NOT FAIR!" My voice was louder and clearer than I had expected it to be.

No one moved towards me, but my mom spoke to me shakily. "I know, honey, but sometimes things aren't fair. Death is not fair. That doesn't change what happened, though, Casey." She took a step toward me. "I know this is hard, but you can't think like that. Remember how when Grandma died, we had to remember that it was her time to go?" Was she seriously comparing her son dying in a car accident to when her mom got cancer? This was nothing like that. She had gotten the chance to live; Cooper had never even fallen in love.

I held my hand out in front of me to stop her advance. I was tired of people trying to make this okay. None of this was okay. "This is nothing like when Grandma died. We got to say goodbye to her. We were prepared. She was fifty-five, and we were children. I hardly knew her. Cooper was my brother and one of my best friends. He was only eighteen!" Tears, which I thought I was out of, rolled down my face, but I didn't stop. "Stop trying to make this normal. Nothing about you having to bury your son is normal. Isn't that what you always told me? That parents should never outlive their kids? So why are you acting like I'm overreacting right now? Don't we have a right to be mad?" She was silent while she fought back tears.

"Of course, you do, Casey. You have the right to feel whatever you want to feel," Ray told me soothingly. In my anger, I hadn't noticed him picking up the pieces of my phone from off the ground.

"Stop! Are you trying to replace him? Trying to be a good big brother? Is that why you're here? You see that I'm down a brother, so you're trying to take his place?" I knew what I was saying was harsh, but why else would he be here? "Look around you, Ray! Everyone else here is family, except for you!" It was a low blow, but it was true. He might love them like his brothers, but they weren't his family. And I sure as hell am not his little sister that needs him to take care of her.

"I'm trying to take care of you, Casey, because that's what your brothers would want me to do." There was hurt in Ray's eyes, but we were all hurting right now. I had no reason to feel bad for him.

"I don't need you to keep looming over me like I'm some little girl who needs to be protected." The bitterness in my voice must have finally gotten my point through Ray's head.

"Fine, but I'm not leaving, Casey. They might not be my blood, but they are my family; whether you like it or not. Now, I'm gonna go get a cup of coffee." He turned his back on me and headed down the hallway to the cafeteria.

My mom put her hand on my shoulder, and I brushed it off. "Don't, Mom." I knew she was about to tell me to apologize to Ray.

"I wasn't going to say anything other than maybe you should get some rest. I'm sure Belle and Danny are going to be with Carson for a while, and Cam's going to be in surgery a while longer. Dad found out that his leg was practically shattered in the accident. You need sleep, honey. We all do." She looked exhausted. She was makeup-free, and I couldn't remember seeing her like that in years. Me throwing a fit was the last thing she needed right now. "I'm sure your dad could get you into an on-call room for a little while if you want."

"It's okay, Mom. It's not like I could sleep anyway. I guess I should clean that up." I gestured to my phone. "I'm sorry." She pulled me into a hug.

"It's okay, sweetie. You have no idea how badly I would love to break something too. We're all angry, love, but that doesn't change what happened. We just have to accept it." I fought back another round of tears as I nodded. My mom let go of me as my dad walked away from the front desk.

"They should be done in about an hour. They have to put in a few more screws and then close. He's going to need a lot of physical therapy, but except for a minor concussion, he didn't have any other injuries. He was lucky it was just his legs."

I made my way back to the chair I had been sitting in before my outburst. Ray came back into the waiting room shortly after, but he didn't sit next to me like he had before. Instead, he sat across the room and stared blankly at his phone. He looked just as exhausted as my parents did. Part of me wanted him to sit next to me again, but another part of me was still mad at him for trying to take care of me like Cooper and Camden would. I sat there conflicted a few minutes more before Belle and Danny came back to the waiting room. Belle had clearly been crying at the sight of her son on life support, but she still tried to force a smile.

"He's in pretty rough shape, but he's going to be alright. He's strong. You kids should probably go home for a little while and get some rest."

"Cam's still in surgery; we can't just leave him," I protested, getting to my feet. They're my family too. She can't expect me to leave either one of them.

"Honey, Cam is going to be asleep for a few hours after his surgery. Go home and get some sleep. Ray can bring you back during visiting hours." My dad was using his patient voice on me. It was the one he used when he needed to deliver bad news but still keep patients calm.

"I'm not going anywhere. You can't..." Ray cut me off in the middle of my sentence as he walked up to where we were all standing.

"My dad's house is five minutes from here. We can go there, get some sleep, and I'll bring you back first thing in the morning. I already talk to him about me staying there; I'm sure he won't mind you being there too." I really didn't want his opinion or his help right now.

"I'm not leaving!" I stomped my foot like a toddler, and Ray rolled his eyes at me.

He grabbed my wrist and pulled me aside. "Casey, your parents don't need to deal with you throwing a tantrum right now. You are coming with me, and you are going to get some sleep. Okay?" His voice was more stern and severe than I had ever heard it.

"I'm. Not. Leaving. You can't make me leave." I kept my voice from shaking and glared at him.

"Really?" He threw me over his shoulder. I tried to fight him, but he didn't put me down. "I'll make sure she gets some sleep, and we'll be back in the morning." He gave my mom and Belle a quick side-hug and shook my dad and Danny's hands. "Keep us updated, and try to get some sleep yourselves."

"We will, Ray. Thank you for watching out for her. She's lucky to have you." I rolled my eyes at my mom's comment. She is probably one of the biggest supporters of 'Raysey,' and no matter how many times I tell her we are just friends, she always thinks we're secretly dating.

Ray carried me all the way out to his truck before setting me down. "Get in," he ordered as he opened the passenger door. I shook my head at him. "Casey, please, I'm tired, and I don't want to fight you on every little thing. Just get in the damn truck." Before I moved, he walked away from me. I climbed in as another round of tears started to fall. "Case?" His voice was softer now, concerned instead of angry.

"I don't want to leave them. What if something happens? I already wasn't there when Cooper..." I couldn't finish the sentence.

Ray started the truck and tried to take my hand, but I pulled away from him. "Casey, you being there wouldn't have changed anything other than your parents would have one more kid in the hospital. Just like you being at the hospital all night won't do anything other than make your parents have to worry about you on top of everything else. Let them take care of Carson and Cam, and for God's sake, let me take care of you."

When I didn't answer for a minute, he started talking again while we pulled out of the parking lot. "I promised them I would take care of you. Sam agreed to it too. It's part of being one of the brothers. We are all supposed to watch out for you and Jess." They seriously made some stupid secret pact to make sure I was taken care of. It sounded exactly like something my brothers would do. They were always protecting me. I can't believe one of them is actually gone for good. "It was his idea, you know?" Ray said, interrupting my thoughts. "Camden might be the more responsible one, but when it came to protecting you, Coop was always ready to fight for you. I want to scream, and cry, and throw things too, but this is what Cooper would've wanted me to do." His voice cracked, and I heard him swallow hard to fight back the tears. "So, will you please just let me do what he would want?"

"I'm sorry," I said quietly. I couldn't think of anything else to say, so we rode in silence for the rest of the drive. I was mad at them for not telling me and for not believing that I could take care of myself, but I didn't want to upset Ray anymore, so I sat quietly in my anger.

When we pulled into the driveway, we both climbed out of the truck and walked up to the front door. Even though it was dark, I could tell the house was massive. Ray never talked about his dad, so I wasn't sure what he did for a living, but it must pay well. When his parents got divorced, Ray was young, and he spent most of his time with his mom. I had never seen his dad at anything for him, but I knew Ray stayed with him on the weekends sometimes.

Ray knocked on the door, and the man who answered was the spitting image of him: tall, olive skin, green eyes. The only difference was this man had more wrinkles; he must not be as carefree as Ray. "You must be Casey." He reached out his large hand and shook mine. "My son's told me a lot about you. I'm Adam." I looked at Ray, but he avoided my eye. "Your bed's made up for you all, Ray. If you need anything else, you know where to find it." He turned and headed back to what I assume was his room, so I followed Ray into the house.

He stopped at a large room near the back of the house. The walls were painted light blue, and pictures of sea animals decorated them. "You can have my bed. I'll sleep on the couch." I couldn't tell if he was uncomfortable with the idea of us sleeping in the same bed or just with me being in his childhood bedroom, but his face was flushed.

His dad was already letting us stay here; I really didn't want to add any hassle by taking over his couch too. "Ray, I'm not going to kick you out of your own bed. It's only a few hours, and besides, we've shared a bed before." He looked confused by my sudden change in attitude but shrugged his shoulders in acceptance of the fact. I stood and watched as he started rummaging through his drawers, pulled out a pair of shorts, and walked into the bathroom that was connected to the room.

I pulled the covers back on the full-sized bed and laid down on one side. There was no way I was going to be able to fall asleep after everything I had dealt with in the last few hours. I stared up at the ceiling for a while before Ray finally came out of the bathroom. I could tell he had been crying from the sniffling sounds that echoed through the dark room. He hadn't let himself fall apart yet, at least not like I had. He had been holding himself together for me. I felt like I was invading his privacy by listening to him cry when he had tried so hard to hide it from me, so I closed my eyes and pretended to be asleep. I felt the weight of him next to me as he slowly eased into the bed. I continued listening to his breathing hitch for a minute before I rolled onto my side and scooted closer to him.

"I'm sorry, Case. I didn't mean to wake you." He was clearly trying to hide the sadness in his voice. "Go back to sleep."

"It's okay. I wasn't sleeping anyway." I scooted even closer to him. He gave me a questioning look that I could hardly see in the dark and moved his arm to put it under my head. I curled against him and laid my head on his chest as his other arm wrapped around me. He cried harder into my hair. I stayed silent until he started to calm down.

"I'm sorry," he whispered while his breathing hitched again. His arms fell from around me, but I didn't move away from him. As much as I hated to admit it, I needed him right now, and I hoped he needed me. I didn't respond to him; instead, I continued listening to his heart race. As his heart slowed, so did my breathing. "Goodnight, Casey Jane," I heard Ray whisper through my sleepy haze. His arms pulled me even closer to him and held me in place.

I woke up the next morning disoriented; then, all of the memories started flooding back. It hadn't just been a dream. Tears began to well in my eyes. I reached for Ray's phone, and the time showed on the screen: six-fifteen. We're late. I practically jumped out of bed just as Ray walked into the room with his hands full. "Why'd you let me sleep past six? We're late for visiting," I yelled at him through the tears.

"Quiet down. My little brother is still sleeping. I already talked to your mom, and she said not to rush because Cam needs to sleep for a little longer. Before you ask, Danny and Belle are going to be in with Carson for a while, so you wouldn't be able to see him either." When he finally realized my tears, his voice changed from calm to panicked. "Hey, hey, what's wrong?" He sat down the clothes, coffee, and food he was carrying and grabbed my hand.

"It was all real. It wasn't just a dream. He's really gone." My tears were falling faster even though I was trying to stop them.

"I wish it wasn't real, Case." He sat down on the bed in front of me and dropped my hand. "I wish none of us had to go through this, but we do. And I know that doesn't make any of this easier, but we have to focus on being there for Carson and Camden right now. So, I need you to eat some food, drink some coffee, and take a shower. I borrowed some of my stepmom's clothes for you. Okay?" I nodded as my tears started to slow. He leaned closer to me and grabbed the plate off the dresser behind me. "Eat. I'll be in the kitchen if you need anything."

I scarfed down the breakfast of toast, bacon, and fruit while I drank the coffee. Ray must have been paying more attention to me over the last few years than I had realized because everything was exactly how I liked it: the bacon was crispy, the fruit was fresh, and the coffee had just enough creamer in it. Was that part of his deal with my brothers too? It had to be; why else would he know all of that? I pushed the thought aside and went into the bathroom to shower. My house wasn't small by any means, but it looked like a shanty compared to this one. The bathroom was twice the size of mine at home and was complete with a large marble shower. Two fluffy, black, perfectly-folded towels were sitting on the matching marble countertop. I numbly went through the motions of taking a shower and pulling on the clothes Ray had borrowed for me. I was about to walk out of Ray's room when I heard voices coming from the kitchen.

"How's she doing?" the deeper voice, which belonged to Ray's dad, asked suddenly. I knew they were talking about me.

"How do you think she's doing, Dad? One of her brothers just died, the other one's legs were so shattered that he was in surgery for more than four hours last night, and her cousin is in a coma on a ventilator with severe head trauma." Ray's voice was full of a mixture of sadness and anger. "Her entire world is falling apart around her, and there isn't anything that anyone, including me, can do to fix it. She's angry at everything and everyone, and when she isn't angry, she's crying. I'm doing everything I can to be there for her, but I don't know how to help her through this. Sometimes she acts like I'm terrible for trying to take care of her, and other times she doesn't want me to leave her side. It's so confusing." I heard him huff as something smacked on the counter.

"Are you kidding me, Ray? You think you're confused? Imagine what that poor girl is going through right now. She definitely doesn't need your feelings getting involved in this. She has enough on her plate. You just need to be there for her without over-complicating anything." His dad was angry now, but I wasn't sure what he was talking about. Sure, Ray and I had argued last night, but that was because I was angry, not because Ray had done anything wrong.

"I'm not trying to make this harder for her," Ray objected.

"Well, it seems to me that cuddling with her in your bed could make things more confusing for her. She needs a friend right now, Ray, not a boyfriend. If you are her boyfriend, that's fine, but if not, now is not the time to be changing that." Great, another person who thinks Ray and I are dating. I rolled my eyes at the idea that seemed to follow us everywhere.

"I'm not trying to be her boyfriend. That's just our relationship, Dad. I care about Casey, and I love her, but I don't want to date her. She's one of my best friends." I was tired of listening to their bickering.

"Hey, thank you for breakfast, and thank you for letting us stay here, Adam." I walked into the kitchen and put my hand on Ray's arm. "Are you ready to head to the hospital?" I tried to pretend like I hadn't been listening to their conversation.

"I'm ready to go if you are. Just let me grab something from my room." I followed him to the bedroom.

"So your dad thinks we're dating too?" He jumped at the sound of my voice; he must not have known I was behind him. "I guess that's pretty much par for the course for us now."

"You were eavesdropping on my conversation with my dad? Are you some kind of stalker?" he teased as he picked up his phone and wallet.

"It was kinda hard not to hear it with how loud you all were talking, and by the way, I don't want to date you either." He laughed as he turned back toward me.

"Oh, please. You would jump my bones in a second, just like every other girl at our school." He moved closer to me and grabbed my sides. I knew what he was about to do, but I couldn't move away from his grasp. "Admit it, or I'll tickle you."

"Ray, don't," I warned, but it didn't stop him. A squeal mixed with a laugh escaped my lips. "Ray!" His fingers stopped after a minute of my protesting. Our laughter had left us both breathless, and I rested my head in the crooked of his neck while his hands stayed in place just above my hips.

He dropped his hands suddenly and pulled away from me. "We should get going." He walked out of the room without another word to me. What the hell was that about? That was the first relaxed moment I've had since the accident, and he ruined it. I caught up to him as we were walking out of the house, but he didn't acknowledge me. I climbed into the truck quickly as I started to panic. Maybe he knew something I didn't about Camden or Carson's condition. The five-minute drive to the hospital was silent, and Ray seemed stiff, which only added to my anxiety. As soon as the truck was parked, I climbed out and rushed to the door.

"Cam just woke; we were about to go in and see him. Do you want to come with us?" Was that why Ray was in such a hurry to get here? Because he didn't want me to miss seeing Cam when he first woke up? I nodded slightly to my parents and followed them down the long hallway to Cam's room.

"Hey," Cam greeted with a groggy smile. We took turns leaning in to give him gentle hugs before settling into the chairs had we pulled up to the side of the bed.

"How do you feel, bud?" my dad asked as if he was talking to a random patient rather than his own son. "Do you have any pain?"

"A little bit, but mostly I'm just tired. God, that crash was crazy. The deer came out of nowhere, so I swerved, and the next thing I knew, the truck was flipping. How are Carson and Cooper doing?" There it was. The question none of us wanted to answer. We all looked at each other gravely - wondering who would be the one to speak up.

Finally, my dad did. "Cam, the accident was bad. Your truck rolled down a hill and into some trees. Some of the trees fell on top of the truck, which is what crushed your legs. Carson had quite a few broken bones, and one of his ribs punctured his lung. They were able to fix it, but he's on a ventilator, and he has some pretty severe head injuries, which they're assuming is from his head hitting the window. He's in a coma, and they aren't sure when or if he's going to wake up." Camden paled as he listened. I wasn't sure he could handle this next part, or if I could, for that matter. My mom was already starting to sniffle, and the sight made tears well up again.

240

"What about Cooper? He's alright, isn't he?" My mom couldn't choke back her sobs anymore. "Mom, what happened?" The fear in his eyes made my tears fall too.

"Cooper wasn't wearing his seatbelt. He was thrown around the cab of the truck quite a bit, and when the tree that crushed your legs fell, it made the door cave in on him. He was pronounced dead on the scene." Cam started to cry before the words left my dad's lips.

"No. No. No, he's fine. He's fine! HE'S FINE!" He yelled louder as his sobs came faster. "He-He can't be gone. Mom, please tell me he's not gone." My mom answered by crying harder. "It's my fault. It's my fault. I was-I-I was..." he stammered as his breath quickened.

"Cam, what are you talking about? This is not your fault." My dad tried without success to calm him down. "Cam, you need to breathe. He's having a panic attack. I need a nurse!" He struggled with shaky hands to grab the oxygen mask behind Cam's bed. My mom gripped my wrist tightly. An older lady rushed in to help him place the mask over Cam's face. This was going worse than I had expected it to.

When his breathing started to slow, he pulled the mask down. "I was lecturing him about responsibility, and I took my eyes off the road for one second. It's my fault," he explained through tears.

"It was an accident, Cam. It isn't anyone's fault." It was the first thing I had managed to say since walking into the room, and my firm voice seemed to surprise my family. I was surprised by it too; I had expected to sound weak and quiet from my crying. They all looked at me expectantly to see if I would continue. When I didn't, a voice from behind me did.

"She's right, honey. No one is blaming you. This could've happened to anyone." Belle walked into the room and rested her hand on Cam's shoulder.

"I'm so sorry, Aunt B. If I hadn't been arguing with Cooper, this never would've happened. If I..."

Belle cut him off. "Don't do that to yourself, Camden. You will drive yourself crazy with the "what-ifs." Carson is going to be alright." She turned toward me. "Casey, if you want, you can go in and see him. They're only letting immediate family in until he's more stable, so if anyone asks, Ray is his cousin."

I looked across the bed at my dad for permission to leave. As soon as he nodded, I stood up, squeezed Cam's hand reassuringly, and left the room to go see Carson. Seeing Carson had to be easier than seeing Cam. Right? At least then I wouldn't have to watch his reaction to finding out about Cooper. It was just going to be Carson laying there; how bad could that be?

I navigated my way to his room, and the sight, when I walked in, took my breath away. Carson looked completely helpless with all the wires and tubes connected to him. His head was wrapped in bandages, as was his stomach. This silent, fragile version of him was the opposite of the stubborn, strong Carson I was used to. I sat down in the chair next to his bed and looked at him.

"I don't really know what I'm supposed to say to you, Carson, which I know is ironic because I'm rarely at a loss for words." I laughed weakly at my own joke to keep myself from crying again. "If you could see me right now, you would probably tell me that I'm being a cry baby, and honestly, that would be so much better than you just lying here like this."

"He'd probably be giving us all kinds of shit for being together when the accident happened." Ray gripped my shoulders from behind me. "He'd make it seem like we were in the middle of hooking up." I laughed because I knew he was right. I could never tell if Carson actually wanted Ray and me to date or if he just enjoyed teasing us about it.

"What do you think he would do?" I asked suddenly. I would be lying if I said I hadn't thought about Ray as more than a friend, who wouldn't think about it when it's constantly being brought up, but I always felt like it would be too awkward.

"I think he would probably cry just as much as you have, but he would hide it better." He must not have understood that I was asking about if Ray and I hooked up, not if Carson was awake and I was in a coma. Maybe it was better that we never talked about the possibility of us dating. Ray was a great friend, and I didn't want to ruin that. Did I? "What's wrong?" Ray asked, waking me from my thoughts.

"Nothing. It's just weird seeing him like this." He sat down in the chair next to me and took my hand.

"Yeah, it's like it's him, but it doesn't feel like he's actually here."

"I feel like we're supposed to be talking to him. I mean, that's what everyone does in movies. They talk to the person and hope that they can hear them, but talking to him without his sarcastic comments and everything feels wrong."

Ray turned his attention to Carson without another word and dropped my hand to rest his on Carson's bed. "Hey, man, we really need you to get stronger and wake up. You're not gonna like the world you wake up to, but we need you in it. You have a sister here who can't lose another brother and another one on the way who's going need her big brother to teach her everything, so when you feel strong enough, wake up." I watched Ray with tears in my eyes as we sat in silence. "You would've been with them." He dropped his head into his hands, and his shoulders shook.

"Ray, what are you talking about? I thought you said it was a good thing that I wasn't with them." I put my hand on his back while he continued to cry.

"I've seen pictures of the truck, Case. You would've been killed. The back driver's side was completely crushed." He looked over at me with tears still in his eyes. His voice was more strained than I had ever heard it. "You don't get it, do you?" I didn't understand what was upsetting him so much. I wasn't hurt. There were much bigger things to focus on right now than what would've happened to me. "Casey, you and Carson are my best friends. If something had happened to both of you, I don't know what I would do. I can't lose you, Casey."

"You're not gonna lose me, Ray. I'm fine. I wasn't in the truck. I was with you. You drove me home. I was sound asleep in my bed, remember? You didn't lose me." I put my hand on his wrist, and he stood up abruptly, almost knocking his chair over.

"I'm gonna go call Natalie." He left the room quickly and left me sitting alone with Carson, who obviously wasn't much help explaining the situation. Why was Ray acting so weird around me today? It's like overnight, a switch flipped, and now he's not comfortable with me. Maybe I said something in my sleep last night that had freaked him out. I don't care what happened. I just want to fix it.

Chapter 19 - Natalie

"Hello?" I answered. I didn't recognize the number, but it had a local area code, so I answered it anyway.

"Nat, it's Ray. I'm at the hospital. Last night after the party, Camden, Cooper, and Carson were in a car accident. Carson was hurt pretty bad." Ray paused on the line before continuing. "He's in a coma, Nat." I jumped up off of the couch in the living.

"What happened? I'm on my way. What hospital are you at? Is he going to be okay? He has to be alright." I hung up the phone before Ray could answer any of my questions.

"What's wrong, honey?" My mom asked, standing up in front of me. I really didn't have time to answer her right now.

"Carson's in the hospital. I have to go, Mom. It's bad. I need to go." Tears were rolling down my face before I could finish the sentence.

"Let me drive you," she told me calmly. "Mike! Nat and I are leaving. I'll call you in a little bit!" she hollered up the stairs at my dad as she grabbed her keys from the kitchen. We climbed into the car just as my phone rang again: Aaron.

"Where are you going?" he asked when I answered.

"The hospital. Carson was in an accident." I hung up the phone without any further explanation. I didn't feel like talking to anyone about this until I knew more about what was going on. I knew they were all going to have questions, and I didn't have the answers to any of them.

I rode silently with my hands clenched and tears falling down my face the entire drive. My mom didn't try to talk to me - she knew better than to strike up a conversation when I was upset. When we finally got to the hospital, my mom dropped me off at the front door. "I'm looking for Carson Nixley or Camden and Cooper Johnson," I told the receptionist.

"Camden Johnson is in room three-fifteen," she told me without looking at me. I quickly texted my mom the room number and climbed into the elevator. As soon as the elevator doors opened, I was greeted by Carson's aunt, uncle, and parents.

"Ray called me" was the only thing I could think to say to the four somber faces in front of me. This was worse than I thought.

Alice took me by the arm and led me to the side of the room. "There was a deer. Cam swerved and rolled the truck. Carson had a lot of broken bones, a punctured lung, and some bleeding in his brain. He's in a coma and on a ventilator until his lungs get a little stronger. They are hoping by the end of the day he will be breathing on his own."

I fought tears that refused to stop. "Can I see him? Were Cooper and Camden hurt? I'm sorry, I'm such a mess right now."

"Cam's legs were broken in multiple places. Cooper suffered major head trauma and internal injuries. He was pronounced dead on the scene." Guilt bit fiercely at my stomach as tears pooled in her eyes. I've been bawling over my boyfriend to her when her son had just passed away. I felt like a complete idiot.

"I'm so sorry, Alice." I pulled her into a hug that felt like it was more for me than it was for her.

"No one, except family, is allowed to see Carson until he is off of the vent, but we knew he would want you here." Casey walked into the room with Sam and Jess as Alice finished her sentence. Without excusing myself, I walked away from Alice, headed straight for Casey, and wrapped my arms around her.

"I'm sorry, Casey. I should've just told you about Carson and me. I was a terrible friend, and now I wasn't even here for you when you really needed me. I'm so sorry." After a moment of shock, she let her arms close around me tightly. I felt her trying to choke back tears and squeezed her tighter.

"Well, isn't that a nice sight? You all are finally getting along. Took long enough." Ray stepped between us as we stepped away from each other and pulled us both into a side hug. "I'm assuming you've been filled in on everything." I nodded slightly, and the elevator opened to reveal my mom.

"I should probably go fill her in, though." I quickly pulled my mom aside and told her everything I knew about the accident. She immediately made her way over to Carson's parents and aunt and uncle to offer her condolences. She only knew Cooper from brief passing in the hallway, but that was enough for my overly-emotional mom to burst into tears.

We spent the next four hours making small-talk in the hospital waiting room while people took turns going back to see Camden when he was awake. More than a quarter of the football team stopped in to see how Carson and Camden were doing. Word of the accident and Cooper's death had spread quickly. Messages were flooding into all of our phones to ask questions and offer condolences. My mom had left after a few hours, so I stayed close to Ray or Casey most of the time.

Finally, around two in the afternoon, Dr. O'Neal, who I had been told was Carson's surgeon, came to tell us that he was going to start the process of taking him off the vent. "If he can handle the strain of being off of the vent, we will move him out of the ICU and into a double room with Camden. We should know within the hour whether or not he needs to remain on the vent. I'll be back out to update you soon," Dr. O'Neal explained.

"He's strong," Casey whispered, leaning over to me. I must have had fear written all over my face. I nodded at her without a word, but I wasn't feeling any better. Carson had to be okay, and I had to be able to see him. I needed him to wake up, so I could apologize to him for being so stubborn last night at the party. I needed to tell him that I wasn't mad at him. I needed him to know that I wasn't going anywhere and that I wasn't going to cheat on him. I needed to reassure him that I'm not like Lindsey.

I didn't want to sit here anymore. Half of the people who had gathered in the waiting room were people who hardly knew Carson, including several girls he had slept with him and who were now crying about him being hurt. I glared as a few of them started talking to his mom about if she thought he was strong enough. Instead of screaming at them to shut up like I wanted to, I rolled my eyes and turned my attention back to my phone. I had been scrolling through old pictures for the last hour to keep my mind busy. Every once in a while, Casey would look over and ask about whatever picture I was looking at at the time. I think it was her way of distracting me from thinking about Carson.

"Who's that? He's cute," she said as she looked down at my phone. I smiled at the picture of Landon, my best friend from home, giving me a piggyback ride with my head resting on his shoulder. He was smiling at the camera, and I was smiling at him.

"He's my Ray. He is my best friend at home, and his mom is my mom's best friend. We were raised like siblings, but people always thought we were together." I couldn't pull my eyes away from Landon's gentle smile.

"I don't know why you wouldn't go for him. He's definitely got the whole "boy-next-door" thing going for him with that floppy, sandy hair."

"Well, too late now. He's in San Fransisco. You would like him, though; he was always trying to break me out of my shell." I smiled at the thought of Landon dragging me to my first boy-girl party when we were thirteen. I missed him more than anyone else from home. I swiped to the next picture in my camera roll: Landon kissing me on the cheek. It was from homecoming last year; he had been my date per our moms' requests.

"Are you sure you were just friends?" Casey asked with a laugh. I rolled my eyes at her and continued to swipe. The next twenty-plus pictures were of Landon and me. "Are you all still friends?" I was so busy reminiscing that I almost didn't hear her question.

"We still check in with each other every once in a while, but we don't talk like we used to. I don't really talk to anyone from home anymore."

Casey quickly filled the awkward silence that followed. "What's he like? Is he crazy smart like you? Is he an athlete? Is he a player?"

"He was literally raised on a golf course, so that's pretty much his whole life. He was definitely a country club kid. He's always been too busy for relationships, so he's not a player. And he's had everything in his life handed to him, so he never had to worry about being smart. His dad was our superintendent, which he always used to get us out of trouble." I laughed while I thought about all of the times he had talked me into doing stupid things with him and then talked his way out of trouble when we got caught. "He has an extremely inappropriate sense of humor. We were pretty much polar opposites."

"Sounds kinda like you and Carson." I was about to tell her she was wrong when Dr. O'Neal walked in. Casey and the rest of her family stood up quickly.

"He's off the vent and breathing well on his own." Relief immediately washed over me, but this was only half of the battle: he still had to wake up. "We'll go ahead and move him up, so you all can visit with him." As he walked away, Belle turned to face all of us.

"Once he gets moved up, we'd like to give Camden a chance to see him for a little bit before anyone else goes back. We'll let you know when someone else can visit." I sank back in my chair to wait, but time was crawling now. I could actually go see him now. The only thing stopping me was having to wait my turn.

"I think we're ready for some visitors," Alice finally reported about twenty minutes later. "Let's start out with just a few at a time. Camden is sleeping, so please try to be quiet." A group of seven girls, who I had seen fawning over Carson many times before, stood up to walk down the hallway before I could react.

"Natalie, I'm sure he'd want to hear your voice," Belle called out sternly as she blocked the hallway to Carson's room. I couldn't help but smile smugly as I walked through the crowd of girls. "Go get him," Belle whispered to me.

"Thank you." I kept a strong stance as I walked down the hallway. I wasn't going to fall apart when Carson was already in enough pain. I wasn't prepared for what I was walking into, though. Carson had bandages wrapped around his head and abdomen. Normally, the sight of Carson shirtless would've made me blush, but this time it made me afraid to touch him. I made my way over to him quietly and placed a gentle kiss to his lips. The feeling of him not kissing me back made my tears start to fall. I must've watched too many movies growing up because part of me thought my kiss would wake him up.

I laughed at my own naivety. "You've got quite a fan club out there, babe." I took his hand in mine as more tears fell. "Some of the girls out there don't even know your middle name, and they're crying over you. I guess that's why you liked them, though; they paid attention to you without all the strings. I know it's not nearly as easy with me, but I think what we have is worth it. I really need you to wake up, Carse. I'm sorry for last night and everything I said. I need you to know that. So, please wake up so I can tell you. I know I'm stubborn, but I'm admitting that I was wrong last night. I know you don't want to miss me saying that you were right." I stared at him quietly for a second as if he was going to reply.

"He loves you, you know?" I heard from the other side of the room as the curtain opened. I looked up to see Camden staring at me.

"I'm sorry, Cam, I didn't mean to wake you up."

"It's fine. I've slept most of the day, and it doesn't take long for these beds to become uncomfortable. Besides, I wasn't sleeping anyway. I'm serious, though; he loves you." He pulled himself into a seated position with a grimace.

"Did he tell you that?" Does he really love me? Do I love him? I mean, of course, I care about him, but love is a whole different thing. I don't even know what being in love feels like, and Carson and I have only been officially dating for two weeks. That was too soon to love someone, right?

"He didn't have to tell me. I've known Carson his whole life, and I've never seen him act the way he does with you. I was the only one he told when you two started sneaking around. You know, after your little fort date? I could tell that something was off with him, and when I asked him about it, he couldn't stop gushing about you. He said you were different from any other girl. He tried to talk himself out of going after you, but clearly, that didn't work. Natalie, when you walk into a room, you are the only thing he focuses on; he's never been like that with anyone else - not even Lindsey."

When he brought up Lindsey, a lightbulb turned on in my mind. Last night, Carson had said he was jealous of Zach because the last girl he was in love with had cheated on him. Was that his way of telling me that he loved me? How had I not noticed that? "Thanks, Cam." I sat in silence, holding Carson's hand for a few more minutes while I tried to decide if I loved him or not. When I still couldn't make a decision, I gave another quick kiss before walking out of the room, so the hoard of girls could go gawk at him.

Chapter 20 - Aaron

As soon as I got off the phone with Natalie, I wanted to call Lindsey and fill her in on what was going on, but my dad needed help with my sisters. When Norah got back to the house a few hours later, I already had a missed call from Lindsey and quite a few texts from her too. Norah updated my dad and me on everything that had happened, and I immediately called Lindsey.

"Hey, do you want me to come pick you up and take you to the hospital?" Lindsey asked before I could even say hello. "I'm gonna go either way, but I didn't know if you wanted to go with me." I felt a twinge of jealousy by her planning to go see her ex without me, but I pushed it away quickly.

"Yeah, Nat already headed that way, so I'm good to go whenever you want." As I finished my sentence, I heard a car honking outside and looked out the window to see Lindsey's car pulling into my driveway. I ran out to meet her.

"I was already leaving when you called, so I just headed here first," she told me as I climbed into her car. I could tell from her tear-stained cheeks that she had been crying, even though she was clearly trying to hide it. "I just got off the phone with Jess, and she said they were able to take Carson off of the vent. People are actually able to go back and see him now. He probably won't be awake for a few more days, though." When she finally stopped to take a breath, she looked at me expectantly.

"Yeah, Nat was pretty freaked out when Ray called her this morning. She's been at the hospital all day waiting to see him and making sure Casey is alright." I was desperately trying to drive the subject away from Carson because it was making me uncomfortable and was making her tear up.

"Are they friends again? I thought Casey was still pissed off about Carson screwing Natalie." I glared at her. She knew I hated when she talked about Natalie and Carson's relationship like that.

"They're dating, not screwing, Lindsey. Is that what you tell people about us? That we're just screwing?" She rolled her eyes at my question. I knew she didn't want to have this conversation again; we had talked about this multiple times in the two weeks since Carson and Natalie started dating.

"Of course, it's not, but you're forgetting that I dated Carson. They're definitely screwing. Carson doesn't know how to have a relationship without sex."

"It doesn't matter if they are having sex or not; they are still dating. And you're forgetting that that's my sister you're talking about. Seriously, Linds, how many times are we going to have to have this argument? Because I'm getting really fucking tired of it." Instead of answering my question, she just huffed and drove in silence the rest of the way to the hospital. Real mature.

When we walked into the hospital and up to the third floor, my mind shifted from Lindsey to Natalie. She was sitting in the waiting room with her head in her hands. Sam came up to Lindsey and me before I could find out what was wrong, though.

"Hey, perfect timing. A few people just came out, so you guys can go ahead and go back," Sam told us quickly while Camden's mom ushered a group of girls back toward the waiting room. Lindsey didn't hesitate to lead the way down the hall as soon as they were out of the way. I had to speedwalk to keep up with her.

When we got into the room, Lindsey quickly dropped into the chair next to Carson's bed closest to the door while I made my way over to Camden, whose bed was next to the window. I couldn't stop my jealousy from spiking again as Lindsey took Carson's hand and cried at the sight of him. "How are you doing, man?" I asked Camden as I tore my eyes away from Lindsey.

"I'm tired of laying in this bed. I want to be able to walk around and talk to people, not just wait for them to come to me. I can only watch people cry about Cooper and Carson so much before I get tired of it." He looked directly at Lindsey, who glared at him with her teary eyes. "They won't even let me watch TV or play on my phone because of this damn concussion." He lowered his voice slightly. "Hell, since Carse got in here, you're one of the first people who have actually come in to talk to me instead of just staring at him. I'm assuming you don't have much interest in fawning over your girlfriend's ex?"

I laughed at his question even though he wasn't wrong. "Carson and I can hardly get along anywhere other than the football field. There's no point in me pretending to be his friend just because he's unconscious. I'm here to check on you and Natalie." I looked around to make sure Lindsey hadn't overheard me. I knew she would be pissed if she heard me talking about Carson like that. I'm not even sure why she cared about him so much when she was always talking about how terribly he had treated her. I must have heard her tell me a hundred times that Carson never even held doors open for her, so why did she have to make a big production of crying over him.

"I hate to interrupt your time with him, Linds, but there are other people that need to see him," Jess said from the doorway. As we left the room, I tried to grab Lindsey's hand, but she brushed me away and continued crying. Once we got back out to the waiting room, I made a bee-line toward Nat, who was still sitting with her head in her hands.

"That boyfriend of yours must be really good in bed with all of the girls he's got wrapped around his finger. Hell, after what I just saw in there, part of me thinks Lindsey's still under his spell too." When she finally looked up at me, she was smiling - thankfully, because I don't think I could handle another crying girl in this room.

"Yeah, they're all sitting here boohooing over a guy who slept with them once just for kicks, and I'm trying to figure out if I should even be here. I mean, I'm nothing like those girls. Why in the hell did he pick me?" She gestured at the group of girls that were taking turns hugging Lindsey like she was the one whose boyfriend was in a coma. Normally, it bothered me when she lumped Lindsey in with all the other girls who had slept with Carson, but right now, she was exactly like the rest of them.

"Nat, I know I'm not always the most supportive of your relationship with Carson, but don't you think there's a reason he's dating you, and he just slept with them? You should be here more than any of them should."

"Your girlfriend's a bitch," Casey said to me as she plopped into the chair next to Natalie. "She's acting like she's Carson's widow or something. I honestly think she's cried more than his mom has. Oh, and now she's trying to go back and see him again even though she like just left his room." I turned around just in time to see Lindsey walking back down the hall we had just come from not five minutes ago. "Last time I checked, she was the one who cheated on him, so why is she acting like they're still together?" Casey's mom must not like Lindsey either because she unremorsefully guided her back to the waiting room.

I walked over to her and pulled her into a corner away from the rest of the crying girls. "What the hell is going on with you? On the way here, you were talking about Carson like he's a man-whore, and now, you're acting like he's the love of your life. Which is it, Lindsey?"

"What are you talking about? I'm trying to be here for my friend." She tried to look innocent, but she must've forgotten that I knew her better than all of her friends, who only liked her for her status.

"Are you still in love with him? Don't try to lie to me." My voice was stern but quiet enough that no one else could hear us.

"We dated for two years, Aaron. I'm not just going to toss him aside like that doesn't mean anything. He's hurt and needs people to stand by him right now. Don't be mad at me just because Natalie is acting like a cold-hearted bitch that doesn't care about her boyfriend. It's not my fault that I care about him more than she does." At this point, all eyes were on us, and Lindsey wasn't worried about drawing even more attention to herself. She was talking loud enough for everyone to hear her: including Natalie, who quickly left the room to avoid the staring eyes.

"I think you need to figure out if you're over him or not, and until you know, we need to take a break. I'm not going to date someone who is disrespectful to my family and still in love with her ex. You always paint Carson as the bad guy, but clearly, he couldn't have been that bad if you're still so hung up on him." I didn't waste any time waiting for her reaction; instead, I went to find Natalie.

I found her pacing in the hallway outside of Carson's room. "I'm sorry about her, Nat. I don't know why she's acting like that." She looked up from the ground, and I saw anger in her eyes.

"She literally knows nothing about my relationship with Carson, so she needs to shut the hell up. God, I just wish Carson was awake to make her leave me alone. She actually listens to him when he stands up for me." Tears were starting to fall down her face, and I didn't know what to do to help.

"I broke up with her if that makes you feel any better. I've wanted to be with her since we were kids, but I guess Lindsey's a little different now than she was when we were five."

"I don't think anyone is the same person they were at five. If someone would've told me then that, at sixteen, I would have two half-siblings that I never knew about, I wouldn't have believed them." She gave me a teary-eyed smile and a half-hearted laugh. "I'm sorry about you and Lindsey. I didn't mean for that to happen." I sat down on the floor, and she followed my lead.

"I guess you and Casey were right all along. She's in love with him." I don't know how I didn't notice all the signs. Dating me was just her way of making Carson jealous because he didn't like me.

"Well, she's got a lot of competition because so am I." Anger was creeping back into Natalie's voice, but it didn't distract me from her surprising confession. She had only been dating Carson for two weeks; how was she already in love with him? I've liked Lindsey most of my life, but I still hadn't fallen in love with her in the three weeks we had been dating. I wanted to ask Natalie if she was sure, but I had learned better than to question her relationship.

"I don't think you have anything to worry about." I nodded towards Carson's room. "That guy only has eyes for you." I had initially told her that to make her feel better, but it was true. Even before they were dating, Carson hardly even looked at any girls other than Natalie. Maybe I had been too hard on him from trusting everything Lindsey had told me. I glanced over at Natalie to see her staring at Carson through the open door. I guess she doesn't have eyes for anyone else either.

"Do you want me to drive you home?" I asked her, breaking the silence that had fallen over us.

"No, that's okay. Ray's gonna drive me. He needs me to help him pick out clothes for Casey, so she doesn't have to leave." I almost

261

made a joke about Ray and Casey, but Natalie's sullen face made me rethink that idea.

"Okay. Let me know if anything changes, and you need me to come get you." I stood up slowly and offered her my hand to pull her up.

Once she was standing, I turned to walk away, but Natalie's words stopped me. "Thank you for being such a great brother. I know I've told you that you don't need to protect me, but I appreciate it - even though it doesn't always seem like it."

I looked back at her with tears in her eyes. She reminded me of Ashley with her puppy-dog eyes. "Nat, our family might be screwed up, but we're still a family no matter what. You can always count on me." I gave her a quick hug before walking away. "He's gonna be okay," I told her from the end of the hallway, but she was already disappearing into Carson's room.

December 10th

Chapter 21 - Casey

It's been six days since the accident. I think. Sitting in this hospital every day is making the days blur together. Carson still isn't awake, so I refused to go back to school this week. There's no way I could face everyone. School was canceled on Monday to celebrate the championship win and then canceled again on Tuesday in honor of Cooper, so I've only missed two days, but my parents are worried about me falling behind. I think worrying about me helps them keep their minds off the boys.

We've been putting off planning Cooper's funeral until Carson wakes up, but I don't know how much longer my parents are going to be able to wait. We all need closure, and the grief counselor my mom made us start seeing thinks that will be the best way to get it. I'm dreading the funeral. I'm not sure I can handle any more strangers offering me their condolences - I've had enough of that from people visiting Carson.

Thankfully, the groups of people have stopped coming. My parents are still getting texts constantly, but it's only been close family and friends at the hospital ever since this weekend. Everyone talked to me like a small child when they came to visit. They said things like I was lucky to have such a caring big brother or that he's protecting me from above now. I knew they were all just trying to help, but it just made me even more irritated. Ray told me to think about the fact that every time someone says something like that, Cooper is probably cracking up laughing - that actually did help me.

I don't know how I would've gotten through all of this without Ray's help. I've been staying with him at his dad's house every night, and his arms have quickly become the only place I can fall asleep. Ray has been driving me to the hospital every morning. Then, he goes to school and comes back to the hospital afterward. Natalie has been here every day too. She tried to talk her parents into letting her skip school the last couple of days, but they didn't go for it. Usually, she just sits next to Carson and holds his hand while she catches me up on everything going on at school.

The last few days, all the buzz has been about the accident and Aaron and Lindsey's breakup. I hadn't realized how many girls were into Aaron until Natalie was talking about it.

"It's disgusting. Random girls come up and talk to me about him all the time, trying to find out what he likes. I'm so tired of it. I'm just ready for this week to be over so you can come back and get them to leave me alone." Natalie was pacing around the room like a caged animal.

"Look at it this way, Nat, they could be asking you about how you and your boyfriend are going to have sex now. That's the kind of questions I get." Camden laughed at Jess's comment as he pulled her onto his bed with him.

"No, I just get people who don't even know my name asking me how he's doing. No one has any more information about him than what we knew on Sunday." Not knowing was Natalie's biggest problem with this whole situation. She was so used to being in control of everything that this was making her crazy. Carson would tell her to chill out, but I had a feeling that wouldn't fix things coming from me. Instead of saying anything, I just watched as she continued to pace.

"Natalie, you need to sit your ass down before you make me throw up. I already have to sit in this bed all day. I don't need you to make it worse," Camden told her teasingly.

"Speaking of being in bed all day, did you tell them your good news?" I asked Cam. Ray, Jess, and Natalie all stared at him expectantly. After the last few days of being around each other for four hours a day, we had all gotten really close and even more invested in Carson and Camden's recovery than we already were.

"Dad thinks I'll be able to go home in a few days as long as I can still do my physical therapy from home." He didn't sound nearly as excited as I thought he would be.

"That's great, baby. Why don't you sound excited? Isn't that a good thing?" Jess looked at him with concern in her eyes.

"Yeah, it's good, but it means that I'll have to be stuck in the house for a few weeks. All I'll be able to do is stare at Cooper's stuff. I can't do that. I'll lose my mind. It's going to be hard enough going through physical therapy without the constant reminder that Cooper's gone." Cam's voice made it obvious that he was holding back tears. I hadn't even thought about him going home like that. I thought he would be excited to be in his own bed again. Was this something he had already been struggling with? He had kept a strong face on for the last few days. We all thought he was doing great, or at least I did. "Wow, I didn't mean to ruin everyone's mood." Camden was trying to lighten the mood, but it didn't work.

"You didn't ruin anyone's mood, man. We just didn't know you were feeling like that. Why didn't you say anything?" Ray looked more concerned than I had seen him since the night of the accident.

Camden shrugged slightly. "You all were doing so much better with Cooper's death, and I didn't want to make anything worse. It's really not a big deal. I'm just not super siked about it, you know?"

"Cam, it is a big deal. Your recovery is a huge deal. Why do you think Mom is making you get grief counseling? This type of recovery and physical therapy can make people severely depressed. Why didn't you say anything? Do you think that just because we aren't still sobbing, we don't miss Cooper? We all miss him, Cam," The anger in my voice was rising. I've sat with him in this room for four days straight. The only times I've left his side is to sleep and use the bathroom. How could he not tell me about this?

"I'm not depressed, Casey. My brother died, and my cousin is in a coma. I'm sad. And I didn't tell you because I knew you would make a big fucking deal about it. I'm fine. Just drop it. Okay? And don't you dare tell Mom and Dad, or I swear, I will beat your ass."

I'd love to see him try to beat my ass when he can't even walk around, but I knew better than to say that to him. "Fine, but only if you agree to be honest with me about this stuff. I know I'm not part of y'all's little boys-only club, but that doesn't mean that you can hide things like this from me. It's bad enough that you and Cooper already put protectors in place for me; I don't need you to hide your emotions to protect mine too."

Cam looked directly at Ray, who was standing next to me. "You told her? Why the hell would you do that?"

"It was the night of the accident. She was being stubborn and wouldn't let me take care of her. Sam wasn't here to watch out for her, and it was the only way that I could get her to leave the hospital with me. What else was I supposed to do?" Ray defended himself quickly.

Jess looked between the three of us with a confused look on her face. "What the hell are you all talking about?"

"The guys have a protection pact for me and you to make sure that we are always taken care of, and clearly, they were never planning on telling us about it. I don't understand why it had to be some big secret," I explained to her. I was just as mad about the pact now as I was when I first found out.

"We knew you both would be pissed off about it because you all seem to think that you're big and bad when you can't even kill a spider. And if we're spilling all of our secrets about it, I guess you should know that Natalie is part of it too now - per Aaron's request in Nashville a few weeks ago. That's why Ray didn't hesitate to drive Natalie home on Saturday night even though he knew it would be awkward driving both of you." Ray hadn't told me that part, and by the look on his face, he was hoping Cam wouldn't tell me that either.

I shot him a questioning glance that immediately made him confess. "I was going to tell you, but I didn't know what terms you and Nat were on. I didn't want to upset you more than you already were."

"Why does it matter that they wanted to watch out for us? There's safety in numbers, and they were just using that to our advantage. I think it's kinda sweet." Jess and I stared blankly at Natalie. "Maybe it's because I've only had a brother for a couple of months and am just starting to get used to him being protective, but I think it's nice that, even when I was being a bitch to him, Aaron wanted to look out for me." I had no idea how to argue with her point. I hated when she used logic against me to make me feel like I was being dramatic.

I was about to admit that Natalie was right, like always, when my mom stepped into the room. "Hey, kiddos, what do you all want for dinner tonight?" All of us looked to Cam. We had ordered food the last four nights, and we got what he wanted every time. I guess that's part of him being the one with two broken legs.

"How about tacos?" He raised his eyebrows at my mom.

"Okay, I'll order from the Mexican restaurant down the street. Figure out what you want and let me know." As soon as she left, we all pulled out our phones and started looking at the restaurant's menu to see what we wanted.

We were all silent as we stared at our phones. I heard someone groan, but I ignored it until I heard it again. I looked up to tell whoever was doing it to stop and noticed that they were all staring at Carson's bed. I looked over to see him sitting with his eyes open and looking around at all of us.

Chapter 22 - Carson

"Carson!?" Natalie's arms wrapped around me tightly. I tried to move to hug her back, but pain shot through my stomach, and my head pounded.

"Ow," I winced as she gently let go of me. When she sat back, she had tears rolling down her cheeks and a huge smile playing on her lips. I looked around to see Casey, Ray, Jess, and Camden all staring at me in shock. The first thing I noticed was Camden's legs. He must have gotten banged up pretty bad in the accident. Then it hit me; Cooper wasn't here. Why would they put Camden and me in the same room and not Cooper and Camden? Where was Cooper?

"He's awake!" Ray yelled into the hallway. Within seconds my parents, aunt, uncle, and a large group of doctors and nurses came into my room.

One of the doctors made quick work of introducing himself and evaluating me. "Hey, Carson, I'm Dr. O'Neal. Do you know where you are and how you got here?"

"I'm in the hospital. I was in a car accident. My head hurts."

"I'll get you something for the pain, but first, can you tell me the names of your friends?"

I looked around the room. "Camden, Jess, Ray, Casey, and Natalie. My mom and dad are over there, and so are Mitch and Alice. Where's Cooper?" I looked around to see if I could decipher anything from their reactions. My mom's was the most telling: she started to sob almost immediately. I didn't need any other explanation. I knew he was gone. Tears stung my eyes, but I tried to hold them back until they confirmed my suspicions.

"Patrick, I know it's protocol, but clearly, he's alert and doesn't appear to have memory loss, so can you give us a little bit of time to talk?" Uncle Mitch asked his colleague.

Dr. O'Neal nodded understandingly. "Let me just get his vitals first and get him something for the pain." He quickly checked my blood pressure, heart rate, and oxygen levels and put something into my IV before leading the rest of the nurses and doctors out of the room.

"Honey, I'm so glad your okay!" my mom cried as she hugged me. "I was so worried about you." The painkillers hadn't kicked in yet, so it still hurt when she hugged me, but I couldn't bring myself to push her away; instead, I just tried to hide my grimace.

"Belle, I think you're hurting him. How about we wait to hug him until the drugs have kicked in?" My dad gently eased her away from me. It was strange to see him so concerned about me being hurt since he was usually the cause of my pain. Maybe, having a daughter on the way had changed the way he saw being a parent. If only that could've happened years ago.

I pushed my thoughts about my dad out of my head to focus on my original question. "He didn't make it, did he?" My mom and Natalie squeezed my hands tighter.

"He was pronounced dead on the scene." Camden's words hit me harder than I had expected. I stopped trying to hold back my tears; I let them fall while they all stared at me. The tears I saw in everyone else's eyes made it sting even more; they had been dreading telling me this. Soft sobs shook my body for a few more minutes before Camden spoke up again. "We weren't sure if you were going to make it either, man. You were out for six days." Six days? What the hell happened while I was out? I looked around the room again. Camden and Jess still looked like they were together. My mom didn't have any more of a baby bump than the last time I saw her. The only difference was that Ray was standing behind Casey with his arms wrapped around her. Are they finally a thing?

"What'd I miss?" I asked with a small smile and tears still running down my face. The news of Cooper's death was slowly setting in, and I was trying to hide how much it was affecting me. Crying made my entire body hurt, so I kept trying to suppress the emotions that were flowing through me at full force.

Mitch let out a small laugh. "Not much other than just sitting here and watching you sleep. You've had quite a few visitors and a few that have hardly left at all." He glanced around the room at Casey, Ray, and Natalie. "How are you feeling?"

"Hungry," I told them with a forced laugh. I saw Natalie roll her eyes at me. I love when she does that. If I hadn't been in pain and surrounded by my family, I would've pulled her in for a kiss.

Mitch's voice pulled my attention away from her lips. "Well, I'll have Dr. O'Neal come back in and complete his evaluation. Then we'll get you some food." He looked at the large group of friends and family around Cam and me. "Let's give the doctors some room to work." Before I knew it, everyone except Cam was leaving the room and squeezing my hand or gently hitting my ankle as a form of goodbye.

"Your uncle tells me you're hungry and, with how many visitors you've had, I'm sure you want to talk to everyone, so I'll make this fast. I just need to check your incisions and make sure you aren't having any new issues." Dr. O'Neal started pulling away the large bandage on my stomach. The large purple and red wound underneath took me by surprise. I hadn't realized how bad I was banged up. "This is from where we had to stop some internal bleeding in your abdomen. It looks good for six days post-op." I disagreed. It looked like it was going to hurt like a bitch when I wasn't on painkillers. He redressed the cut and uncovered another one closer to my side. "This one is from where we repaired your lung and ribs." He seemed satisfied by the appearance of the long line of stitches that looked worse than the first ones. "Now, I'm going to check the staples in your head."

"I have staples in my head?" It was the first question I had asked Dr. O'Neal since waking up.

"You had a little bit of bleeding in your brain, but we were able to stop it without any damage. Everything looks good here, Carson. I'll let the nurses know to bring you in some food."

"Doc, no offense, but he doesn't want hospital food. We were actually going to order Mexican. Is it alright if he eats that?" Camden asked though I knew he wasn't going to listen regardless.

"That's fine. Just don't push yourself too hard. You haven't had real food in six days, so your stomach might not react well to it. I'll be back in to check on you in a few hours. Remember to take it easy. The last thing we need is you breaking open your stitches," Dr. O'Neal warned sternly before leaving the room.

"You were on a ventilator for the first day. They weren't sure if you were going to be able to breathe on your own. You had us all pretty worried, man," Cam told me once it was only us in the room.

Ray walked in with Nat, Jess, and Casey following close behind him just as the words left his lips. "He's not kidding, Carse. You were banged up pretty bad, but on the plus side, you had quite a few gorgeous girls worried about you."

Nat had just settled into the chair next to me, and Casey was still hovering close to Ray. I know I've teased them about it a lot, but now it definitely seems like something is going on between them. "Ray, it seems like you got some extra attention too. What's going on there?" I pointed at the two of them and raised my eyebrows as best I could.

Ray wrapped an arm around Casey's waist and pulled her closer to him. "Oh, you mean us sleeping together?" I felt my eyes grow wide. I had expected him to deny their relationship, not admit that they're having sex.

Casey elbowed him in the ribs and moved away from him. "By that, he means literally just sleeping. Some things might have changed while you were out, but they sure as hell didn't change that much." There was the reaction I had been expecting. I laughed as Ray pretended to be hurt by Casey's comment.

"So, did I really have girls all over me?" My question made Natalie roll her eyes again. This time I did reach up and pull her lips to mine. If she hadn't made it clear that she missed me before, she definitely did with this kiss.

"Do we need to give you two a minute alone?" Casey teased as Natalie pulled away.

"Yes," I said at the same time as Natalie said, "No." She smiled at me sweetly. As much as I love my family, I would much rather be alone with Natalie right now than under all of their watchful eyes; after all, Natalie was the only one acting like I wasn't going to fall apart if she touched me.

I spent the next few hours with my friends talking about everything I had missed, which wasn't much other than Lindsey and Aaron breaking up. I'd be lying if I said I hadn't been expecting that. Lindsey is a drama queen, and Aaron has had enough drama to last him a lifetime without her adding to it. At least it didn't take him very long to figure out that she's insane - he was obviously smarter than me.

"We should probably get going," Ray proposed with his hand on Casey's shoulder. "I told my dad we'd be back by eight." They both hugged me goodbye before heading for the door.

"Yeah, I should get home too. Sam said he's going to stop by tomorrow after school, okay?" Jess leaned in and kissed Cam before heading for the door. "I'm glad to see you awake, Carse."

Once they had all left, I turned to Natalie, who was still sitting in the chair beside me. "Are you going to leave me too?" I stuck out my bottom lip in an attempt to make her feel sorry for me. I wasn't ready to be alone with my thoughts. Having my friends around had distracted me from everything, and I didn't want to know what I was going to feel like once they all left. "Or do I get a little bit of alone time with you?"

"Hey, don't forget that I'm here too," Camden teased as Nat stood up and pulled the curtain shut between his bed and mine. I scooted over in my bed and stared up at her.

"Are you sure it's not going to hurt you if I lay down?" I smiled at her and grabbed her hand to pull her down next to me. She climbed into my bed gently, being careful not to touch me. We were both quiet for a minute, and I was starting to worry that I had done something wrong. "I'm sorry, Carson." What is she apologizing for? For me getting hurt? For Cooper dying? Did she think her lying with me was hurting me? Or was she apologizing for something she was about to do?

"What are you talking about, Nat?" When I looked over at her, tears were starting to well in her eyes. I tried to pull her closer to me, but putting my arm over her shot pain through my side.

"I'm sorry, I was being so stubborn the other night. I know I don't always make things easy, but please don't find someone new." Her voice was hardly above a whisper, and it was strangled with tears. "I don't want you to go anywhere." She sounded like a little kid as she buried her head into the side of my neck. I hadn't seen Natalie this vulnerable since the first time we had hung out, and she had told me about her dad's affair. I knew then that I never wanted to hurt her as much as he had.

I ignored my pain and tried to wrap my body around hers. "Baby, what are you talking about? I love how stubborn you are. I'm not going to find someone new. I'm not going anywhere."

She looked up at me with wide eyes. Had I said something wrong? "I love you," she whispered softly. I had no idea how badly I had wanted to hear those words. We had only been together for three weeks, and for one of those, I was literally comatose, but I still knew that this was right - that she was right for me.

I let my lips meet hers for a long, lingering kiss before I responded. "I love you too, Natalie." She smiled against my lips while I kissed her again. She pulled away and laid her head on my chest before I could deepen the kiss. As I looked down at her sweet smile, tears formed in my eyes. Every emotion from today started to rush over me at one time. Fear, sadness, anger, happiness, and love flooded my brain, and sobs began shaking my entire body. Natalie didn't ask what was wrong or try to soothe me; instead, she just kept her head on my chest and stayed quiet while I cried. I know some of my tears fell into her hair, but she didn't care.

Over my own sobs, I could hear Camden doing the same on the other side of the curtain. I had almost forgotten that he was here, but for some reason hearing his cries made me feel better. I had people going through this with me. I looked down at Natalie again; her eyes were closed, but her cheeks were stained with tears. I had family and friends who were feeling all of the same things I was right now. I started to slow my breathing, and I heard Cam do the same, but Natalie still didn't say a word - she also didn't move away from me. She just held onto me like she was afraid that I would disappear if she moved or spoke.

I hugged her a little tighter. "I'm not going anywhere," I whispered into her hair.

To find out what happens next in Casey, Carson, Natalie, and Aaron's stories, keep an eye out for Megan VanLoo's next book – "The Perfect Friend"

Made in the USA
Middletown, DE
15 February 2022